BELOVED ABDUCTOR

Through the actions of Edmund de Vert, Felicia Meriet had escaped her evil cousin. Now she was to discover the high price of her freedom. She was committing herself to a man who had abducted her, a man who had hated her the first time he set eyes on her. To possess that which your enemy most wanted was the perfect revenge, he had told her. And she had played right into his hands by marrying him.

BELOVED ABDUCTOR

Beloved Abductor

by
June Francis

Magna Large Print Books
Long Preston, North Yorkshire,
England.

British Library Cataloguing in Publication Data.

Francis, June
  Beloved abductor.

A catalogue record for this book is
available from the British Library

ISBN 0-7505-1300-4

First published in Great Britain by Mills & Boon Ltd., 1987

Copyright © 1987 by June Francis

Cover illustration © Len Thurston by arrangement with
P.W.A. International

The moral right of the author has been asserted

Published in Large Print 1998 by arrangement with Judith
Murdoch Literary Agency

Magna Large Print is an imprint of
Library Magna Books Ltd.
Printed and bound in Great Britain by
T.J. International Ltd., Cornwall, PL28 8RW.

CHAPTER ONE

Felicia Meriet's eyes watered as the smoke from the cooking-fire weaved its uncertain way about the unfamiliar hall. The room was crowded with men, and the clamour of their voices bounced against her ears in undulating waves. She rubbed at the knot of pain spreading between her dark brows and longed for the quietness of the bedchamber that had been allotted to her. How long she would possess its solitude she did not know.

She glanced at her cousin Philip sprawling in the canopied chair next to her. He was darkly handsome with high prominent cheekbones and a full sensuous mouth. His nose was thin and straight like that of all the Meriets, and once Felicia had thought herself in love with him. When his eyes caught hers, they glittered in a predatory fashion as they ranged over her. She lowered her gaze swiftly, in seeming modesty, knowing it would do no good to let her cousin become aware of her fear and dislike.

Why had he brought her here to the manor of de Vert? He had said it was for her own safety in these perilous times when England simmered on the verge of civil war again in this year of Our Lord, 1265. She doubted the truth of his words. Could she be safer so near to the northern border with Wales? If it was her safety Philip was concerned about, he should have left her on his own manor in Leicestershire. Even better, he should have allowed her to return home to her manor of Meriet, which was a little north of Ludlow.

Felicia sighed. What a fool she had been to have gone with him in such a meek fashion that day more than a year ago! He had come to tell her of the deaths of her father and brother Mark at the Battle of Lewes, which had taken place a few days before. She had barely taken in his suggestion that he would deal with her affairs and that she should go with him to his manor. He, her close male kin, the son of her father's brother who was long dead, had appeared to be kind. In her grief, she had wanted to believe that he meant to do the best for her and that he cared. Only later had she caught the look of triumph on his face when they had talked of her father and brother dying on the battlefield. Much later, when it was too late. Her mother had died in childbed six years earlier, so when Philip had said that she would benefit from the comfort of an older woman, his wife, she had thought there was some truth in his words.

Still, she had felt the need of someone she knew, and asked if she could take her cousin Joan with her. He had brushed her request aside, saying that his wife Matilda would be company enough. To some extent that had been true, since Matilda had been pathetically eager to be friends with Felicia. She was a gentle creature who feared her husband greatly and often tried to disguise the marks of his ill-treatment. Felicia closed her eyes briefly, remembering. The friendship had not lasted long. Her throat moved convulsively as she seemed to hear the long-drawn-out scream and the slithering and thudding of Matilda's body as she tumbled down the stone steps. Felicia had come running out of her bedchamber to see her cousin standing at the top of the stairway.

'She slipped,' Philip murmured, his eyes dangerously chill. 'My poor wife. Now I must find another.'

Felicia had whirled round and locked herself in her bedchamber. Never even in the privacy of her own room had she voiced her suspicions to herself. The days had passed into weeks and often she had begged Philip to allow her to go home, but always he had put forward some excuse.

Gradually the suspicion that he did not intend ever to let her go took root in her mind and grew until it shadowed all her thinking.

'More wine, coz?'

Felicia lifted her head and hooded her eyes swiftly, nodding meekly. Philip's smile was contemptuous as he snapped his fingers. A serving-man standing just behind them stepped forward. He was soberly clad in a black tunic, and seemed to have been awaiting her cousin's call. Briefly she caught a glimpse of frosty grey eyes, an aquiline nose and a long-lipped mouth before his too long tawny hair swept forward and hid his face from her, and her cousin's, eyes. The man poured wine into the large silver chased cup. Philip drank deeply before passing it to her. She was careful to sip only a small amount, and not to drink from the same spot as he. She might need her wits this night.

Her cousin let out a growl. 'God's blood, woman! You must drink deeper than that. More wine, and perhaps you will have a bit more warmth in you.' He snapped his fingers again and bade the servant fill the cup once more.

Felicia felt a surge of anger, and her fingers twisted tightly about the cup's silver bowl. Her mouth set firmly, and she watched impatiently as the man filled the cup to the brim. She was aware again of his gaze upon her. His eyes washed slowly and with a cool deliberation downwards, lingering where the blue silk of her undergown moulded her well-formed breasts. Even as she flushed, her blue eyes sparked. For a brief second surprise gleamed in the servant's cool eyes before they darkened into charcoal slits. He straightened, and stepped back out of her vision.

Felicia's temper seethed. How dared he look at her like that! Did she not have enough to put up with from her cousin with his advances and innuendoes? To have a servant study her with such arrogance, openly calculating the charms beneath her clothing! Were all men beasts? Did they think, every one of them, of nothing but gain, power and bedding a wench? Not to mention drinking and filling their bellies! She picked up the silver cup, and defiantly gulped down half its contents before disdainfully passing it on to her cousin, knowing she might regret the act later. Wine swiftly went to her head.

'Would you think it rude in me if I begged to be excused, Philip?' she asked. 'I am weary after the long journey from Leicestershire.'

His eyes glittered with annoyance. 'I will not have you retire so early, Felicia.' Philip had a strange way of biting his words off short when he was annoyed. He did so now. 'I miss the presence of a woman since my wife so unfortunately met her death—but I am thinking of remedying that as soon as the mourning period is over.'

Felicia's heart seemed to miss a beat. Did he mean to have her for wife? 'But I have the headache.' She let her hand rest on the wide scarlet linen sleeve of his cote-hardie. 'Please, Philip?' She gazed at him with limpid eyes.

'It is my wish that you stay.' Philip's hand rested heavily on hers and he toyed with her fingers, pressing each one hard until it hurt.

Felicia made no sign of discomfort. She knew he was warning her, but was also aware that it was best to show no pain. The longer he thought her amenable to all he said and did, there was a chance that one day he might slacken his guard over her. Was that why he had brought her here? He had left few men at his Leicestershire manor when he had departed unexpectedly three weeks earlier, and sooner or later her chance to escape their surveillance would have come. When she did not wince or remove her hand, Philip lifted her fingers to his lips and kissed each one.

'You will stay,' he said emphatically.

Felicia nodded, letting her hand lie a little longer in his before taking it away. She watched him as he drank. If he took enough, sleep would come, and she would be able to leave the hall.

No sooner had he emptied the cup than he beckoned the servant forward again. With a barely audible sigh, Felicia took it once more and gulped down enough of the wine to satisfy Philip. Over its rim her glance roamed the hall. So many men and so well armed, even here at the feast to celebrate her cousin's taking this castle. The drawbridge was up and men guarded the walls. Was he expecting trouble? She supposed he would be a fool not to anticipate some retaliation after slaughtering the household of the knight who had owned this manor. Sir Gervaise himself and his sons were also dead, so Philip had informed her. Still, they might have allies, and England simmered uneasily beneath Earl Simon de Montfort's rule.

Few believed that Henry III, and his son the Lord Edward, were kept so closely guarded purely for their own protection. Even Felicia had heard the rumours that Edward chafed beneath his uncle's restraint, and that many of the barons were growing restless of Earl Simon's dictates. Her cousin was for the Earl. His star had risen with the Montfort's, and he had grown powerful and rich in a land torn by conflict. Her father and brother had fought on the King's side at the Battle of Lewes, despite not having always agreed with Henry. Yet, having sworn fealty to the King, they had not been men to go back on their word.

Felicia felt the pain tighten in her head, and she wondered how much longer she would have to stay in the smoke and noise. Several tumblers had risen from their places at the far end, and one began to somersault up the centre between the tables. There was a ripple of taunting laughter as he slipped on the rushes scattered on the stone floor and he grinned self-consciously, gaining his balance, and other tumblers joined in. A juggler followed, and after him a minstrel in a red surcote over a yellow tunic, who approached the high table and began to sing a slow ballad. His voice was pleasant, not too deep but musically low, inducing relaxation. He played a mournful tune on his lute and sang a lament about Arthur and his final battle against Mordred. Felicia gave a yawn, and rubbed a hand across her eyes as his yellow-and-red-clad figure seemed to recede into the distance, only to appear nearer next time she looked. She would have to go to bed.

She turned to look at Philip slouched

against the cushions behind him, whose eyes were only slits as he gazed at the minstrel. She rose to her feet, thankful when Philip took no heed of her. The room seemed to tip sideways, and she had to cling to the arm of the chair. At last she managed to stand upright and, taking a shaky breath, walked to the rear of the hall and thence into the courtyard. She took deep draughts of air as she stood for a moment, and her head felt less confused. Then the mist that was clogging her thoughts descended again and she stumbled along the rear wall of the keep. She rounded a corner and neared the stone steps that led up to her bedchamber.

A shadow moved beyond the stairway, but Felicia did not pause, thinking it was her imagination. Her body felt as if it would float, and on reaching the bottom step, she tripped and slid. She lay there, thinking it best to wait a little while before attempting to climb to bed. Instantly the shadows seemed to merge into one oversized dark cloud, and all awareness fled.

A figure detached itself from the dark bulk of the keep, striding towards the hunched-up shape. The man stooped and slid his arms beneath Felicia and lifted her limp body against his chest. For a second, starlight gleamed dully on his tawny hair and then he moved back into the gloom. Conscious of the guards watching high on the outer walls, he melted swiftly into the darkness and began to retrace his steps to the rear of the keep. It had been easier than he had expected, and Meriet had not recognised him despite their brief encounter two weeks ago. When he came to the buttery, there was just space enough behind its walls and the outer walls to worm his way through. He raised a hand to protect Felicia's head as he stooped beneath a low branch, walking alongside the outer wall. At a postern gate, he slung her inert form over his shoulder, fumbling at his waist for the key. The door opened to reveal the river, and, stepping carefully, he walked halfway down the steps, which he had cleared of trailing weed the night before. Fortunately none of the guards watched in this direction, thinking themselves safe because of the river. He leapt.

He walked easily along the grassy path that followed the river bend. His horse whinnied as he approached and he hushed it, easing Felicia's quiescent body on to its back. The girl half lifted her head while he swung into the saddle behind her, and he put out a hand to steady her as she murmured and then slipped into unconsciousness again.

Only once did he turn and gaze back at the castle. Dawn was not so far off, and it was a good hour's steady riding to the charcoal-burner's hut in the forest.

Felicia groaned and turned over. Immediately she was aware of the hardness of the pallet beneath her. She screwed up her face in bewilderment, reaching for her covers and wondering why it was so stuffy in her bedchamber this morning. Her fingers grasped fur, and she caressed the edging of the cloak in surprise, then her fingertips scraped the earthen floor of the hut.

'I'm not in my bedchamber!' The words were forced from her as she lifted heavy lids and stared up at the smoke-darkened rafters, where hung a haunch of salted pork and several bunches of herbs and onions. She sat up abruptly, wincing and putting up hands to hold her head steady.

At a stir of movement to her right, she eased her head round carefully. A man sitting on a three-legged stool watched her. His eyes were grey; his brows, straight and thick, several shades darker than his tawny crop of hair. The jaw was firm with no sign of thickening, and his mouth was long-lipped. She guessed that he was some ten years older than she, and she would be eighteen at Martinmas in November. An attractive man, if the chill in his glance had not seemed to freeze her senses. Her heart gave a sudden lurch.

'Where am I? Who are you?' she croaked.

He did not speak, but rose and went out. Felicia glanced about her swiftly and at once regretted doing so. She shut her eyes again, trying to think—to reason why and how she had come to this place. Only when she felt the wooden rim of a cup against her chin did she realise that he had returned. She opened her eyes and summoned all her strength to grip the cup, managing to lift it to her lips. She drank the water slowly, not looking at him, setting her will not to be daunted by his silent presence. She drained the cup and handed it back to him.

'I would like some more,' Felicia demanded huskily.

'Later,' he said in an offhand manner. 'I wish to speak with you.'

'I do not feel like talking at this moment,' she murmured truthfully, giving a yawn. 'I have the headache.'

There was a short silence.

'I did not ask you to talk with me, Mistress Meriet. I said I wished to speak to you. The two are different.'

'How do you know me? Who are you? It—it was you who gave us the wine last night, wasn't it?' she muttered fretfully. 'You put something in it, didn't you? But why?' Fear twisted her stomach, and she felt sick.

'Ay! Poppy syrup. It was easy enough done.' His voice held a hint of derisiveness. 'Your cousin's men are not so careful for his safety as he would have them be. They were not choosy when it came to forcing peasants to leave their labour in the fields and to help in the preparing of his feast. He lost men also, it seems, when he killed by treachery those who gave him and his train hospitality.' His tone had deepened with anger by the time he finished speaking.

'But you are no peasant! Peasants would not behave in the way you have done. Are you one of Sir Gervaise de Vert's allies?'

'I am kin to him. My name is Edmund de Vert. Let that be sufficient answer.' He scowled.

'But why drug my wine, and why have you brought me to this hovel?' She eased herself into a sitting position, resting her back against the wattle and daub wall.

There were several long moments of silence while he stared at her, an impatient frown puckering his brow.

'At first I thought of killing your cousin. You must know of all that he has done to this manor? The pair of you are as close

21

as hand in glove, if the gossip is to be believed,' he sneered.

'Gossip? You speak in riddles, and still you do not tell me why you have brought me here. What have I done that warrants an abduction?' There was the barest hint of a tremor in her voice.

His expression was glacial. 'You are the one possession your cousin holds dear above all others. All the signs are there to be read.' He rose to his feet. 'I overheard his men talking as we prepared the feast. They say he intends to wed you.'

Felicia gasped, 'No!' despite her awareness that what he said was true even though Philip had never spoken his mind to her. But she was remembering Matilda's long scream, and her cousin's words afterwards. Still she said, 'You have read the signs wrong.'

'I have watched you together and seen how he fondles you. But only yesterday I heard that they reckon he murdered his wife and that you were there when it happened. Did you arrange it between you? You are young to be a murderess and a wanton! What are you—seventeen, eighteen summers?' He flung the words at her, his face hard set.

'They are wrong! You are mistaken!' Her words were but a thread of sound. 'The lady Matilda slipped.' Even as she spoke, some of her uncertainty and anguish showed on her face.

So the lady was not as innocent as she looked, Edmund thought savagely. Perhaps she had not struck the blow, but she knew something. 'Slipped?' His voice was contemptuous.

'I do not know.' Her voice was ragged and her head downcast. 'I had no proof. Now it is too late to do anything about her death.'

He did not hear the regret behind the words; to his ears, they seemed to be only an excuse.

'Too late for her, perhaps,' he rasped. 'Too late to fix guilt where it belongs. But it is not too late for him to regret all that he wrought on this manor.' He paused and took in a deep hissing breath. 'Your cousin raped my mother and caused her death. Also the deaths of—of the lord of this manor, Sir Gervaise de Vert, and of his sons John and Henry.'

Felicia glanced up swiftly, trying to say something, anything, but she could think of nothing. She was certain it was all true.

'There is no mistake,' he said swiftly, misinterpreting her glance. 'I was there. Three of Philip's men held me and knocked me senseless before they set fire to her house.' His voice was bleak, and only by the set of his jaw did she know of the rigid control he held over his anger. 'The blow almost killed me, as they intended. The fire was to make certain, I presume. Thank God they did not stay to see it burn to its end but left to wreak more mischief and destruction elsewhere. I woke to smoke and flames, but managed to get out of the house before it collapsed. Although God in his mercy saved my life, my mother, whom I dragged out with me, died in my arms two days later. All my skills were useless to save her. I buried her in the forest where we took shelter.'

His words caused a chill of apprehension to tauten Felicia's stomach. 'What has it to do with me?'

'Surely you know?' he said softly, giving her a calculating look. 'Revenge on your cousin.'

Felicia flushed suddenly, and she was aware of her vulnerability as she sat on the floor. She began to push herself up, her hands climbing the wall behind her slowly. He made no move to prevent her, smiling sardonically, the deep grooves in his cheeks deepening. Her fingers suddenly reached an obstruction, and raced tremblingly over a pot that hung on the wall. She lowered her eyes, swiftly praying that hope had not shown in her face. She had acted the part of a timid and submissive maid for months, for safety's sake. Twice she had resisted her cousin's advances when Matilda had been alive, had shown her repulsion for him. Almost he had lost his temper with her but for some reason had held back.

Perhaps it was his wife being alive? After Matilda's death, she had realised more than ever just how unstable and violent was Philip's nature. She had no desire to meet the same fate as Matilda, so had pretended to be that which she was not. Surely she could play the same game now?

Even though she expected him to move, Felicia jumped when he reached out and grabbed her about the waist. She drooped. It was not the first time she had been manhandled and she had no intention of provoking a swifter, perhaps more violent reaction in an unequal struggle. He had not hurt her, so far.

'They say revenge is sweet,' Edmund muttered. His lips nuzzled her ear. 'What better way of taking it than by possessing that which your enemy holds most dear?'

'You are mistaken,' she said in a shaky voice, looking up into his grim face. For a moment she wondered if she was imagining what was happening. Some remnant of the drug, perhaps, made her feel a little lightheaded. Then his mouth came down over hers—hard and slightly moist. A shiver passed through her. This was reality. Thanks to his actions she had escaped her cousin, but the price she was expected to pay for such freedom was too high. Rape! Apprehension curled in her stomach. He might have just cause for wanting revenge, but she was no common whore to be treated in such a way, and he seemed insensitive to anything she said. To ask his help to get to Meriet was laughable, and he would treat any request as such. Only her own wits would gain her freedom.

Her lips trembled before yielding to his, causing him to lift his head and look at her. Her eyes were shut, dark thick lashes washing the upper curve of her flushed cheeks. Despite what he had heard, he had expected her to struggle in his arms. Experimentally he kissed her again. She smelt deliciously of lavender, and her body was soft and warm. His hands moved upward in a slow caress and his fingers sought the fastenings of her gown.

She jumped violently as he undid the first one, and he stopped. Not so quiescent, after all! The unbidden thought surfaced in his mind ... What if the rumours were not true? Suddenly he could almost hear his mother's screams of protest, and his breathing quickened, his fingers curling against Felicia's breasts.

She was aware of his distraction and at a loss what to do. Was this the moment when he would move her away from the wall to the floor? She would have no defence then, so she acted in the only way she could think of to hold his attention; deliberately she pressed her body against his. She shivered as he let out a scornful laugh, hating him in that moment for thinking she was so acquiescent, but she responded to his kiss, not resisting as he tugged several more of the fastenings undone. As he began to nuzzle her throat, she opened her eyes, slightly shaken. The unwelcome thought that here was the man who could have ... remained unfinished, swiftly quashed. He wanted to use her for his own ends as surely as Philip did, and she would be better rid of both of them. She swiftly lifted the pot from the wall, and before Edmund could realise what she was about, brought it down on the side of his head.

When he let out a groan and slowly crumpled to the floor, Felicia was completely taken aback, not expecting him to collapse so instantaneously—if at all. She hesitated, then realising that now was not the time for second thoughts, for surely he would be even more angry when he woke, she dragged her skirts free from his outflung arms and made for the door.

It opened quickly to her fumbling touch, and she tossed a thankful prayer heavenwards as she came out into a sunlight that winked and flickered through the golden-green foliage of massive trees. She sent a jerky glance round at the oaks and hornbeams that seemed to march on and on, with no end in sight. Which way? She must go swiftly before Edmund regained his senses. Not towards the castle: any place, rather than back to her cousin. There was no sound of huntsmen or forester to guide her, no sign of peasants coming to gather kindling for their cooking-fires. Even the birds did not sing here. Where was she? How deep in this forest?

Her eyes fixed on some shadows beneath the trees. Because of the sun's brightness she had not seen the animals at first, and raced over to where they cropped the grass. Her legs were shaky, and her heart was jerking in her breast. There were two horses: one, a chestnut, a lovely beast; the other dun coloured. She spoke soft words as she approached them. The chestnut backed away, snorting, and without hesitation she turned to the other. Her breath was jagged as she heard the sound of scraping feet coming from the cottage, and with a determined hand she grasped the horse's mane and dragged herself up.

Edmund caught but a brief glimpse of shapely white legs as he stumbled out of the hut, and then she was gone into the cover of the trees. He wiped the back of his hands across his cheek, where blood trickled. A bitter smile twisted his lean face. She had tricked him properly! He whistled, and the chestnut lifted its head and came trotting to him. His head was still muzzy from Felicia's blow, which had landed on the still sore wound inflicted by Philip's men two weeks back. Swinging himself into the saddle, he urged his horse across the clearing.

Felicia found it difficult at first to prod her mount into anything more than a steady trot, however hard she dug in her heels. God only knew where the horse would take her. She glanced about her, searchingly, fearfully, knowing herself completely lost. Here and there the summer sunshine reached down, lighting bluebells, now fading from their blue intensity. As a low-hanging branch loomed in front of her, she ducked, swaying slightly, fastening up her gown. Her cheeks burned as she remembered how he had touched her.

Hoofbeats sounded behind, and she urged the horse on. The man was not going to take her against her will without a mighty effort. Her days of being meek

29

and mild were over! The ground began to flash past more swiftly, as, heedless of the danger, she whacked the horse on its flank. Branches caught at her veil and greening brambles snatched and rasped her skirts. The trees seemed to go on endlessly, and she heard the clear piping of a blackbird near at hand. Then more birdsong, and the snuffling of swine as they delved for food. The trees began to thin out. Felicia's heart lifted. She was safe. Safe from her abductor, and from her cousin Philip.

Blinking in the bright sunshine, she saw ahead the waste and pasture where cows grazed under the watch of a cowherd. A village huddled not far from a river. Approaching across the waste were a handful of men and, beyond them, the towering grey-white walls of a castle. Frantically she tried to wheel about as the men in red livery with a black saker hawk clearly displayed on their surcoats fanned out so as to cut her off. A sob rose in her throat when a mailed fist snatched at her horse's mane. Before she could utter a word of protest, she was surrounded by her cousin's men. Her mount had returned to its home village.

Edmund brought his horse, snorting and blowing, to a hasty standstill amid the trees. He saw Felicia being surrounded, and knew in that moment that the wiser course would have been to lose himself in the forest. She would tell them what had happened to her at his hands, and they would come searching. Still he did not move, trusting to his greater knowledge of the manor to deal with that eventuality should it arise. He was surprised when the whole group of men gathered and took her back towards the castle. His brow puckered and he ran a thoughtful hand across his stubbly chin. Once more the lady had surprised him! He dismounted and took some salve from his saddlebag to deal with the cut on his head. His eyes never moved from the men going towards the castle, as he wanted to be sure where they were taking Felicia. Come nightfall, he planned to enter the castle grounds again.

The spidery shapes of watchmen took form as Felicia and her escort approached the castle walls. The drawbridge was down over the water-filled ditch. Cold despair, heavy as iron, weighed on her spirits, and apprehension tensed her muscles. Yet she held her head high, seeming, to the men who surrounded her, to be unaware that she was her cousin's prisoner once more. She clattered ahead of them over the drawbridge and on beneath the stone archway of the gatehouse, ignoring their presence. Unaided, and without waiting for them, she dismounted, giving the horse into the hands of a young groom, who stood gaping at her.

'See to him,' she called briefly before moving slowly in the direction of her bedchamber. The courtyard was busier than any courtyard should be at that hour in the morning and she gazed in bewilderment at what was going on. Men were dragging lances and shields from the store beneath her room. The air was filled with shouts and the rumble of wheels as sacks of flour and haunches of meat were loaded into carts. As she ran a hand jerkily down one of her braids, her spirits rose slightly. It seemed that her cousin was on the move again. She forced a path between the bustling men towards the stair that led to her chamber, intending to change her clothes before she confronted Philip. Reaching the foot of the steps, she bunched her skirts in one hand and ran up, wondering how much grace she would be allowed before he demanded her presence in the hall. By the time she had pushed open the heavy wooden door, her breath was uneven. She stepped over the threshold, and came to a halt.

'Well met, coz!' The figure in the blue linen surcote dropped the scroll he had been reading on to the chest at the foot of the bed.

Felicia stared at him, and the room seemed to swirl, causing her to put out a hand to the door jamb to steady herself. It was quiet, after the noise in the courtyard. At last she moved slowly forward, her gaze not leaving Philip's face, waiting for him to pounce.

He stretched out a hand and plucked a leaf from her veil. His eyes glittered as he spoke. 'Where have you been? Not romping in the hay?' His voice was silky.

'Hardly—not as early as this, Philip.' Felicia forced down her fear. She least trusted her cousin when he was at his most amiable. 'Haymaking is not until the end of June—as you would know if you spent more time on your manors!' She made to go out again, but he grabbed her sleeve and jerked her to a halt.

'I said, where have you been? Do not play games with me. Your bed has not been slept in, nor were you to be found anywhere in this castle or its grounds this morning.'

Felicia remained silent. His nails bit into her skin through the fabric of her sleeve. She was uncertain whether the truth would perhaps serve her best. Fleetingly she recalled what the man had said about her cousin, and the expression on his face when he spoke of his mother's rape and death. Then, without fully understanding why she did so, she lied.

'I have been somewhat anxious about my complexion lately,' she murmured, a bland smile upon her smooth oval face. 'I rose early, wanting to wash in the dew. You know, Philip, it does not have the same magical powers later in the year. So, you see ...' Her voice faltered as his eyes gleamed wrathfully. His jowls were just beginning to thicken and there were pouches beneath his eyes. How had she ever thought he was handsome? Or ever been in love with him? The memory of a lean face and compelling grey eyes flickered in her mind even as Philip's fingers tightened on her arm.

'You lie! You have a lover, haven't you?' Felicia caught her breath as his fingers pinched her flesh cruelly. 'I left you too long alone after Matilda's death, answering Montfort's bidding.' He shook her violently.

'I do not!' she shouted. 'You are hurting me, Philip!' She stamped her foot. 'I am not a serf to be treated so,' she added in a furious undertone, her control snapping.

'Why, you bitch!' His mouth twisted unpleasantly, and he slammed her in the face with his fist.

Felicia fell back against the chest,

stunned. The taste of blood was in her mouth and her ears were singing. She stared at him in disbelief. In the past she had tolerated his advances, sensing it was better to do so. She had heard much about his cruelties, but never had he hit her so hard before. Squeezed and pressed as though he were playing some game with her, but never this. She now realised that her danger was very real at his hands.

'I shall treat you in any way I wish,' he declared, leaning over her, his hands clamping on her shoulders. 'Your father and brother can no longer protect you. Always I regretted Mark being born, and I was glad when your mother and her baby died.' He laughed unexpectedly. 'Did you know, dear coz, I grew up with Meriet's praises sung in my ears? My father loved the place. Now it is yours, and I would have it.' His hand slid up to her throat, and tightened. 'I would wed you, dear coz.' His voice was almost gentle.

'That is impossible,' gasped Felicia. 'For cousins to marry is against the law and the teachings of the church.'

'So it is,' Philip frowned slightly. 'But there are always those who are willing to go against such laws—for money or for advancement.'

'No!' she cried, attempting to pull herself from his grasp.

'No?' His grip tightened. 'You were willing to belong to me once, sweet coz, yet you showed no sign then of the woman you are now. A pity.' He bit her neck. 'Now tell me,' he murmured, 'where is this lover who has followed you here?'

'There is no lover.' She choked as his fingers clamped round her throat, trying to stare at him steadily. Her throat hurt, her face throbbed, and her lip stung. 'How I hate you!'

Slowly, surprisingly, he loosened his grip. His eyelid twitched several times and absently he lifted a hand and rubbed it, before releasing her. 'At last the gloves are off!' he laughed. 'I thought there was more to you than the insipid maid you have appeared to be these last few months. I still remember how you returned my kisses.'

'That was a long time ago.' She coughed, easing her throat. 'I was but a child who had listened to tales of romance and brave deeds performed by knights. I did not know you for what you are. My brother Mark soon disillusioned me, telling of your whoring and cruelties on your manors.'

'Dear Mark! But he is dead, and so is your father. You would be wiser if you did not make me angry.' His dark brows furrowed. 'Learn well, and I think we could deal well together, sweet coz. They say hate is akin to love. You were in love with me once. I shall make you love me again. I mean to have you, and I must make sure of you before I leave this place.'

'Leave?' Felicia's eyes flew wide.

'Do not look so pleased, Felicia. I shall definitely have to make sure of you before I go to Worcester. Earl Simon has sent for me, but I will make time for you.'

'What do you mean?' Her throat was suddenly dry.

Philip moved more swiftly than she could think—or dodge his groping hands. He forced her backwards until the wooden frame of the bed pressed against her hips. She gave a cry as he suddenly released her, causing her to overbalance and fall on the bed. For a moment she was paralysed, watching as he approached, but as he took hold of her skirt she kicked out at him, only to have him grasp her ankles, pressing her feet down. He knelt on them, before stretching himself out on her.

Searing panic seized her. She twisted her face away from him, gritting her teeth as he bit her neck and fondled her. She could smell his over-sweet perfume, and his sweat.

'Relax, coz,' he whispered against her cheek.

'I hate you, and I would rather die than submit to your will,' she said stonily. 'You are a beast that you would force yourself on me.'

'A beast?' He shifted his bulk and stared down at her. 'You would be wiser keeping your mouth shut, coz. Any other maid I would not have delayed so long in the taking—but, believe me, I have feelings for you that at times cause me pain. I do not really want to hurt you.'

'I find that hard to believe.' She looked up at him, her eyes hard blue.

'It surprises me, too.' He laughed, and unexpectedly rose from the bed. 'To show you that I am not the beast you think, coz, I shall not take you swiftly like the beasts in the field, but shall woo you this night. Montfort can wait a few hours more.'

She made no answer, but rolled off the bed and got to her feet. She met his gaze as she smoothed down her skirts.

'Prepare yourself for me,' Philip said with a sudden frown. 'I shall soon banish the thought of any other lover from your mind. I shall bed you tonight, and wed you on my return. If you fight me, that will make it only more exciting for me, coz—but painful for you.' He turned and went out of the room, taking the key and locking the door from the outside.

CHAPTER TWO

Felicia stared at the door. She felt as though in some nightmare. Her limbs were without form, filled with black ice, unable to move. The thump of Philip's feet receded down the stone steps, and they seemed to come from a great distance. At last she stirred, reaching for the cloth in the pouch hanging from her girdle, and dabbed at her cheek and mouth, staring as a crimson stain spread on the linen. She sank slowly on the bed and gazed unseeingly up at the ceiling. Slowly her thoughts began to take shape; they whirled frantically in her head, searching for a way out of her predicament.

Why had Philip not killed her as he had Matilda? He would have inherited Meriet then. Could there be any truth in his words? Did he care for her—was that what he meant by having feelings for her? At least she knew now why he had killed Matilda. He wanted Meriet—and her! Tentatively she felt her cut cheek, and fear clutched at her stomach. Why could she not have run the other way from the hovel in the forest! For a moment she thought of the man she had run from and wondered where he had gone when she had been taken. Fled, most likely—yet he did not look the sort of man who would shrink from danger. How had he got her out of the castle? She began frantically to think—to seek some way out of her terrifying situation—but she had little hope.

Shadows, like grey veils, gathered in the corners of the room. Only the light penetrating the narrow window opening enabled her to see the sewing she worked at to take her mind off the fearsome thoughts that plagued her. It was quiet outside, except for the occasional call from a guard on the walls. She had changed into a yellow silk undergown with long sleeves and a high neck, over which she wore a dark brown linen surcote. About her throat she had fastened a long veil that also covered her head. As she pulled the thread through the fabric, she took deep steadying breaths.

The sound of heavy feet on the steps brought her heart into her mouth. Her fingers trembled as she stabbed the needle deep into the cloth before putting it aside, and her fingers slid down the riband on her girdle. Swiftly she cut off the scissors that hung there and slipped them up her sleeve. Men's voices sounded outside.

'I do not wish to be disturbed. Tell the men to pay no heed to any noise from this chamber.' There was a harsh laugh from her cousin.

Feet clattered down the steps as a key grated in the lock, then the door crashed against the wall. Her cousin stood swaying slightly in the doorway, his bulk a deeper blue shadow against the darkening sky. He lurched into the room and pushed the door to clumsily. It did not quite shut.

'Here I am, coz!' The words were slurred as he staggered towards her.

Felicia did not reply. She slid the scissors carefully into her palm, surprised that her cousin was so drunk.

'Would it not be best to wait, Philip?' Her voice quivered. 'If you gave me more time, I might be willing to do what you wish.' She pressed herself against the wall furthest from the bed and slid along it away from him. There was a slight flurry of cool air against her ankles as her skirts fluttered.

'Liar!' he muttered. 'Do—Do you think you can dissuade me?' Philip's bulk was threatening as he followed her. He lunged, and caught hold of a fold of her skirts, and his arm held her waist. Twisting, she lifted the scissors and thrust them down into his arm.

Philip let out a screech that seemed to

hit the stone walls as Felicia tore herself from his grasp. Without hesitating, she flew across the room and out of the door. He stumbled after her, clutching his arm, but she was too quick. Out she went, pulling the door shut and turning the key before he could reach it.

Felicia fled down the steps, barely seeming to touch the stone. Without pausing at the bottom, she darted into the shadow of the keep and stood there, her heart pounding, listening to Philip hammering on the door and cursing her. She glanced up at the walls and saw men's head turn but they made no move to go and see what the noise was about. She realised why, and sagged against the wall, laughing silently, her hand against her mouth. She laughed until the tears ran down her cheeks. How long she stayed there like that she did not know, but at last the storm of tears and laughter ceased. She stood thinking.

Earlier, there had come into her mind a blurred vision of a darkened river. Had Edmund taken her out of the castle that way? Was there a door in the wall in the direction of the river? Perhaps she could find it if she were left undiscovered long enough. How soon would her cousin give up knocking at the door—perhaps he would bleed to death, or at least fall into a stupor. He seemed as drunk as he had been the night before, but that had been the drug. Maybe his slow reaction recently was because he had finished off the drugged wine. She smiled to herself and began to creep along the keep wall, glad that there was no moon. When she turned the corner and neared the buttery, the rear door in the keep suddenly opened, and before she could step back a man came out. She tensed, praying that he would not see her.

'Hurry up with that ale, Ned!' A tousled dark head peeped out of the doorway, and an arm holding a rushlight.

'I'm doing my best, Peter. Hold that light a little higher. It's dark out here.'

The blood pounded in Felicia's ears as the man held up the light, and she shrank against the wall. The movement was only slight, but it was enough to send the light fluttering as the man turned in her direction.

'What was that? I thought I saw summat.'

The man called Ned turned, swinging the pitcher he carried.

'Hold that light a bit further this way. I thought I saw ... There, I saw it again! Quick!'

Felicia darted away as he made a grab for her, but Peter had already sprung forward. He grasped her shoulder.

'Let me go!' she hissed, spinning round and holding aloft the scissors.

He stepped back hurriedly. 'Now take it easy, Mistress. I don't mean you any harm.' He held up his arms as though to ward her off, and glanced quickly at his mate. 'Weren't you saying this one was a witch, Ned?' he muttered. He crossed himself swiftly and made a circle with his finger and thumb.

'Dunno,' said Ned uneasily. 'She might have got out of this pile, last night, but she was captured easily enough this morn. But what's she doing here? I thought the master was ... You know.' He lunged forward suddenly as Felicia turned her head in her effort to keep her eye on both men.

Ned grabbed her wrist and twisted it until she dropped the scissors. 'We'll have a reward for this, Peter,' he laughed, pinning Felicia's arms behind her back. 'Don't know how she escaped him, but ...'

'I beg you,' she pleaded, struggling to no avail. 'Let me go. I could reward you if you helped me to escape.'

' 'Twould be more than our lives were worth,' he growled. 'Peter, you'll have to get the ale. I shouldn't be too long.'

'Very well.' He took the pitcher and turned towards the buttery. But as he reached the building a black figure sprang out of its shadows and, before Peter could do anything, he was sent sprawling to the ground.

'Hell!' Ned whirled Felicia about, trying frantically to tug the dagger from his belt. Suddenly he let her go and pushed her at the figure coming towards them. She collided into the man, who grabbed her as they both went stumbling backwards.

Edmund let out a hiss of breath and managed to regain his footing, then he spun Felicia round and put her behind him. He did not know what she was doing out here by the buttery, but she was obviously attempting to free herself from the man. He pulled out his sword and swept it in a glittering arc in front of him.

Ned stepped back in surprise, and his dagger clattered to the ground. He turned and ran, shouting as he did so.

'Damn!' Edward grabbed Felicia's hand, dragging her with him. The other man was just getting to his feet, nursing his jaw. Edmund slowed, then kicked him in the stomach, sending him sprawling back against the buttery door. Felicia was pulled, resisting, behind the buttery, and Edmund turned to face her. They could barely see each other's faces.

'Don't have second thoughts now, Mistress Meriet! I value my life too highly.' His fingers tightened about her hand and he hauled her on into the darkness.

She went without a struggle, knowing she had no choice. The fingers of her free hand touched coarse stone as she stumbled through the long grass against the outer wall. A tree loomed up in front of them, its foliage wide-spreading and black against the sky. Then she was pulled into a space so narrow that she could barely squeeze through. There was wood beneath her hand, a key turned, and then came the slight click as a latch was lifted. The door opened silently, and now she felt cool air and could see the faint glow of a luminous darkness. Urged on by Edmund, she stepped out, while he locked the gate behind them. She gazed down at the glitter of stars on the river and had a brief flash of recall. It was he—as she had thought!

Edmund gave Felicia no time to speak, but dragged her down the steps. From the distance came the faint sound of men shouting. Before she realised what he was about, she felt a brief painful tug on her arm as he leapt from the steps, then his hands slid about her waist and he swung her down beside him. He began to run, pulling her along, and she kept up with him as best she could, often slipping or stumbling. But always he managed to keep her on her feet by the iron-like firmness of his wrist. At last, when the breath was burning in her chest, they came to where she could see a horse outlined against the sky.

'Up with you!' he commanded, his eyes gleaming brightly.

Felicia hesitated, looking up at him, remembering. 'I do not want to go with you,' she said breathlessly. 'I am grateful that you rescued me from those men, but our paths part here, Master de Vert.' She attempted to tug her hand from his grasp.

'Don't be foolish!' he rasped. 'What do you think I was doing within the castle walls but looking for you? You will pay for that blow you dealt me, Mistress Meriet.' His fingers tightened about her waist. 'Now, up with you.'

'Let me go!' she panted, struggling in his hold. 'I will not go with you.'

He paid no heed, but lifted her and flung her on to the horse. Before she had a chance even to raise her head, he was in the saddle, his hand pressing firmly on the middle of her back. When the horse began to move, she had to cling to the skirt of Edmund's surcote. The breeze that rippled the grass caught her veil, fluttering it out like some giant moth. She attempted to smooth it down, but was forced to abandon her efforts and renew her hold on his surcote. The ground flashed beneath her and she shut her eyes swiftly, her heart in her throat, having visions of falling. But the hand on her back grasped the fabric of her gown more firmly when she thought herself most likely to slip off. They came to the forest.

Felicia wriggled, lifting her head as the horse slowed its pace. 'Where are you taking me?' she gasped.

'Does it matter?' he mocked, holding her more tightly. 'The outcome will be the same.'

'At least let me sit up!' she cried. 'I—I feel sick!' The pressure on her spine lifted, but he still held her as she carefully eased herself upright. Immediately his arm went round her, causing her to stiffen. Anger stirred within her. It seemed that she had exchanged one form of captivity for another.

The horse walked on, and her nerves tightened as they entered the dark confines of the forest. An owl hooted. Never had she been in the forest at night before. All the tales of hobgoblins, demons, wolves and witches that her nurse had told her long years ago were vividly real in her mind. Trees swayed and creaked overhead; the undergrowth rustled and shifted. She gasped as she caught the gleam of eyes in a tangle of leaves, and shrank against Edmund. He, at least, was flesh and blood. She shut her eyes tightly and weariness swamped her, yet she remained rigidly upright and wide awake as they went on further into the forest.

A lavender-scented curl tickled Edmund's chin and brought him out of his reverie. While they had been out in the open he had given Felicia only scant thought: all his concentration had been on getting under cover, for at any moment he expected the drawbridge to rattle down and to hear the thunder of hooves. It had not happened, and now he relaxed; instantly he was aware of the girl. Against all his inclinations, his senses were stirred. Her head rested under his chin. How stiff and silent she was. Incredibly, he felt like laughing, having expected her, now that they had seemingly escaped, to try to persuade him by any means within her power that she was innocent of all that he had said about her and her cousin, and to make excuses for having hit him that morning. Perhaps she would do so when they reached the cottage. It was not much further now.

It was black as pitch inside when Edmund pushed open the door and, with a mocking bow, bade Felicia enter. She walked in slowly, her hands clasped tightly against her chest. The room brightened as he lifted the iron-domed cover from the fire. When he held a rushlight to its smouldering embers, the light caught and flared, lighting the room even more. The smell of rancid mutton-fat came faintly to her as he set the light on the table.

'Sit down, Mistress Meriet.' His eyes gleamed in the flickering light, which darkened the hollows beneath his cheek-bones.

'I do not wish to sit down.' Her voice quivered.

He moved towards her, and all Felicia's former trepidation rose, causing her to sink swiftly on to a stool. He brought his own close to hers, and their knees touched. She lowered her gaze, conscious of his eyes upon her mouth.

'Look at me,' he ordered, putting a hand to her chin. She tried to pull away, but his fingers were insistent. He scrutinised her face and then touched her cheek gently; he was infinitely more tender than she would have thought possible. Even so, she winced. 'Who did this to you? It wasn't those men?'

Felicia shook her head, surprised at the hint of anger in his voice. His hand ranged the full extent of the blow her cousin had dealt, then the tip of one finger ran gently over her swollen lips. Her mouth quivered slightly. She found that sensitive touch, even though it hurt, evocative.

'Who, then?' He released her chin and went over to the door, picking up the saddlebag he had dropped when entering.

'My cousin Philip,' she replied unsteadily.

He frowned down at her and pushed back his coif, revealing his untidy mass of tawny hair. He seemed less forbidding thus. Again he seated himself close to her, in his hand a small jar. 'Why do you suffer him to treat you so?' he grunted, taking off its top.

'I had little choice,' she replied tersely. 'Just as I had little choice when you abducted me after drugging the wine.' She toyed with her fingers, looking down at them.

'That was different.'

Before Felicia could resist, he took her chin again and raised her face, so that she had to look up into his eyes. She found the experience unnerving.

'How is it different?' she asked in a stiff voice.

He began to smooth salve on her cheek. 'I did not hurt you. All I did was to ...' Before Felicia could draw back, he brushed her swollen lips gently with his own.

She stiffened instantly. The gentleness of the caress filled her with confusion and uncertainty. Without realising she had done so, she had begun to relax, but now she was on her guard again.

'Your intentions were not to stop at a kiss, Master de Vert!'

'You were not averse to my kisses, Mistress Meriet. Or so it seemed to me.' His mouth twisted sardonically. Slowly he trailed salve across her lips, watching the flush that rose to her cheeks. 'Does your cousin stop at kisses?' he murmured, straightening up.

Felicia gave an angry gasp. 'I suffered your embraces, Master de Vert, thinking it the only way to lull you off your guard! And it worked!'

'So it did.' He touched the sore spot on his head. 'But it would not have, if your cousin's men had not hit me so hard.'

'Then the saints were on my side, Master de Vert.' She raised her chin. 'I am not to blame for what my cousin did to you, or to your mother, although I am sorry for—for what happened.'

'Sorry?' Edmund was suddenly angry. 'Who are you, Mistress Meriet, to think that the saints are on your side? A whore and a murderess, that is what they say about you in your cousin's household!'

'It is not true!' Felicia sprang to her feet

and glared at him, angry tears filled her eyes. 'It—is—not—true!'

'Isn't it?' He rose to his feet slowly. There was a long silence.

'What are you going to do with me?' she asked brusquely, lacing her fingers.

'At this moment I do not wish to do anything with you, Mistress Meriet.' He turned and rammed the jar back into his saddlebag. 'At this moment I am hungry and wish to eat. Are you not hungry?'

Felicia did not answer, surprised by his words. She watched him lift the blackened cooking-pot over the fire. Her nerves were taut, and she wondered how long he was going to play the waiting game. Perhaps his aim was to make her more amenable to his advances. She sat down again, determined to make him see that what he planned was just as wrong as what Philip had done to his mother.

'Would your mother, whom you seem to have cared much about, have wished you to seek revenge in such a way, Master de Vert?'

The directness of her question made him still as he took bread from a crock. Setting it on a platter, he began to cut it with the knife from his girdle. He stared at her, but did not reply. Since seeing her face, his previous plans had been overturned at the sight of the bruising and cuts on a countenance that had been beautiful that morning.

Felicia let out an infuriated sigh. 'I am innocent of all the blood that my cousin has spilt on this manor!' she cried, her hands clutching the edge of the table. 'Why do you think I was struggling with that man? I was fleeing my cousin's attentions.' She paused, drawing a shaky breath. 'He wants Meriet, the manor that came to me only after the Battle of Lewes last year.'

'You talk of innocence, and my mother—do you not consider her innocent? I came from Chester, having not seen her for many months, but was too late to save her from your cousin's attentions. I deemed her safe, despite the uneasiness of the times, because my—my lord Gervaise had her welfare much at heart. I never thought to encounter such treachery or cruelty as that dealt out by your cousin!' He rammed the knife, point down, into the table with such violence that Felicia jumped back.

'Why do you not vent your anger upon Philip? It is he who is the guilty one.' Her blue eyes flashed. 'Soon it will be too late for you to do anything to him, for he has orders from Earl Simon de Montfort to go to Worcester. God willing, he will have little thought to spare for me. A quick search of this manor, perhaps, and then he will be on his way. When Earl Simon calls, Philip goes. You know the way into the castle,' she said rapidly. 'Surely you could get in again? You could drug him and have him brought to justice!' Her face was hard, and her fingers tightened once again on the table. 'You seem to know much about potions and lotions.' She smiled derisively.

'You talk foolishly!' He pushed the platter across the table, and went over to a far corner of the room, bringing back a flask and two horns. 'Even if it were possible, I have other plans.' His brow furrowed. 'Think, my fine lady. The castle would be no safe place now to try and gain entry. It will be teeming with men in search of us and our way out.' He paused and took a gulp of ale, meeting her gaze and trying to work out if she disliked her cousin as much as she claimed. It was not unusual for lovers to fall out. 'Besides, if I had wanted to deal with your cousin in such a way, I could have done so. By taking you instead, I sought to make your cousin suffer.' His voice was bitter, and his brow had darkened.

'Suffer? You think my cousin will suffer because I am missing?' Felicia threw back her head and laughed, albeit a mite hysterically.

'You think not?' His voice was quiet. 'They say he killed to have you.'

'Have me? Ay!' The laughter died in her face, and tears glistened in her eyes. Suddenly it was all so unreal, talking to this man she barely knew, and who planned revenge. She looked down into the liquid gleaming in the flask on the table and poured ale into a horn. Since morning she had gone thirsty. There was no point in affirming her innocence. Let him think what he liked, this—abductor! She did not care.

Edmund moved abruptly. He had expected her to deny again her involvement in the death of Philip Meriet's wife, and was irritated that she had not done so. Taking a cloth, he removed the pot from the fire, setting bowls on the table, and spooning out the hash of peas, barley and onions.

'Eat!' he commanded, holding out a wooden spoon.

She looked up then. Her shoulders sagged wearily, and the bruise showed vividly on her face beneath its smear of salve.

'I'm not hungry.' She took another gulp of ale.

'I said—eat!' He took her hand and pressed the spoon into it. 'We have a journey before us on the morrow, and there will be no hot food on the way.' He sat down opposite and took up his own spoon.

Felicia looked at him. So they were not staying here, after all. Her spirits rose slightly, and she dipped her spoon into the food. He hardly seemed aware of her now.

'We go south,' he said roughly, breaking bread and mopping his bowl with it.

'South? Not to Chester?'

'Didn't I say so? Drink up, Mistress Meriet. There will be no more ale after this, and who knows it might help you to sleep ... although I have not drugged it.' There was a hint of mockery in the softly-spoken words.

She flushed, wondering if his intent was to get her drunk so that she would not resist him. Yet surely he knew that she could offer little resistance this night, being completely in his power. Why were they to go south? She picked up the horn, tossing off the rest of the ale. Already her pain seemed less, but her fear was not.

Edmund studied her. When he had first heard of the lady Felicia Meriet she had been but a name behind which stood a shadowy figure, a voluptuous wanton with hard eyes and a cruel mouth, who had planned the death of his wife with the bestial man she had given herself to. She had in no way resembled the girl in front of him. As he stared at her, she blinked drowsily back at him. God's bones! he thought. She looks so vulnerable: like a

57

kitten rescued after being half drowned.

'You can sleep on the pallet in the corner,' he muttered, putting down his horn. 'There are some blankets in the chest.'

Felicia did not move. Surely she had misunderstood him? She stared at him bemused.

'Well?' he rapped in a harsh voice. 'Go and rest. I shall wake you just before dawn.'

'What?' Felicia rose in one swift movement, relief showing in her beautiful eyes. 'You ... You aren't ...' She halted, unable to go on. The colour rose in her face as their eyes held.

'Go to bed, Mistress Meriet.' Edmund rubbed a tired hand over his face. 'You will be perfectly safe this night.'

Felicia could think of nothing to say, so she turned and walked slowly towards the chest he had indicated. She lifted the lid, pulled out a blanket and wrapped it carefully about her before going to the pallet to lie down. She watched him replace the cover over the fire and blow out the light. For a moment her heart quickened its beat as she heard his stool creak, but he did not come over to her. Slowly she relaxed, and before she could ponder long over the change of heart in her captor, she was asleep.

CHAPTER THREE

Felicia groaned and would have turned over, but whoever was gripping her insisted that she woke, and she sat up. Shivering, she lifted heavy lids and was immediately aware of her surroundings. It was cold in the hut with the chill of early dawn.

'Come! We must go now. If we wait any longer, we risk being caught by Philip's men.' Ruthlessly Edmund pulled the blanket from her and pulled her to her feet. 'My horse cannot travel so swiftly with two of us on its back, so we must go by ways unknown to your cousin.'

Felicia could barely see his face in the dim light that penetrated the opening in the thatch. She yawned by way of reply.

'Here!' He pulled her by the hand over to the doorway and pointed to the pail of cold water. 'Rinse your face, and you will soon wake up.'

She hesitated, and then seeing his look of impatience, took a deep breath and plunged her hands into the water and splashed her face. She gasped, but repeated the action before taking the cloth he held out. Quickly she rubbed it over her face before handing it back. He put it in his saddlebag.

'Let us go. I thought I heard movement outside earlier on, but when I went to look, it was only my horse stirring. It could have been someone spying on us from the village. Not everyone there regrets that Sir Gervaise de Vert has been replaced by your cousin.'

He swung the saddlebag over his shoulder and, turning the key in the door, pulled it open. He went out before her, scanning the clearing before beckoning her out. In no time at all he had lifted her on to his horse. This time, it seemed, he planned for her to ride pillion, although there was no proper pillion seat, only a small firm cushion. Felicia grimaced. It was not what she was accustomed to, but she was not going to complain. She was certain he would not care about her comfort. He swung himself up in front of her and urged his mount across the clearing in a different direction from that they had taken the day before.

The forest seemed to have no end, and the sun had risen high before they reached its limits. She wondered again why they were going south and where their destination was, but did not ask him. Surprisingly, this morning she was no longer so anxious, accepting that she had no choice but to go with him. At the back of her mind was the hope that she might have the chance to gain her own manor of Meriet, which lay to the south-east, between Shrewsbury and Ludlow.

They travelled on, seeing no one, which was fortunate since they were poorly armed to defend themselves against outlaws, or worse. The thought that Philip might still discover them had not completely disappeared from Felicia's mind. She glanced about her, gripping more tightly the straps that fastened Edmund's cloak. The horse climbed a steep hill that ran alongside a deep narrow valley, picking its way delicately until it reached the crest, where they paused. The lowlands of Shropshire could clearly be seen and, in the distance, water. A breeze rippled the grass and the tops of the trees. The sky had clouded over after a brilliant start to the day.

Edmund clicked his tongue and flicked the reins. The horse began to edge its way through scrub and scree down a barely discernible path. Trees grew thickly on either side of them, and their way seemed often to lie in deep shadow. Felicia found herself thinking that there was something sinister about the place, or was it only that the sun had once more disappeared behind thickening cloud? She shivered as a chill wind blew.

'If you are cold, unfasten the cloak and put it about you.'

She was surprised that her captor had even noticed her reaction to the change in the weather, but did as he suggested and began to unbuckle the straps that held the cloak.

Suddenly there came an unexpected snarling that seemed to rumble on without pause, and her heart leapt. She had heard the sound only once before, and it had cost her the life of a favourite hunting-dog. As the horse reared, she snatched desperately at a fold of the cloak and began to slide backwards while Edmund fought for control of the panic-stricken animal. Then she saw the wolf.

It crouched over a dead hare, and its rough grey-black fur stood up about its neck. Its ears were pricked, and its lips were pulled back in a grimace that showed yellow fangs.

Felicia slid forward again, jolting hard against Edmund's back as he brought the horse down and hard over to the right. It pranced nervously, tossing its head and whinnying. She shut her eyes and sent a prayer winging to the heavens. As she waited for the wolf to leap, she heard the rasp of metal as Edmund unsheathed his sword. She opened her eyes again.

The wolf made a sudden movement towards them, and leapt. Edmund twisted in the saddle and, driving hard down with all his strength, thrust the sword into one of the wolf's eyes. The impact sent a shudder through not only him, but the horse and Felicia. Even as the noise of the wolf's distress rasped in its throat, Edmund rammed the blow home more deeply. The wolf flipped back, and he tugged out his sword. Felicia had no opportunity to see what happened to the wolf, for the horse gave vent to its terror and started to race down the hill. She was bounced about on its rump, clinging desperately to the straps about the cloak. Edmund fought for control, having no chance to sheath his bloodied sword. Trees flashed by dizzily as they approached a bend, tearing round a stand of trees at an incredible speed as Felicia felt the straps sliding through her fingers. Frantically she made a grab for a safer hold, but the cloak came away in her hand and she went tumbling from the horse. She landed on her back and lay gasping, staring blankly at the clouded sky. After what seemed an age there came the sound of running feet, then the sky was blotted out, and dark grey eyes gazed down with concern into her face. She tried to speak.

'Save your breath.' Edmund's voice was terse as he ran a hand over the back of her head. 'You are fortunate indeed, Mistress Meriet.' There was a barely perceptible quiver in his tones. 'Don't try to move.' He began to pull at her veil, tearing it in an attempt to unhook it from numerous thorns. Growling in exasperation, he eased it from her head and left it pinned to the brambles, then without more ado he took her arms and ruthlessly dragged her out of the blackberry bush, tearing her linen surcote as he did so.

For a moment Felicia stood there, slightly bent over, leaning on Edmund's braced arms. She let out a reluctant laugh, glancing up at him, her face pale. His arms slid about her as she crumpled.

'Damn!' The word seemed to come from a long way off as she fought to stay conscious. Waves of ice-cold sickness swept over her. 'Take deep slow breaths,' commanded the voice.

She obeyed, and gradually the world began to take on form again. She could hear the wind in the trees and feel its coolness. Then she became aware of a warmth beneath her hand and cheek. Its firmness somehow steadied her, and her head stopped spinning.

His hand caressed the nape of her neck in a gently soothing manner, causing her to relax against him. She felt unexpectedly safe, and had no wish at that moment to move away from the security of his arms. His heart beat rapidly beneath her ear, and a seam on his surcote dented her cheek. It hurt. She moved her head into a more comfortable position and took another deep breath.

Perhaps there was something in the sound that told Edmund that Felicia was recovering from her faintness. His caressing fingers stilled, and there came a tug on one of her dark braids, which was hard enough to compel her to lift her head. Edmund stared down at her. His eyes, the grey of wood-smoke, held a caring expression that surprised her. Then they flicked into a sharp awareness, which seemed to reach out and touch her, causing an answering stir of emotion.

She felt an unexpected surge of excitement stretch tingling fingers along her nerves. Her face flushed, and her eyes were a bemused iridescent sapphire, without guile. She moved slightly, brushing against him with an uncalculated allurement.

Edmund's hands moved restlessly the length of her back, coming to rest on her hips. In that moment he found it hard to resist the temptation to kiss her. There was an expression in her face that drew him, making him forget, and her body was warm and pliable beneath his hands. He half lowered his head, then suddenly he was aware once more of the cut on her face, the slightly swollen mouth, and of how she had come by them. Her eyelashes twitched, and she seemed to be pleading with him.

Had this tug of attraction he felt been the same as that which had caused her cousin to kill Matilda, his wife ... tempting him, leading him on in a desire to possess this woman in his arms? Edmund's mouth tightened and the smoky eyes became charcoal. The moment passed; then the light died in her face and she moved away from him as his arms slackened.

Felicia made to pick up the fallen cloak, and gave a cry.

'What is it?' Edmund whirled round towards her.

'Nothing!' she said in a gasping voice.

'Nonsense!' He saw the agony in her eyes, and his arm slid about her waist again and he gave a piercing whistle. 'I am sorry, but we shall have to ride on,' he murmured, frowning, as he glanced at the threatening sky. 'I think we are in for some rain. Is it your back?' Felicia nodded. 'It will be painful, but if you go before me, I can act as a support for it.'

She pressed her lips firmly on the pain that shot up her spine as he lifted her on to the horse. She clutched its mane, watching Edmund put the cloak about his shoulders. He climbed up behind her, easing himself as close as possible before wrapping the cloak about her. When he clamped his arm round her waist, the act sent a quiver through her, and he half smiled.

'There is little I can do to you on horseback, Mistress Meriet,' he murmured against her hair. 'The journey is too long for you to sit so rigidly.'

'Where do we go?' The first jolt of movement shuddered up her spine, and she almost screamed.

Edmund hesitated. 'Shrewsbury.' His arm tightened. 'I would not choose to take you there, but I have friends who will give us shelter and not ask too many questions.'

'They must be friends indeed, if you can arrive, unannounced, with a strange woman, Master de Vert. What will they think?' Her spirits had lifted at his answer, and its effect showed in her voice.

'Do not think yourself free from me already, Mistress Meriet,' he replied. 'They are old friends, and whatever they think, they will at least pretend to believe what I tell them.'

Felicia fell silent, unable to understand why he was taking her south with him—why he should choose to take her to his friends' house. His actions confused her. If he wished to make her cousin suffer, surely he should have let Philip know that he had taken her?

It did not take them long to descend the rest of the hill, and they travelled along lower ground for what seemed painful hour upon hour. It was well into evening when they came to a mere, which swiftly spotted as the rain that had been threatening began to fall, gently but relentlessly. Briefly Edmund pulled up his horse, and they eased aching backs and shoulders, gazing at the stretch of water with its fringe of rustling reeds and water iris.

'It is said to be bottomless,' he murmured against her ear.

Trepidation quivered in Felicia's stomach. 'You—You are not thinking of throwing me in, Master de Vert? For I tell you now that I can swim.'

'Throw you in?' He let out an exasperated breath. 'I have no desire to kill you, Mistress Meriet. Perhaps you, though, would like to join the sirens that, they say, live in this mere?'

'Sirens?' Felicia brushed a flurry of raindrops from her cheek, and gazed at the grey surface.

'Mermaids.' His breath warmed her cheek, and she was suddenly conscious of his arm about her. 'I've always wanted to meet a mermaid.'

She made no answer, thinking it was a strange conversation to be having when the rain was starting to soak them.

'Mermaids, who would lure fishermen to their doom with promises of gold. Different sirens use different lures. You use your beauty, I suppose—in exchange for what, I wonder, Mistress Meriet?'

'I do not understand your talk of mermaids and sirens, but if they are a kind of wanton, Master de Vert, you insult me!' she said in a heated voice. 'Why do you take me south? Why can you not let me go? Set me free so that I can go home to Meriet?'

'We go south in search of that justice you talked about, Mistress Meriet,' he replied brusquely. 'I have an uncle who will advise me—and I take you with me because that is my desire.'

'But it is not mine,' she said in a low voice. 'Please, I am not the maid you think I am.'

'So you say.' There was a long silence but for the noise of rain dripping on leaf and twig, grass and flower. Edmund found himself wanting to believe her. 'We shall see,' he said. For a moment his hand rested on hers, and then he removed it before urging his mount on.

Felicia sighed deeply, but said nothing.

She gazed at the looming night clouds, tinged with orange and silver in the west. 'I am curious, Master de Vert, about how I am going to address your friends—and should I not know more about you if we are travelling together?'

'We are going to the home of Richard Mortimer, an old friend who is now a wool merchant, and his sister Nell Seisdon lives with him. She is recently widowed, and has a young son, Harry.' He hesitated. 'I shall tell them that you are the daughter of an old friend of my mother—and that I am escorting you to your home before I continue south. I think that might be feasible.'

'But why should I be in need of your escort—and, also, how will you explain my lack of baggage?' asked Felicia thoughtfully.

He gave an exasperated snort. 'I shall think of something. You do not need to say much. In truth, it will be best if you say little. Now be quiet, Mistress Meriet; I wish to think.'

'But you have not told me anything about yourself, Master de Vert,' she insisted. 'You said you were kin to Sir Gervaise de Vert—yet your mother did not live in the castle. I remember your saying that Philip set fire to her house.'

'So I did,' he said drily. 'You have a good

memory, Mistress Meriet. My mother and my lord's wife did not always agree—so, my—Sir Gervaise deemed it wiser that they occupied separate dwellings.' His words were true enough, but they did not begin to explain the relationship between his mother and Sir Gervaise—or his own. 'As for myself, I am a physician and spend most of my time in Chester. Although, recently, I have been in Italy and the East to study the work of physicians there—in the hope of improving my understanding of the ills that plague people.' He paused before adding softly. 'Does that answer your question?'

She nodded, and they fell silent, busy with their own thoughts. Soon they were crossing a loop of the Severn, hearing the swift surge of rushing water beneath the bridge. Green lush meadows lay on both sides of the road, which suddenly met with another. Not far ahead lay the walls of Shrewsbury. The turrets of the castle showed grey and misty in the murky twilight as they approached and passed through the gates into the town. Had they arrived later, they would not have been allowed in.

Felicia tried to straighten her aching back, pushing at the wet tendrils of hair that fell into her eyes, and she glanced about her as the horse clip-clopped on the cobbles. They passed along a narrow street

71

with upper storeys close overhead on either side. She jumped as a cat darted from beneath the horse's hooves and melted into the shadows, its eyes gleaming amber, the only sign of life in the gloom. The scent of wood-smoke, rotting offal and vegetation came to her nostrils. Another sign of life, she thought. At last they came to the market square and halted outside a large house. The shutters were all fastened, but a sliver of pale yellow light filtered through a crack to the right of the door.

Edmund dismounted, leaving Felicia hunched over the horse's neck. He strode up to the door and banged it hard with his fist. She could not resist a guilty glance about the square, expecting shutters to fly open as the noise vibrated. All was quiet, despite a feeling of being watched. Edmund hammered on the door again and, after several moments, it opened and a man stood there. Holding a candle in one hand and a staff clasped tightly in the other, he surveyed the tired figure before him. 'Who is it that comes disturbing the peace at this time of night?' he demanded in a deep musical voice.

Edmund threw back his hood. 'Do you not recognise me, Dickon?'

'By all that is holy—Edmund!' Dickon let out a delighted laugh. 'I did not think to see you until the fair in July.' He stepped down, and the two men, who were much of a height, clasped each other's shoulders. 'Where did you spring from, Edmund? How was it on your travels? It is good to see you.'

'It is a long tale, and one best told over a cup of ale—and a meal, if you can spare it out of your meagre wealth. I hope your fire is blazing, although it is meant to be summer. Can you give shelter to two poor soaked travellers, Dickon?' Edmund's voice was suddenly serious.

'Two?' Dickon's eyes lifted to the huddled and bedraggled figure sitting upon the horse. 'Good God! A lady, my friend?' His voice was low as he cocked a curious eye at Edmund. 'Here is a tale indeed! I don't know what Nell will say. And, speaking of Nell ...' They both turned as the pat-patter of feet sounded just inside the doorway.

'Who is it?' demanded a sharp voice.

Felicia lifted her head and peered through dripping hair at the woman standing on the threshold. She was tall, and her hair, which was unbraided ready for bed, fell in long rippling waves.

'It is Edmund.' Dickon turned towards his sister. 'Nell ...' he began, but he never finished.

Nell swooped on Edmund, holding out both her hands to him. 'Edmund! We have missed you so! But we did not think to see you yet. Come in!' She grasped his hands tightly, and he could only smile down at her. In that moment he forgot Felicia.

'How are you, Nell? And the boy?' He raised her hands to his mouth, and kissed each one in turn.

Felicia gazed dully at them both. She lifted an unsteady hand and removed a sodden lock from the cut on her cheek. Anger stirred inside her as weariness and pain forced her to let go her grip on the horse's mane and she slithered slowly to the ground. Searing pain shot up her legs and back as her feet slid from beneath her on the glistening cobbles. She gave a cry and tried to rise, but with a groan fell back again.

'Did you fall?' Edmund, who had turned, knelt on the cobbles beside her, leaving Nell staring down at them both in surprise.

'I tired of waiting,' muttered Felicia in a furious voice. She pressed her lips tightly together as Edmund ran a hand carefully over her lower limbs.

'That was foolish!' He gazed down at her, an impatient look upon his face. 'Pray God, I do not think you have broken any bones—but this extra fall is bound to cause us more delay.'

'I am wet, tired, hungry, and in

74

considerable pain, Master de Vert,' she whispered angrily. 'And not in the mood to be blamed for delaying you. I would remind you that I would not be in this condition if it were not for you!'

'You would rather I had left you warming your cousin's bed?' he taunted, his voice equally furious.

Felicia flinched. 'Take your hands from me! If you do not, I shall yell to the heavens the kind of man you are!' Her voice shook on the words.

'You will not be able to walk a step, my fine lady!' He was just as heedless as she of the listening ears of Dickon and Nell.

'I will!' Her mouth set determinedly, and her eyes sparkled amid the glistening raindrops on her face.

Edmund was suddenly unsure if it was only rain wetting her cheeks. He hesitated, still gripping her arm. Felicia glared at him and began to push herself up from the ground. With an exasperated growl he released his grip on her, and she tossed him a grim little smile as she attempted to walk, but took only one step before giving a whimper of agony.

Immediately he slipped an arm about her waist and swung her up against his chest. 'Pride and pain do not go hand in hand!' he said vehemently.

Felicia did not answer but pressed her

lips tightly together on the words and the pain. She averted her face from Nell's frowning gaze.

'Who is she, Edmund?' Nell gave a reluctant laugh that held a touch of pique. 'I know that you are not averse to picking up a lame person or two and helping them—but never have you brought a lady to us!'

'Ask no questions now, dear Nell—I shall explain later. Rather let us come in out of the rain.'

Nell gave him the tiniest of smiles, and shrugged. 'So be it then, Edmund. But leave your cloak just inside the doorway; it is dripping wet.'

'So are they,' murmured Dickon, his voice quivering slightly. 'And he will have a job taking it off, Nell, for his arms are rather full! I shall do it for him. Then, Edmund, I shall stable your horse.'

'Thank you.' Edmund tossed his friend a grateful look and stepped over the threshold with a very silent Felicia in his arms.

Dickon took the cloak from Edmund's shoulders. He gave Felicia a curious glance, and she flushed. Then he was gone. Edmund swung her round to face Nell, and she was suddenly, embarrassingly, aware of her dishevelled state and the bruise and cut on her face. She lowered her lashes as Nell's cool stare surveyed her.

'Edmund, now tell me who she is.' Nell's controlled amusement did not quite hide her impatience.

Felicia looked up at Edmund's wet face. He seemed tired, and she suddenly realised that the journey could not have been easy for him, either. Yet as he smiled at Nell, his weariness seemed to vanish. Felicia felt a twinge of irritation as he began to speak in a light, slightly conciliatory voice to explain what had happened. None of it was true, except for the part where she had fallen from the horse, and she had to admire the way the lies fell so easily from his lips. It was amazing; she would not have thought he possessed so much imagination! What would Nell think of him if she knew the true story? At that moment, Felicia had no intention of telling her. There would be little point, if Edmund did as he said he might and let her go. All the time Edmund was explaining, the pair of them were dripping water on the floor, and she was very much aware of it. After that first swift glance at Nell, she had kept her eyes downcast, not wanting her hostess to see her face too clearly. Edmund, she noticed, had made no explanation of her injuries. When he came to the end of his tale, she could not tell whether Nell believed it or not.

'There is only one problem, Edmund,'

said Nell, smoothing a fold of her bright green silk skirts. 'Will Mistress Meriet be content to share a bed with me? Harry also sleeps in my chamber in a truckle.'

'If you would prefer it, Mistress Seisdon,' said Felicia in a cool voice, 'I could go to the lodging hall at the abbey. My father knew the abbot well, and I would not like to inconvenience you.'

'No, you cannot,' interrupted Edmund hastily, frowning at her. 'We have travelled too far this day as it is, after your fall. Besides, I have no intention of going out in the rain again.'

'It is of no consequence your staying here, Mistress Meriet,' retorted Nell, stiffly polite.

Felicia felt Edmund's arms tighten about her, and the look he gave her contained a hint of warning. 'Then I accept your offer with much gratitude,' she said promptly, and just as politely as Nell. 'But I must apologise for dripping all over your floor, Mistress Seisdon. The journey was long and wet.'

'Of course,' said Nell. 'The floor is of no matter. The serving-maid will see to it in the morning.' She frowned. 'But you cannot go to bed in that condition, Mistress Meriet. Whatever Edmund says, you should be in bed.' Her face lightened. 'I shall take you up now and find you something to wear. It is very unfortunate that your baggage-horse should have bolted when you were attacked by the outlaws.'

'Very unfortunate,' murmured Felicia, a slight tremor in her voice as she darted a glance at Edmund's face. 'But we were fortunate to escape with our lives.' She saw a muscle twitch in his cheek, and an imp of mischief caused her to add, 'You have never seen such bravery, Mistress Seisdon. How many of them were there?' She paused, aware of Edmund's eyes on her face. 'Was it four, or was it ... six ... and Master Edmund and my groom fought them off. It was a pity we had to leave Edgar behind to have his wounds tended.' She gasped as he suddenly pinched her side.

'A very great pity,' said Edmund drily. 'But that is enough of my bravery! Let us do as Nell suggests. I shall carry you to the chamber and leave you in her capable hands.' He smiled sweetly down at her, and Felicia smiled just as sweetly back. She knew it was all pretence, but she could not help wishing that it was not.

They left the candlelit hall at its rear, passing into a narrow passage and thence through a door that led outside. Felicia could smell the sweet damp odour of rain-sodden roses, but the rain had stopped. A flight of wooden steps led upward at the back of the house. As Edmund carried her up their slippery treads, Felicia clung to him. Her hands were feeling even colder and wetter as she clasped them tightly. In that moment, she feared falling again above all other fates.

Nell opened the door, and walking ahead of them both she crossed the bedchamber. A candle in a stand showed that the room was empty. They passed through, and Nell pushed open another door at the far end, where she stood aside for them to enter. In the room stood two beds. In the smaller lower one could clearly be seen the huddled shape of a sleeping child.

'My son,' she whispered in a voice that trembled slightly. She touched the curls that were all that showed above the covers. 'We must take care not to wake him, Mistress Meriet.' She turned and faced them, lifting worried brown eyes to Edmund. 'He has had the fever, and still tires easily.'

Edmund nodded, his face concerned. 'Do not fret so, Nell! He is a fine healthy boy.' His voice was soothing, and Felicia saw Nell visibly relax. 'I doubt he will have a relapse as Seisdon did, if that is what you fear.'

Nell smiled and touched his arm briefly. She went to a large carved oak chest, lifted the lid, and drew out an undergown of pale blue.

'Do you wish me to help you to undress, Mistress Meriet?' Her smile did not quite reach her eyes. 'If it is as Edmund says, you will be unable to do much to help yourself.'

Felicia was almost tempted to declare that she could manage perfectly well by herself, but even before she opened her mouth, Edmund spoke for her.

'That is good in you, Nell.' His voice was warm, almost a caress.

Felicia shot him a glance, and experienced a sudden sense of depression. 'You can put me down,' she said fretfully.

He gave a casual nod and carried her over to a carved chair that had a cushion to soften its hardness. 'I shall come up later with some poppy syrup. It will help you to sleep, and ease the pain.'

'I will manage without, I think,' she muttered, as he settled her on the chair.

'Don't be foolish!' For a moment his bulk hid her from Nell's gaze, and he still held her. 'Do not attempt to enlist Nell's aid in escaping from me,' he murmured. 'If you told her the truth, she would come to me for verification and I would tell her you were given to fantasies, having listened to too many romantic and adventurous tales in your younger days.' His face was but a few inches from her own.

'I do not doubt you would!' Felicia's voice was icy despite its breathlessness. 'Now will you take your hands off me?'

'Certainly.' His eyes glinted and a corner of his mouth tilted up attractively. 'And then I shall take your hands off me!' He reached up and prised her cold stiff fingers from about his neck. Felicia flushed as he held them, warming them between his own for a moment before he straightened and turned away. Felicia lowered her head, not looking up even when he spoke to Nell and went out of the room. She could not understand her feelings. She had not thought that an unwelcome, unsought, warmth of feeling towards her abductor could cause such turmoil within her.

She wished she could shut out all thought for a while. She had been going to refuse the poppy syrup, but now realised that she would sleep better with it, if for no other reason than to drive from her thoughts Master Edmund de Vert—physician. Nell turned to her with a satisfied smile that did not make her feel any better. Perhaps Edmund has kissed her, she thought irritably. She did not like accepting her help in undressing, but had to make the best of it. Fortunately Nell was not inclined to indulge in light conversation at that hour, and neither was Felicia. She accepted the assistance with a murmur of thanks before stumbling painfully across the room and sinking into bed. She was thankful when it was accomplished.

'I shall bring you some food,' said Nell, gathering up the damp surcote and undergown, and leaving the room with a flurry of skirts. Shortly after, she returned with a tray upon which was a bowl of soup, a platter of bread and a cup from which steam curled.

'You are to eat, and to drink all the potion down.' Nell placed the tray across Felicia's lap, and sat down on the edge of the bed, after taking a swift look at her son. 'Edmund will not be coming up again to see you this evening. He has much to talk about with my brother, what with the uprising in the Severn valley and all.'

'Uprising?' Felicia glanced up swiftly over the rim of the cup. She took a sip of the still hot liquid. It tasted of fruit and spices and was unexpectedly delicious.

'Ah! You have not heard, either.' Nell shrugged her silk-clad shoulders and toyed with a large ruby ring on her finger.

Felicia put the cup down on the tray. 'Heard what? What is this about an uprising?'

'The Lord Edward has escaped, and the men of Shrewsbury have been ordered to form themselves into constabularies by

Earl Simon.' Nell sighed. 'You had best eat your soup first, Mistress Meriet, it is cooling fast. That is the problem of serving food upstairs. One has to bring it outside up those long steps.' She fell silent, not realising that her news had pleased her unwilling guest.

'Where is Lord Edward now?' Felicia picked up the bread and dunked it into the soup. She began to eat hungrily, not put off by the coolness of the food.

'If I knew that, I would know more than the whole force of Earl Simon de Montfort.' Nell's voice was tart. 'One moment he is reported to have been seen here—the next, somewhere else. No one knows where he is, and perhaps it would be best if Edmund stayed here instead of chancing the road south.' A slight smile curved her mouth.

Felicia flicked an impatient glance at Nell's rapt face. 'And what does Master Edmund say to that?'

'He gave no answer.' Nell gave a shrug, and rose to her feet. 'But that does not mean that he will not stay.' She smiled again. 'You may leave the tray on the stool beside the bed. I shall return for it later.' She paused a moment, gazing down at Felicia. 'Tell me, Mistress Meriet, how you came by that cut on your face? I thought you fell off the horse backwards.' Felicia involuntarily touched her cheek, glad that the one candle in the room was not bright enough to show up her swollen lips.

'I twisted, and a loose bramble scratched me,' she murmured.

'Oh, I see. Edmund gave me no answer when I asked him. For a moment I thought someone had hit you! When I suggested it, he gave such a scowl, almost as if I were suggesting it was he! As if I would think such a thing! Edmund is the kindest of men ... if a mite hasty and quick-tempered at times.' With these words, Nell turned and left the room.

Felicia stared after her. She suddenly had the strangest desire to laugh; then her thoughts sobered and she began to eat the rest of her food slowly and painfully. So the Lord Edward had escaped ... That must have been the reason for Earl Simon's order to Philip to report to Worcester. It was unlikely, then, that her cousin would spend much time in hunting for her.

Meriet—if only she could get home! What would Edmund do? Despite Nell's words, she did not think him a man who would shirk danger at a woman's bidding, whatever his feelings towards her. It was true that there was always danger at times of conflict: bands of men made it an excuse to loot, rape, and burn what they did not want, just for the joy of destruction.

Suddenly Felicia felt a chill at her heart. Meriet was not so far from the reported uprising. Joan, her cousin, would still be there. She was only sixteen, but fair and a virgin. Surely she would be safe? Philip had made no mention of ridding Meriet of Sir William, her own steward, although Felicia had never received any answers to the letters she had sent by messenger. Still, Joan should be in no danger.

She drank the rest of the potion. Then, with painful difficulty, she moved the tray on to the stool before relaxing against the pillow. In the shadowy room there was no sound but the soft even breathing of the boy. Then she slipped over the borders into sleep so swiftly that she was unaware even of Nell coming to collect the tray.

CHAPTER FOUR

'Good! You are awake at last!'

Felicia jumped, and opened her eyes, slanting a sidelong glance in the direction of the youthful voice. A small boy sat cross-legged on top of the truckle bed, gazing at her out of large brown eyes. He was a small replica of his uncle, although Dickon did not have so many freckles.

Neither did his hair curl so riotously about his ears.

'I shall go and fetch Master Edmund,' he said, not seeming put out at all by Felicia's stare. 'He told me to let him know when you woke.'

'Stay a moment,' Felicia said with a smile. He uncurled his thin wiry body in its blue tunic, then looked at her enquiringly before springing off the bed. He stood straight, his feet firmly planted a little apart. 'I must go now,' he said patiently. 'Master Edmund said he would give me a penny if I did so.'

'Wealth indeed! You must certainly go, then, but tell him I am very hungry and likely to faint away if I am not fed before long.'

He grinned as she had intended, and gave a wave of a grubby hand before going out of the room. There does not seem much wrong with that young man! she thought, looking about her.

The walls were washed white and several tapestries covered their bareness. Most depicted flowers and fruits in shades of yellow, red and green, and one had a unicorn in the middle worked in cream and gold. She could not but admire the skilful needlework; Nell must have great patience. It was not a virtue that Felicia would have thought she possessed. The shutters had been flung wide, letting in not only the warm morning sunshine but also the sounds of vendors proclaiming the goodness of their wares in the market square below.

The door opened, and Felicia's eyes flew to it with unusual eagerness. Her disappointment was out of all proportion to what she knew it should be when Nell entered instead of Edmund, carrying a bowl of water. Behind her came Harry, clutching a towel of creamy linen. 'I am sorry to cause you so much bother, Mistress Seisdon.' Felicia's voice was stiffly apologetic.

'It is of no consequence.' Nell placed the bowl on the stool next to the bed. 'Harry, leave the towel and go and fetch the tray.' She held out a slender hand and took the towel from her son, smiling her thanks as she did so. She watched him leave the room before turning to face Felicia. 'Do you feel any better? I would have brought you water to wash in last night, but I forgot. Would you like to sit up?'

'I am not sure,' said Felicia reluctantly. 'I tried before, and it hurt.' She smiled at Nell, enjoying the picture she made. She wore a deep blue undergown, which was fastened snugly at her waist by an embroidered linen girdle. Her gleaming auburn hair was plaited and coiled about her ears beneath a gossamer-fine veil. This was topped by a coif patterned with the same embroidered colours of purple and pink as the girdle.

'Edmund says it is unlikely that you will be able to travel for several days.' Nell passed Felicia a small square of linen which she had dampened. She moved away from the bed and walked with a smooth grace over to the window. 'Have you known him long?' Nell's tone was casual.

'Not as long as you, I think,' replied Felicia quickly. She wondered what question would come next.

'I think that is likely to be true,' Nell said thoughtfully. 'Edmund and Dickon were taught by the monks, and Dickon often brought Edmund home.' Her eyes softened in reminiscence. 'There were few moments of laughter in our home after my mother died. Yet when Edmund, Dickon and Steven came, even Father found it hard not to be amused by their ploys and nonsensical talk.' Her voice, which had been animated, suddenly took on a bitter note as she carried on talking. 'They were so unlike Father, you see. Perhaps it was Mother dying so young that changed him. Money became more important than people to him.' Nell came slowly over to the beds, and sat down on her son's truckle. She smoothed its coverlet with an unsteady hand. 'I was fifteen when he wed me to Seisdon, who was the same age as my father. But he was very rich, you see, and that mattered more to Father than the fact that I cared for another, who returned my affections.'

Felicia rubbed her hands meticulously with the cloth, not looking at Nell. 'This other ... This other ...' she began. 'Was he ...'

'He was not poor.' Nell looked across at her, puckering her brows. 'He had a good future ahead of him and an income from his father.' She twisted her fingers in her lap. 'He was as fair as an angel, exciting and unpredictable—and with a fierce temper. Father considered him not only too poor, but also dangerous. He had ideas that were strange to my father—and I admit I thought them somewhat odd. He thought that all men should be free to go where they wished and have a say in the ruling of the realm, regardless of their station. After I married Seisdon, he followed Earl Simon, thinking he would bring about God's kingdom here on earth.' Nell let out a low laugh. 'Of course, it never came!' She fell silent.

'It must have been hard for you,' said Felicia in a low voice, folding the cloth carefully. She wondered if the 'fair angel' was Edmund, but did not like to ask. If he was, did it mean that Edmund and Nell would marry now that she was free to do so?

'It was hard,' murmured Nell.

Felicia lifted her head. 'Yet surely, sometimes, such a marriage like yours can work out?'

Nell shook her head, a bitter twist to her mouth. 'Seisdon wanted me only for my beauty and to bear him children. He liked dressing me up like a doll, and trying to begat sons. As it was, I was a sad disappointment to him for many years. I lost three babies before Harry was born. After he passed his fifth birthday, life became a little easier.' Nell shrugged, her eyes hard.

There was a look upon her face that Felicia understood. She had often seen that fearful apprehension and uncertainty in Matilda's eyes, and felt a sudden overwhelming sympathy for Nell. 'I'm sorry you have been so unhappy,' she murmured.

Nell shrugged. 'It is nothing to do with you. I do not know why I tell you this ... Perhaps it is because I have never had another woman to talk to. My life was not all gloom. Harry was, and is, my delight, and compensated for much unhappiness. After he was born, Seisdon did show me a little more consideration.' Suddenly her

91

face glowed. 'He is a fine boy, do you not think?'

Felicia nodded. 'He is—and clever, I should not wonder.'

'That is true.' Nell beamed at Felicia. 'Dickon would teach Harry all concerning the wool trade when he is a little older, but I would like Harry to be a scholar. He knows some Latin already.' Her smile faded, and she plucked at the bedcover. 'Dickon is not so keen on such a path. He is good and kind, my brother, but I have had enough of living with a man I cannot agree with on so many things. I have enough money for my needs, and more. I would choose a husband for myself now: one that would suit me and Harry.' She gave Felicia a brittle smile. 'I suppose you think me ungrateful to my brother?'

Felicia shook her head. 'It is good that you can choose.' She fell silent, feeling again that sense of depression.

Nell picked up the bowl and the towel. 'Edmund has gone to the herbarium at the abbey. He said to tell you that he will not be gone long, and to remember all that he told you.' Her eyes were curious now, but Felicia had no intention of enlightening her. She might be surprised at how unangelic her fair lover was, if she knew the truth!'

Nell gave a sudden exclamation. 'Your

92

breakfast! What is that child up to now, I wonder? You would not believe the mischief a boy of eight can get into when one is not watching.' So saying, with a swish of skirts she swept out of the room.

Felicia stared unseeingly at the unicorn on the wall as the door closed. She found herself marvelling at the duplicity of men, and of one man in particular.

There came a tap on the door, and a few seconds later it opened.

'I pray that you have not fainted away through lack of nourishment!' said Edmund politely, his eyes gleaming.

Despite all her intentions, Felicia smiled a welcome.

'I have brought you some bruisewort. You might know it as comfrey. After you have eaten, you are to drink it all down, and pray it does its work swiftly.' Edmund perched himself on the side of her bed and placed the tray across her knees. 'How is the pain this morning?' He smiled down at her.

Felicia gave a wry smile back and lowered her eyes to the tray. There was no doubting his attraction. He had changed his garments and now wore a white under-tunic of linen under a scarlet surcote with yellow embroidery on the wide sleeves. His tawny hair had been shorn and now curled neatly to just below his ears. He had also shaved. Was all this for Nell's benefit, she wondered.

'The pain is a sore point, I see. I warned you! Are we speaking this morning?' he asked politely, when still she remained silent. 'Did you have much to say to Nell?' There was an edge to his voice.

'I see no point in discussing my pain if you know all about it, Master Physician.' She lifted a morsel of bread to her mouth and began to chew slowly before swallowing, aware of his eyes on her face. 'As for Mistress Seisdon—she did most of the talking, not I. As you said, she would not believe me if I told her that I was your prisoner.'

'You told her?' His face tightened and his eyes narrowed.

'I told you that she did most of the talking,' retorted Felicia scornfully. 'She seems to think much of you ... She thinks that you will stay longer. If we do, she just might begin to suspect how it is between us, Master de Vert. You—You cannot keep me a prisoner for ever, you know.' Her voice was derisive as she looked into his face, despite her racing heart.

He smiled sardonically, lifting dark gold brows. 'To keep you for eternity was never my intention.' His hands moved towards the bareness of her throat, revealed by the low neckline of the blue undergown. She did not realise it, but the blue exactly matched her eyes at that moment.

Felicia flushed at the probing expression on his face. She was suddenly unable to speak, experiencing again that excitement of yesterday. He caressed the column of her throat with the balls of his thumb before taking her face between his hands and kissing her gently, but at some length. She gave a trembling sigh, her eyes softly moist and dazed. A muscle moved in his throat, and then his lips twisted into a smile.

'You are a witch, Mistress Meriet,' he muttered in a strained voice. 'Eternity! I never gave thought before to how I would like to spend it.' He rose abruptly and strolled over to the window.

There was a long silence, in which Felicia tried to gather the shreds of her pride and suppress the voice that kept speaking of his kindness and not his duplicity.

'Did Nell tell you of the uprising?' Edmund said at last.

'She did.' Her voice was controlled, almost emotionless.

'It is probably the reason for your cousin being sent for by Earl Simon.'

'I thought that might be so, myself. What do you intend?' She reached out a steady hand and picked up some more bread. She was no longer hungry, but meant to eat, if only to keep up her strength. If the opportunity came, she would run as far away from him as she could.

'What do I intend?' He turned to face her. 'I shall carry on with my original plan, with some differences.'

'And what are they? Are you going to free me?' She picked up the cup, and her hands shook slightly. All her nerve-ends seemed to be stretched, waiting for his answer.

'If Earl Simon is sending out messages for aid, so will the Lord Edward. He will need men if he is to win this fight.'

'You will go and join the Prince?' Felicia's voice could not hide her surprise. 'Why? And what of me? *Will* you let me go?'

'Where would you go if I did?' He gave a tight-lipped smile. 'You cannot run back to your cousin.' He sat down on the chest.

'So you still do not believe me innocent?' Felicia's fingers tightened on the cup. 'He is the last person I would run to! Do you think me some sort of dolt?' She touched her cheek with a shaking hand. 'I would go to Meriet, as I told you. I would go home. I have not seen it for over a year ... not since Philip came with news of my father's and brother's deaths at Lewes.' Her voice tailed off and she stared angrily into the cup of ale, swirling it round violently.

'I did not know you had lost menfolk!' Edmund exclaimed in a startled voice.

'What? The gossips never told you that?' Her voice mocked him. 'Is it that they do not know the truth concerning me, after all?' She placed the cup on the tray with a thud. 'I am weary and would like to rest.' She leaned back and shut her eyes. It was partly true.

'Not until you have taken your medicine, Mistress Meriet.' She heard the slight creak of the floor as he came towards her. 'And why do you not tell the truth and say that you are weary of me and would be rid of my company?' Unexpectedly there was a meekness in his voice that she had never heard before. She opened her eyes as the large bed sank beneath his weight.

'Because I am a lady, although you think otherwise!' she told him tersely.

'Are any of us what others think we are?' He moved the tray and put it on the floor, handing her a small silver cup. 'Now drink it all.'

'You are very imperious!' There was a sparkle in her eyes as she took it. 'Does it taste vile?'

'Don't all the best medicines taste so?' He smiled as she took a cautious sip before drinking all the potion down. Their fingers brushed as she handed him back the cup.

'How is it that you became a physician?' she asked, hiding her hands beneath the coverlet. 'You said that you were kin to Sir Gervaise—and that your mother lived at his manor. I would have thought that meant you would have been his steward.'

He hesitated before answering. 'I am surprised that you are interested in the likes of me, Mistress Meriet.'

Felicia flushed. 'I need to know more about you in case Nell asks me further questions. Besides, I have nothing else to do this morning.' She smiled sweetly at him.

'I see,' he said good-humouredly, stretching out his long legs in their red hose. 'My mother was a wise woman. Not only did she have a gift of healing, but she knew the names of most plants and what they could do. She could read, and sought cures in learned books. Since boyhood I followed her about the manor, helping her by day and by night.'

'But that would not make a physician of you. Did your father help you?' asked Felicia, thinking he was going to be silent after a stilted but encouraging start.

Edmund absently traced the engraving on the small cup with the tip of a finger. 'Sir Gervaise saw to my education.' He straightened his shoulders and tilted his head. 'I went to the monks—to my uncle Walter, who is the abbot of a monastery in Worcestershire. After that I went to Oxford. I was there when the King stood before the assembled magnates at the Easter feast several years ago, and later that summer, when the provisions were announced. Much talk was bandied about. It was said that the King should accept advice from a council of fifteen.' He paused, not seeing her in that moment. 'Some said it was time for the King to have deep speech with his chief men. Some called these meetings parliaments. It was a good idea.' He grimaced, and his eyes met and held Felicia's. 'Some of the changes called for did take place, but not enough. So much fell apart when the barons themselves would not have their own actions dealt with. Justice, it seemed, was still to be only for the rich and powerful and not for the lesser orders, as I think was intended.' He paused.

'The Lord Edward stood against the King, alongside his uncle the Montfort, then,' said Felicia, filling the silence. 'He asked that the barons fulfil their oaths to support knights like my father. They were called bachelors, and helped to bring in some reforms.'

'You have listened to your father, I

think.' Edmund smiled.

She wrinkled her nose, and went on, 'I have the gist of it, but I do not know or understand it all. My father was in agreement with the Lord Edward and Earl Simon at that time. Then later he thought the Earl's stand too rigid, saying he expected change too swiftly. To expect men used to ruling to give up some of their power immediately, making room for the merchants and landowners, was a lot to expect. In truth, my father said it was a huge step and one some will never be happy with.'

Edmund nodded, staring at her thoughtfully. He had not expected a woman to be interested in such matters. 'Some of the problem lay in the ill-feeling between the King and Earl Simon himself. Despite Earl Simon's wife being the King's sister, they have never agreed. Earl Simon despises the King because he is not a fighting man: he would rather make buildings than war.'

'Ay, but my father said that the Earl wished to be able to call the council in the King's absence and to exercise the King's functions when he was not there. There was bound to be discord.'

'Did your father follow the Montfort or the King to war?' Edmund leaned a little closer to Felicia. 'The Earl was a great man. He had vision, and he roused men's finer feelings and gave them hope, for a while. Dickon, Steven and I followed him for a season.' Edmund's smile faded. 'Then Dickon and I realised that he was just a man like any other—and did not understand freedom as we saw it.' He sighed, and ran a hand through his hair, raising it in a crest.

Felicia nodded. 'True freedom is not gained so easily. My menfolk died fighting on the King's side. They had given him their allegiance because he was the King.' Felicia pleated the coverlet with a careful hand. 'It could be that the Prince will send word to my manor at Meriet. Sir William, my steward, fought on the King's side. He might have news, if ...' She paused. 'Have you ever met the Prince? Why do you think of joining him if you were for Earl Simon?' She lifted steady eyes to Edmund's face.

He laughed suddenly. 'What have I ever had to do with princes? But I have seen the Lord Edward—and heard that he cares for his friends and other men not so well born. In that lies my hope.' He shrugged broad shoulders. 'I think, if he is not killed first, he will possess more wisdom than his father when he comes to be King. Besides, he and I are much of an age, and perhaps this country needs young blood. Your cousin also fights for the Montfort; that fact alone would ally me to the Prince's cause!'

Felicia saw that his face had hardened at the mention of Philip. 'You say that in the Lord Edward lies your hope. What hope?' She moistened her mouth nervously. 'Could it be that you have thought of seeking justice from the Prince?'

'Perhaps,' he said, rising to his feet. 'It is unlikely that I would seek it from Earl Simon while your cousin has his ear.'

Felicia winced as she moved uneasily in the bed.

'Are you uncomfortable?' He noted her pain.

'I shall have to suffer it.' Felicia made a face. 'Did you give young Harry his penny?'

Edmund nodded. 'He would go with me, I think, to seek out the Lord Edward, thinking it a great adventure. Dickon says he himself might come with me. He has wool interests in the Cotswolds.'

'But Nell said ...' Felicia hesitated.

'Said what? Tell me.' He folded his arms across his chest and looked at her thoughtfully. For some reason she had blushed.

'Nell said that you might stay here. That she might be able to persuade you. But I do not think you a man to be so easily persuaded. I did not think you a man so easily scared of danger.' She lowered her eyes.

'Nell says many things! But I do not intend to dally in Shrewsbury,' he said softly, 'however pleasant you might think I would find it.'

'Why should I think of your pleasure at all, Master de Vert?' She yawned, thinking he had answered part of her question—but not all of it. Yet he could hardly take her to war with him, surely? She eased herself down in the bed and shut her eyes. 'Now really I would like to rest, if you do not mind leaving me,' she murmured dismissively.

'Of course. There is much I have to see to myself, besides dancing attendance on you.' His voice was cool.

Felicia swallowed her reply, and did not watch him go. The day stretched before her with expected tedium. She swallowed the sudden lump in her throat and turned on her side with painful difficulty. She had a deep yearning for the peace and comfort of her own home, Meriet. If only she could go there! She shut her eyes and tried to think of a sensible plan.

Edmund shut the door of her bedchamber and went swiftly across to the room he shared with Dickon and out of the door at the other end. For a moment he stood at the top of the stairs, looking down at the sunlit garden without seeing it. For a while, back there, he had almost believed her innocence ... that she hated her cousin as much as he did. Slowly he began to walk down, his face creased in thought.

'Edmund! How is Mistress Meriet?'

Edmund met Dickon's lively gaze. He paused on the bottom step. 'Still in pain, although she bears it bravely.'

'She is a pretty maid, despite that cut on her face and the swollen mouth—her eyes are beautiful ... So Nell says.' Dickon's own brown ones twinkled.

'Does she!' Edmund gave him a resigned glance as they began to cross the garden.

'Ay, she is jealous, I think—but honest with it.' Dickon put out a hand, preventing Edmund from opening the door into the house. 'Let us not go in yet. Do you not think you should tell me the truth about Mistress Meriet? Surely you cannot think I have fallen for the tale you told Nell? We have been friends too long for me not to know when you are lying!'

Edmund's eyes narrowed and he would have shrugged off his friend's hand. Then his mouth eased into a smile. 'I never could hide much from you, could I? Let us talk, then, but not here where Nell might overhear. I think I would enjoy a stroll down by the river.'

104

'So be it; I must go there anyway. Nell is missing Harry and thinks he might have gone fishing. I must teach that boy how to swim, and then she will worry less.'

It was pleasantly cool beneath the trees on the bank.

'Well?' Dickon leaned against the trunk of a massive oak, watching Edmund's face as he flipped a pebble into the water. 'Since we left the house you have not spoken except to enquire the price of wool. Is this secluded enough for you, my friend?' He folded his arms. 'What is it that worries you?'

Edmund turned to him. 'Mother is dead. She was murdered by Sir Philip Meriet—Mistress Meriet's cousin. He also murdered, or had murdered, my father and half-brothers.' His fingers tightened on the pebble he still held.

'Good God!' Dickon's face was suddenly bleak. 'Tell me all! And tell me what it has to do with Mistress Meriet.'

Slowly, his face grim, Edmund began to tell Dickon all that had happened. 'I came back from Italy, as you know, three months ago—after you sent word that Master Seisdon had died. I planned to come here after sorting out my affairs in Chester and seeing my mother and father.' He drew breath. 'I guessed there was something wrong before I reached the village. There were no workers in the fields, but as I approached, several peasants came running towards me. They paid no attention when I called, but I recognised one of them and shouted his name—we had fished the river when boys. He told me to flee, that the lord, lady and their sons were dead, and that the swine responsible were slaughtering and raping in the village. I lent him my horse and packhorse—he had small children—and said that, if things went well, I would see him again at the charcoal-burner's hovel in the forest.' He paused and cleared his throat. 'There were horses with trappings outside Mother's house. I did not stop to think, but went in. He was striking her, so I went for him, only to be seized from behind. I struggled and fought as he raped her, but there were three of them and I was hit over the head. When I regained consciousness, the house was on fire. We only just managed to escape.'

'By "he"—I presume you mean Philip Meriet?' said Dickon.

Edmund nodded. 'For two days I kept her alive, but, despite all my attempts, she died.' His eyes were suspiciously bright. 'I was told by that same villager to whom I lent my horses that Meriet was going to have a celebration feast and was seeking helpers at the point of a blade. I seized my opportunity and became a serving-man. I was going to poison him at first—although that seemed too easy a death for him, but I just wanted to wipe him off the face of the earth. Then when I was in the buttery I heard about Mistress Meriet ... That she was being brought to the feast, that Meriet was mad with love for her, that she was his mistress and had plotted with him to murder his wife, and that despite her being his cousin, he planned to marry her.'

'God's bones!' Dickon stared at Edmund. 'You believe that of her?'

Edmund's mouth tightened, but ignoring Dickon's question, he went on. 'I still had a key to the postern gate—or I knew where it was hidden. John, Harry and I often used that way in and out of the castle, long after they built a sluice-gate for the mill and the water ran too shallow for boats. I drugged Philip's wine, and hers—and I abducted her.'

'What! To what end? No wonder you did not wish to tell Nell the truth!'

'I do not think she would approve, do you?' Edmund said stiffly.

'Of abduction? Neither do I—and I do not think it is your custom, either, Edmund!'

'Seeing one's mother raped and beaten to death changes one.' Edmund's jaw set rigidly as he returned his friend's look.

'What do you intend to do?' Dickon's face softened, and he placed a hand on Edmund's shoulder. 'Whatever your plan, surely you are not going on with it?'

'I have not decided.' Edmund scowled. 'Even when I first thought of abducting Mistress Meriet, my plans were confused. What I did depended up to a point on Philip Meriet's reactions. Before I heard of the Lord Edward's escape I thought to use her to bargain with, thinking it unlikely that I would get justice under Earl Simon any other way. I am my father's only living offspring. There is a possibility that I can lay claim to his manor, but it would be easier if Meriet had not taken by force what could be mine.' He paused.

'De Vert manor in exchange for Mistress Meriet—was that your plan?' asked Dickon, frowning slightly.

Edmund nodded. He had no intention of telling his closest friend any more than he had. He felt uncomfortable about his thoughts of revenge now.

'You should return Mistress Meriet before you do anything more you might regret,' said Dickon. 'You mentioned Nell. I am her brother, remember. And while she and I do not always see eye to eye, you must have guessed that she is looking in your direction for a husband now that Seisdon is dead.' They began to walk.

'I will not deny that it was the thought of marrying Nell that brought me home before all this happened,' said Edmund. 'But I know, if Steven were at hand, I would not stand a chance.' He came to a halt and gazed towards the bridge, looking for a sign of Harry.

'And now?' Dickon gripped Edmund's arm and stood in front of him. 'I will not have you play fast and loose with Nell. She is fond of you, and already jealous of Mistress Meriet. If you would wed my sister, set Mistress Meriet free.'

Edmund stood unmoving. 'What of Steven?' he said abruptly. 'You have never had word?'

'Of his whereabouts? None since our parting in Oxford. God only knows how long ago that is now! Whether he still follows Earl Montfort I do not know.'

'You know that is was always Steven that Nell wanted. If she accepted me, it would still be second best for both of us.'

'But you are the better man,' insisted Dickon, his face brightening. 'If it is justice and de Vert manor you want—let us seek it together. Forget your previous plan, Edmund, and together we shall go and find the Lord Edward. It will be like old times.'

'You think so? We would need Steven for it to be the same,' Edmund said lightly.

'Let us go along to the bridge, as I think I see Harry there. If he has been lucky, it will be fresh fish for supper.'

Dickon opened his mouth to speak, to press for a more satisfactory answer, but his friend had that set to his jaw that boded ill for any who pushed him too far. He was not happy. Suddenly he decided that he must make the better acquaintance of Mistress Meriet. Perhaps then he would understand Edmund's reluctance to give him a definite answer.

'It is kind of you to visit me, Master Mortimer,' said Felicia, easing herself against the pillows a little more.

'You will not think so when you see that I have brought you another dose of Edmund's poison! If it does not kill you, it should cure you!' Dickon twinkled at her and pulled a stool up to the bed. 'He has gone to see a sick child, the daughter of a friend. Nell is busy in the buttery, and I said I would do this task for her. A pleasant one, I might add.'

Felicia's cheeks dimpled. 'That is most kind of you. I am not used to lying abed, and even when I was in my cousin's ...' She paused uncertain how to go on, wondering if Edmund had told Master Mortimer more than he had told his sister.

'Your cousin?' prodded Dickon, stretching out his legs.

'I ... I have two cousins,' said Felicia brightly, clasping her hands on the coverlet. 'Joan ... and Philip,' she went on hurriedly, sensing the gleam in Dickon's eyes that he had heard of Philip. 'Joan lives with me at Meriet. She is my mother's sister's daughter—but her parents are both dead and she was left with little. Father invited her to come to live with us before he died. She is like a sister to me, and I miss her greatly.' She fell silent, realising she was getting on to dangerous ground again.

'Why does she not travel with you?' asked Dickon, thinking that when Mistress Meriet blushed she was exceedingly attractive.

'Because ...' She let out an impatient breath. 'Because, Master Mortimer, when my brother and father were killed at the Battle of Lewes, my cousin Philip took me to live with him and his wife. He was determined to cut me off from all those who would comfort me—or help me. Has ...' Her hands twisted on the coverlet. 'Has Master de Vert told you anything about me? I think he might have, from the look on your face.'

Dickon nodded. 'I cannot think you a murderer's accomplice, Mistress Meriet.' He leaned forward and patted Felicia's hand. She had to swallow the sudden lump in her throat.

'I thank you for those words, Master Mortimer ... It is more than Master de Vert believes of me.'

'Edmund has been through much lately.' Dickon squeezed her hand comfortingly, thinking he heard the sound of a door being opened.

'But he is oblivious of all that that is seemly or chivalrous!' Felicia's sapphire eyes widened with entreaty. 'Master Mortimer, do you think ...' At a sound at the door, she looked away from Dickon startled. Her eyes met Edmund's.

'I see you are getting better acquainted with each other,' drawled Edmund, his eyes as hard as flint.

Dickon turned his head and smiled. 'I brought Mistress Meriet her medicine.' He raised Felicia's hand to his lips and kissed it with obvious pleasure. 'She is my guest. I thought I should come and see if she has all she needs.'

'Of course.' Edmund folded his arms across his chest, leaning against the door-jamb.

'But I shall now leave you, as I have a customer to see. Mistress Meriet, perhaps I can come and see you again later?'

'I would like that,' murmured Felicia, smiling sweetly at him. Her guileless blue

112

eyes met Dickon's amused brown ones. She pulled her hands from his and gave Edmund a defiant glance.

Dickon straightened and looked into Edmund's set face. By all the saints, it could be that Nell had better look elsewhere for a husband, unless he was much mistaken!

CHAPTER FIVE

Edmund shut the door firmly behind Dickon before turning to face Felicia. There was a flush on his cheekbones. 'If you propose, Mistress Meriet, to try your tricks on Dickon, I advise you to think again!' He kept his back against the door. 'He has broken more hearts than you would credit. He was a minstrel in his younger days before he decided to settle down and take life more seriously, and he knows exactly how to woo a lady! I doubt the woman exists who could captivate him, however alluring.'

'If he is up to all the tricks, I do not know why you need to worry about your friend!' retorted Felicia.

'He has a soft heart.' There was a sardonic twist to Edmund's mouth as he strolled forward and rested his hands on the carved wooden foot of the bed. 'Did you look at him out of those beautiful eyes of yours and plead your cause?'

'He believes me innocent of Matilda's blood,' she said angrily, 'which is more than you do! And if I am the sort of woman you seem to persist in thinking me, surely your friend will sense it if he is so wise in the ways of women?' She looked away from him, her eyes fixed on the unicorn on the far wall.

'I did not say he was impervious to a woman's charms,' he murmured, his grey eyes narrowing as he looked at her bruised face. The swelling had gone down about her mouth, and the bruise was purpling. 'Perhaps you could—persuade—him to help you. What would you offer him besides your hand—your lips next? And then your body? Is that how it started with your cousin?' He flung the words at her; some devil was forcing them out of him.

Felicia's face whitened. She struggled to sit higher against the pillows, and glared at him. 'How dare you! Do you know what it is like to be held prisoner by a man you suspect of murder? Do you know what it feels like to go in fear of your own life—to see no way of safety? You begin to think like a hunted animal. You want to run and run, but there is nowhere to run. You hide

114

the real you behind a mask in order not to appear a threat. Hence, no danger to be disposed of!' She paused and took a shaky breath.

Edmund went to speak, but she held up a hand. 'When I ran with you, unwilling though I was, I thought that I would be safer with you than with Philip. Yet it seems you regard my feelings as little as he did. You would use me also for your own ends. I wish you would go away and leave me alone—for I find I do not wish to see you.' She twisted her head on the pillows and closed her eyes tightly on the tears that were near.

There was a long silence while she fought back her tears, and Edmund battled with a conflicting storm of emotions: fury at her comparing him to Philip; guilt because some of what she said was true enough to hurt; and an overwhelming desire to take her in his arms and beg her forgiveness. He turned at last and walked swiftly away from the room, slamming the door behind him.

Felicia raised brimming eyes and stared at the closed door. A sob burst in her throat and suddenly she could no longer bear to lie passive in the bed. Painfully she pushed back the covers and with great determination swung her legs over the side. She heaved herself up and stood swaying for a moment in aching discomfort as she struggled to force limbs that seemed as stiff and uncontrollable as the wooden joints of a child's toy. She shuffled across the floor in slow agony towards the door, and carefully opened it. The other bedchamber was empty. Gradually she managed to make her way across, clinging to chest and bed in glad respite until she reached the outer door. She put a hand out and attempted to open it. It gave, and she clung to the door-jamb, breathing in the sweet fresh scent of roses and gillyflowers as they bloomed in the warm evening air. Then she sank to the floor, too weary to move another step.

It seemed an age before she heard footsteps on the stairs, and then it was the running feet of a boy. They looked at one another as he reached the top, and Felicia attempted to smile from her position on the floor. She was slumped against the door across the threshold, and he could not pass without stepping over her. He showed only the barest quiver of surprise at the sight of her.

'I—I felt like a breath of air,' she murmured. 'Could you help me back to bed, Harry? I find I cannot get up again.'

He made a clicking noise with his tongue and teeth, scrubbed at his chin and screwed up his face. 'Don't know, but I'll try.' He dropped on one knee and held out a hand. Felicia took it, not sure if he could take her weight. But the thought of sending him to fetch help made her grit her teeth, and by edging herself up with her elbows against the door-jamb, and with the aid of his surprisingly strong young hands, she managed to get to her feet. Slowly they made their way until at last they reached the further room, and Felicia was able to sink thankfully on to the bed.

'Thank you, Harry. Can this be a secret between you and me? The others would be angry if they knew that I got out of bed—especially Master de Vert. But it is tiresome lying here with nothing to do but think.' She dimpled at him, and he grinned back.

'Master Edmund already has a face as dark as a thundercloud!' He bounced up and down on the bed. 'Mother sent me up to ask if you are able to do a little mending. Your surcote is dry, but it needs stitching.' He sprang suddenly down and did a somersault across the wooden floor. 'Also ...' he panted, wobbling slightly, 'would you like fish for supper—or eels? I caught them in the river with my friend Sam.'

'I would like both! I mean the sewing— and the fish or the eels. I do not mind. Is it lovely down by the river? Did you catch many fish and eels?'

'Six eels and four fish. Sam caught ten eels but no fish.' He grinned again. Two of his front teeth were missing. 'We were even, although my fish were bigger than Sam's eels.'

'Do you swim?' Felicia gave a sigh. 'How I would love to swim now in cool water.'

'You swim!' Harry looked impressed. 'I cannot swim yet. Uncle Dickon is going to show me how. He would have done when I was smaller, but my mother and father were always scared I would catch a fever and die. Oh! Uncle Dickon asked if you would like some wine. He took delivery of some from France only a week ago.'

'I would. Give him my heartfelt thanks.'

'All right!' Harry gave her a wave and went out of the room, leaving the door ajar.

Felicia started to wonder how often the outside door was left unlocked. Or had it been so that evening only because Edmund had left her in such anger? How would she face him when next he came? They did not seem to be able to have any discourse that did not cause disharmony. It would be best, perhaps, if they saw less of each other. Yet, should he come, she would behave in a cool and aloof manner.

But Edmund did not come that evening, or the next day or the next. At first Felicia was glad. Her mixed emotions settled down. She often felt low spirited, but she told herself that that was only to be expected after all she had been through. Nell, Dickon and Harry visited her, bringing her food and drink, medicine, and work to do with her needle. Her bruises began to change colour, and her pains eased. Each day, when the others were not around, she would rise from her bed and stretch her limbs, taking short walks about the two rooms. She did not ask after Edmund, because she knew what he was doing without having to mention his name. Nell and Dickon told her that he spent time with the almoner at the monastery, and visiting the sick. She did not need Nell to tell her that she had been spending time with Edmund. Each evening Nell came to bed with such a 'cat got the cream' expression on her lovely face that it irritated her unbearably.

When on the third day Edmund did not come to visit or even send word enquiring after her health, her pent-up anger grew and bubbled over. She determined to escape from the house and make her way across the river to the abbey. She would seek the help of the abbot there to reach Meriet. The sooner she was away from Master Edmund de Vert, the quicker she would forget all about him. It would be best to wait until supper-time, when most of the household would be in the hall. Dickon had even asked her if she would like him to carry her down that evening. She had put him off, saying she still did not like sitting for long periods. Her supper was brought up; an excellent meal of chicken and herbs, followed by a fruit pastry. With little appetite, she barely touched it. She dressed in her own clothes and braided her dark hair, which she had left loose for days. Her only regret was that she could not say goodbye and thank you to the family who had shown her such warm hospitality. A more painful regret she would not admit to feeling.

She crept down the steps with a stealthy awkwardness. It was a warm, golden June evening, and its beauty led her to pause. Her heart ached strangely at the sight of all the fertile loveliness of the garden—but she must escape before she was discovered. Making her way between beds of roses, gillyflowers, cabbages, onions and herbs, and past a handful of squabbling fowl scratching in the earth, she went out through a wicket gate.

Drawing a shaky breath, she began to walk, rather stiffly, but with more ease as she went along, towards one of the bridges that crossed the Severn. Fortunately she had visited Shrewsbury often, and knew her way about its streets. It did not take her long to reach the river. She paused for a moment on the bridge and nestled her chin upon her arms as she rested, gazing down at the swirling water, trying to shrug off her depression. Then she began to walk again towards the abbey, and had reached the other side of the river when she heard a splash and a child's sudden scream, that was abruptly cut off.

She turned round on the path and looked towards the water. As she stared intently, a head broke the surface, and her heart seemed to stop beating as she recognised the curls. Without pausing to think, she began to move down to the water's edge, forcing her idle muscles to strain and stretch as her hands beat the air.

A lad—straight-haired and with a chubby face—whirled round as he heard her coming. His face was strained but resolute, and he had already stepped into the water, hoping to reach his friend.

'Are you Sam?' panted Felicia. The boy nodded. 'Go! Go and fetch Master Edmund the physician and Harry's mother. You will do little good with that stick.' Felicia tore at the fastenings on her surcote, kicked off her shoes, and within seconds had plunged into the water, not waiting to see if the boy did as she had bidden.

Already the current was taking Harry away from the bank. Felicia struck out towards him and went with the current. She caught a glimpse, and then saw him gasp air before sinking below the surface. Frantically she beat the water with her arms and legs, cursing her hampering underskirts. She dived. It was green, foaming and swift beneath the surface. She saw a twisting form and struck out towards it. Her hand hit flesh and her fingers twisted about cloth. Her lungs were bursting as she sought air above, dragging her burden. She bobbed up like a cork, wrenching Harry with her. She drew air into her lungs and felt with desperate fingers for Harry's face as she turned on her back and went with the current again. She caught glimpses of people on the bank, some running. Then ahead of her she saw men in the river, and a boat. Within moments she reached them, and several pairs of hands grasped her and held her safe as Harry was lifted from her arms.

'Now, missy, you lie still. We've got the lad. Half filled with water he is, but still alive.'

'Thank God! Thank God!' she gasped, allowing herself to be helped from the river.

Someone sat her down on the bank, and she began to shiver with cold and reaction. An elderly man with white whiskers offered her a flask, which she would have refused, but he insisted.

'Now you don't want to go down with the fever, missy. Take a swig. 'Twill do you good.'

Fever? Master Edmund! What had she done? She must go. Go to the abbot. She struggled to rise, but was forced down.

'Now then—now then! Don't be so hasty, little missy. You must rest, or you'll swoon on the way home, I wouldn't wonder. Now here's my good lady. She'll take care of you. Don't fret.' The man moved back, and an ample-bosomed female with several chins and dressed in sensible brown homespun knelt down beside Felicia.

'Now m'dear! It will do you nothing but good to have a little drink of this. It is of my own making.' The voice was kind and brooked no argument. Felicia gave in and did as she was told, resting against the plump arm supporting her shoulders. She took a cautious sip of the spicy burning liquor, then several more as warmth began to course through her veins, relaxing her cold body. Within minutes a sweet warm languor filled her and she ceased worrying. She snuggled against the comforting pillow of the bosom next to her cheek. The voice murmuring gently in her ear, and the bosom, somehow made her feel safe. She began to think of her old nurse and how she had whispered stories to help her to sleep after her mother had died. What was it she had been worrying about? Felicia found she could not remember. She shut her eyes and gave in to the weariness that weighed down her limbs.

Edmund listened with only half an ear to what Nell was saying. He stared down at the chessboard as a sense of boredom overwhelmed him. It was his own fault that he had to listen. He had encouraged Nell to talk, and she had talked in the last few days, to show her great interest in proving something to himself.

Dickon plucked idly at the strings of his lute, and Edmund felt his nerves stretch and tighten. Suddenly he rose to his feet. It was no use—he had to make an excuse. He could say that it was time they were on their way if he were to take her to Meriet first. He would pretend that he did not know how she was getting on. Surely she should be on her feet more by now? Was she perhaps staying up in the room to avoid him?

Nell looked up at him, startled by his abrupt movement. 'Where are you going?'

124

Edmund bit back a curse and smiled at her. She was looking lovely in a green undergown of cotton embroidered with silver thread, yet she did not cause his senses to stir. 'I thought I would go and see how Mistress Felicia is faring. I have been busy the last few days, and would like to see for myself if her condition is improving.'

'I shall come with you.' Nell got up. 'I want to see if Harry has gone to bed as I told him to. He should not have stayed out so late last evening.'

Edmund forced himself to return her smile. 'Of course. Come, by all means,' he said stiffly, aware of Dickon's eyes upon him. Before he could move, there came a loud hammering. He lifted a startled eyebrow and glanced at Dickon, who rose and went over to the door. The banging increased.

'I'm coming!' shouted Dickon. 'Don't knock the door down.' He flung it open, and Sam fell forward into the hall. He was tugged up quickly by Edmund.

'Sam! What is it, boy, that you make such an uproar? Have you caught a giant fish and wish to tell Harry about it?' Dickon cried.

Sam shook his head. His face was flushed, and sweat ran in rivulets down his neck. ' 'Tis awful! Harry's in the

125

river and likely drowning! A maid went in after him and told me to fetch the physician and his mother.' Sam would have sunk to the floor but for Edmund's steadying hand.

'What? I don't believe it! It cannot be!' Nell's face was drained of all colour.

Edmund's eyes went to Dickon. 'Best you see to Nell. I shall go with the boy. There might be some mistake.'

'I should go,' insisted Dickon, going over to his sister. 'Good God, Edmund, it is my place!' He slipped an arm under his sister, smoothing back her hair and veil. 'The boy is supposed to be in bed.'

'He *is* a boy, isn't he?' Edmund smiled grimly. 'Your place is with Nell. What can you do that I can't? I am the physician.' Dickon nodded, his expression strained and uncertain. 'Don't start worrying before you have to—it sounds as though Harry had a rescuer, and the riverside is seldom empty of folk on such a fine evening. But build up a fire and get out some dry clothing—perhaps a hot tub.' He turned to the boy. 'Can you still run, lad?'

Sam nodded, and dashed away a smutty tear.

'Come on, then, show me which part of the river. Make haste!' Edmund and he rushed out.

A crowd was just coming across the

126

bridge as they reached it. They were murmuring and chattering excitedly, seeming in a good mood. Edmund seized one of the men's arms.

'It's Paul isn't it?' Edmund jerked the man to a halt. A small circle gathered about them. 'Tell me, man, is the boy safe? Have you seen him?'

'Oh! 'Tis you, sir.' Paul grinned and scratched his nose. 'He's safe enough, albeit he's coughing up half the river! I saw some of what happened from the bridge. Some young maid went in after him and brought him to the surface. They were carried by the current, but she was fetched ashore with the lad by several of the men. Plucky deed! Risked her life to save young Harry's.' He touched his forelock and went on his way, leaving Edmund and Sam staring after him.

Edmund felt a tug on his shirt and slowly looked at Sam.

'Can we go and find Harry? Just to see if he is all right, really. And the maid—I hope she's all right. She looked as scared as I felt!'

'Did she, Sam?' Edmund smiled down at him. Thank God, he would not have to go back with dread tidings to Nell and Dickon.

They made their way across the bridge in the direction whence several stragglers were still coming. Sam pointed to the spot at which Harry had fallen in, and Edmund remembered Dickon's words about teaching him to swim. He would have to teach the boy now—unless his dip in the river had put him off water for life! At last they came to a small group of people on the bank. Harry was sitting up. His clothes still dripped water, and a plump, motherly-looking woman sat on the grass nursing a huddled bundle clad in a yellow undergown that clung to a shapely figure. Edmund felt a strange sense of apprehension. He quickened his pace. Surely it could not be—yet Harry should not have been here either!

'Master Edmund!' rang out Harry's trembling voice. It drew his unwilling attention. 'It is Mistress Felicia, and she saved my life! Now she will not answer when I call her.'

'Tush, boy, she ...' began the woman who cuddled Felicia.

Edmund did not hear the rest of the words. He stared with dread into Felicia's face. River, trees, sky and earth seemed to blur into a oneness before they shifted and separated again. Suddenly he realised that her breast was rising and falling with a steadiness that showed she was very much alive. He went down on one knee beside her. How had she come here, he wondered, reaching out an unsteady hand to touch the fading bruise on her face. Had she been escaping from him? A muscle quivered in his cheek.

'She's all right, sir,' said the woman. 'Just worn out, and a little tipsy, perhaps.'

Edmund barely heard her speak. He was wondering if the last three days had been Felicia's pretence to conceal that she was getting well.

'She's only tipsy, sir,' repeated the woman.

This time he took her words in. 'Tipsy?' Edmund gave a sigh of relief. 'What did you give her?'

'Only a drop of this, lad.' The bearded husband thrust the flask in Edmund's face.

Edmund took it and pulled the stopper, sniffing it before taking a cautious sip. 'God's blood! No wonder she's sleeping.'

'It won't do her any harm, sir.' The woman's voice was anxious. 'She was shivering so much that we had to do something.'

'Of course,' said Edmund hastily. 'I understand.' He unfastened his surcote. 'Here, let me take her.' He turned his head slightly. 'Sam! You give Harry a hand up, if he is fit.' He did not wait to see if Sam was doing as bidden, but eased Felicia on to his outstretched surcote, then slid his arms beneath her and lifted her, wrapping her in it.

Her eyelids flickered, then opened. She winced, then glanced up at Edmund. 'I ... I thought ... I heard your voice,' she said drowsily, 'but thought it a dream. You have not been to see me for—oh! so long. I dreamed Harry was drowning, and I couldn't reach him.' She yawned and clutched Edmund's tunic. Then her eyes widened as she looked about her.

'You are not dreaming—but you did reach Harry, and he is safe,' Edmund murmured in a reassuring voice.

'I did?' She gave a great sigh. 'I'm not dreaming, and you are not angry with me?'

'Not at the moment!' He grinned, and rose to his feet. 'But the swifter you and Harry are in bed, the better I will like it. Put your arms round my neck if you can. I can carry you more easily like that.'

She stared up into his smiling face and blushed. 'There is no need for you to carry me. I can walk, Edmund. It is Harry who needs looking after.'

'Fiddle! Harry can look after himself. He seems to have got rid of most of the river he swallowed. He has Sam to help him.'

'But ...'

'No buts! You will do as you are told.' He swung her round so that she faced

130

the couple who had helped her, and he thanked them both.

'It was our pleasure, sir.' The woman gave a bobbing curtsy. 'I am certain the young lady will take no harm. Would you like to take the flask with you?'

'That is kind of you,' replied Edmund hurriedly. 'But I am a physician, and shall be able to prescribe a remedy of my own.'

'I do thank you both,' interrupted Felicia, smiling at the couple. 'It warmed me so, and I feel much better than I did when I came out of the water. Thank you again.'

The husband muttered some words in a gruff voice that were incomprehensible. Then he doffed his cap, and he and his wife turned away and began to hasten up the river bank to the bridge.

'Will I go and fetch the lady's surcote, sir?' piped up Sam. 'She left it down by the river where we were fishing.' He stared up at Edmund and Felicia, his eyes shining brightly. His arm was about Harry's shoulders.

'Can you swim, Sam?' said Edmund sternly.

'Ay, sir. My brother taught me.'

'Go, then—but be swift about it ... Hey, Harry, not you—you stay with me. I'm taking no chances!' Edmund frowned down at him as Sam scampered off. 'If you are lucky, Harry, you just might get away without the hiding you deserve! I doubt that your mother could bear to see you walloped, but I am certain her cosseting and insistence that you stay in bed for the next day or so will be punishment enough. And, doubtless, there will be no more fishing until you learn to swim! Now—march!'

Harry pulled a face, but marched.

'Very right and proper too,' murmured Felicia, a quiver in her voice. 'You remind me of Father when he used to bark at my brother Mark. But his bark was worse than his bite, too!'

'You believe that of me?' Edmund's voice was low and intense. 'Yet you were running away, I gather ... From me?'

There was a short silence as he stepped over a tree root and his arms tightened about her. Felicia's heart jerked against his ribs. His face she could not see clearly now that they were beneath the trees. She wished she could, for then she might know how best to answer his question.

'I was only running as far as the abbot's lodgings. I know you have been too busy the last few days—too busy to dance attendance on me.' There was the slightest echo in her reply of the last words he had spoken to her three days earlier.

'You told me to go away, so I did. Surely you have not been lonely? You have had Dickon to dance attendance on you.'

They came out of the trees, and Felicia looked up at him. Did he really think that she and Dickon ... What of he and Nell!

'Without Dickon, Nell and Harry, I might have run earlier,' she murmured coolly. Her fingers tightened on his neck, as his face stiffened.

'I see,' he said with controlled calm. 'But there was no need for you to run at all.'

'You don't see ...' she retorted. 'You still think ...' Before she could finish, they had come to the bridge, and Sam came running up breathlessly, holding out Felicia's surcote.

'It is a bit dusty, but unharmed.' He held it up to her, but Edmund told him to hold on to it.

'You have done well this evening, young Sam.' He smiled down at the boy. 'Do you think that you could go ahead with Harry? His mother will be pleased to see you both, although I think that Paul will be before you with the news.'

The boy nodded, and Harry gave a groan of apprehension. Then they both ran ahead over the bridge. When Edmund and Felicia came to the other side, she was

133

suddenly aware of the curious glances of the constable's men as they passed.

'You could put me down now. I think I could walk as far as the house,' she whispered.

Edmund gave no reply, or move to do as she asked.

'Surely you do not think I will attempt to run away now?' She struggled in his grasp.

'Keep still! It is not that,' he said sharply. 'You have had a shock, and how do you think you will look, walking the streets in that damp gown? If you wear my surcote you will attract even more attention. It is a little on the large side!'

The corner of his mouth tilted up, and Felicia was suddenly aware that the surcote was slipping from her shoulders. Instantly she was conscious of just how damp and clinging her undergown was, and looked hurriedly away from Edmund's interested gaze. 'I did not thank you for coming so quickly,' she said, in an attempt to change the subject.

'I did not know it was you. I was just on my way to see you in the bedchamber and to tell you that, when you are able to ride again, I shall take you to Meriet.'

'You—You were?' She smiled dazzlingly up into his face. 'Does that mean you believe me at last?'

Edmund halted. They had come to the market square. 'It is because I realise that I was wrong in the way I acted. You were not to blame for what your cousin did. I was angry with you for saying that I used you in the same way as your cousin did. If you think that is so, Mistress Felicia, I am sorry.'

There was a flush on his cheekbones, and in that moment Felicia realised what it had cost him to say the words.

'Perhaps I was too hasty,' she murmured. 'If you had not abducted me, I think I would still be my cousin's prisoner. Instead, I shall soon be on my way to Meriet.' She laughed. 'I thank you for that much, Edmund.'

He inclined his tawny head, and smiled. 'Then, as soon as you are fit, we shall ride to Meriet.' He began to walk again across the square to Dickon's house. 'Will it be soon? Sam said he thought you were trying to run. How long have you been practising your steps?'

'Practising?' Felicia lifted delicately curved eyebrows. 'I assure you that was the first time. I walked very slowly and painfully at first. I could not let Harry drown.' She flushed at the gleam in his eye. 'And if you had not quarrelled with me and swept out of the room in a rage, I would not have got out of bed and

135

discovered that the door to the garden was left open. Really, I could no sooner lie meekly back after that than you could stay here, as Nell said, in safety and not go and seek out the Lord Edward.'

'I was not the one who was angry—and you will pay in the morning for running off.' There was a wicked satisfaction in the smile he gave her. 'It might mean that we shall be delayed again, but it seems, Mistress Felicia, that the safe, the easy way is not for either of us.' On those words he carried her into the hall.

Screens had been set about the fire, and although there was no one in sight, they could hear the sound of voices coming from beyond the screens, as well as the splash of water. A serving-maid bustled in with a pail, and slopped water on the floor, barely noticing Felicia and Edmund as she retreated behind the screens.

'Good! Nell did get the tub out. A hot bath is just what you need. It will loosen any stiffness and chill from your bones.'

'But ...' began Felicia, when she was interrupted by an unearthly yell and the sound of tippling water.

'No more, Mother! No more! All this water cannot be good for me. Look! My skin is changing colour!'

'And a good thing too,' said Dickon

sternly. 'The worry you caused your mother, my lad! You stink of the river and fish, and goodness knows what else.'

'Don't shout at him, Dickon,' came Nell's flustered voice. 'He has had enough of a shock. But God only knows how we shall get the mud from his hose.'

Felicia and Edmund exchanged glances, and she wrinkled her nose. 'I suppose I, too, stink of the river,' she whispered.

Edmund smiled, but made no answer.

'And where did you leave Edmund and Felicia, did you say?' came Dickon's voice again. 'I wonder if I should go to look for them, Nell.' He sounded worried.

'We are here,' called Edmund. He edged round the screens, and Felicia was instantly aware of several pairs of eyes upon her.

Nell stopped rubbing Harry's hair and dropped the cloth. She moved forward swiftly, her hands outstretched. 'I do not understand how you did it, but I am in your debt for ever for saving Harry's life.'

Edmund set Felicia on her feet. 'Now is not the time for questions, Nell,' he said hurriedly. 'As soon as Harry is out of the tub, Mistress Meriet must go into it.'

'Of course!' Nell smiled her heartfelt thanks and gazed at Felicia with sympathy. 'But you are so wet ... And your hair! We will chase these men out and fill the tub again. I have a herbal mixture that will be just the thing for you.'

'Thank you,' murmured Felicia, not sure how to cope with Nell's effusive gratitude.

'Mary!' Nell turned to the serving-maid. 'You will prepare Master Harry's bed before you fetch some more water to be heated. Ask Paul to help you ... Dickon, could you help me to lift Harry out of the tub?'

'Of course, sister.' Dickon moved swiftly. He cast a smile towards Felicia. 'Paul told us that Harry was safe, but he could not tell us that it was you who did the saving, as he did not know you. You will always have our sincere gratitude. Harry is a ruffian, but he is all we have.'

'Ruffian, brother?' Nell sounded half annoyed, half amused. 'It must be the company he keeps. Sam—and all those brothers of his.'

'Sam is a good lad,' said Edmund, giving Nell a glance that contained a hint of rebuke.

'Ay, he would have gone in to help Harry,' put in Felicia.

'Sam can swim, Mother,' said Harry, poking a ruffled head from beneath folds of rough linen. 'He is my friend, and I intend to stay his friend.' His mouth set mutinously.

'I can see you are all against me!'

Nell looked annoyed. Then she looked at her son and laughed unexpectedly. 'I understand. I do not forget what bonds of friendship boys forge. It was so with Dickon, Edmund and Steven. Always they defended each other.' It seemed to Felicia that she would have said more as she gazed about the circle of faces. 'But what am I thinking of—talking so at such a time as this. Edmund, shoo! Dickon, as soon as Harry is dry and dressed for bed, you will carry him up for me. I do not want him overtaxing his strength.'

Harry let out a groan, but his mother only gave him a loving hug. 'If we do not hurry, Mistress Meriet will be spending several more days in bed instead of going home. So let us move.'

Harry, Edmund and Dickon moved.

It was hot in the fragrant water. Felicia sighed in sheer pleasure, and held up a glistening shapely leg above the surface. It did not hurt, and she felt as if suddenly she had come through a baptism and was cleansed. The firelight made the water appear to be shot through with yellow and silver. Beyond the screens the candles glowed softly, and there seemed to be a kind of enchantment about bathing in such a light.

But it was getting late. She stood up, beginning to squeeze water from her long

139

dark hair. Nell had gone to fetch her a clean gown. Her own had been washed in the tub, and Mary had hung it out in the warm night air. Felicia was so intent on trying to dry her hair that she did not hear the soft tread of feet on the rushes beyond the screens. She reached out to take one of the linen cloths that Nell had left, and swung her hair down in front of her face. Carefully she gathered all the strands together in its folds before twisting it and wrapping it about her head. She was just about to lift her head when she saw the feet. Slowly, almost unbelievingly, she raised her head.

Felicia blushed, and the heat of it seemed to stretch from the roots of her hair to her toes as Edmund's gaze lingered on her. She could not move her eyes from his face, and did not know what to do. Her hands were still upstretched, clasping the towel to her head. She licked her lips nervously.

'I always wanted to meet a mermaid!' His voice was barely audible. 'But you will catch cold if you stand like that much longer.'

He moved forward and picked up the other towel. Before she could protest, he shook it open and held it out in front of her, shielding her from his eyes. As though in a dream, she stepped out of the tub.

He wrapped the towel about her body and began to rub her firmly.

Felicia's heart began to hammer. His harsh caress with the towel had set her skin tingling, filling her with excitement. 'No! Please!' she whispered, lowering her arms and clutching at the towel with trembling fingers.

He stopped, but still he held her between his hands, and she was instantly aware that he was shaking. He pressed his lips against her bare shoulder, bringing her body closer to his with hard insistent hands.

'No!' she said huskily, as she lifted her mouth to his kiss. His lips fastened possessively over hers with a hungry fierceness that set her blood on fire. Their lips parted only to be drawn irresistibly together again. Felicia knew that she should try to stop him, to fight him, but it was as if her body was no longer under control of her will. It seemed to have a life of its own, wanting to reach out to the vitality that was so much a part of the man who held her, and join it. Her body arched against his, and he lifted her off her feet and buried his head between her breasts, murmuring unintelligible words against her sweet-smelling, still damp skin. Her arms had gone, of their own accord, round him, and with one hand she caressed the nape of his neck beneath the newly trimmed

141

hair. She could not understand her own longing to be so close to this man who had abducted her, or her hunger to be wanted by him, and for him to go on wanting her. For him to love her, even—the thought trickled through into her consciousness. No! That was impossible!

Felicia began to shiver. She moaned as he caressed her taut nipples with warm, searching fingers. The towel had slipped from her hair, sending damp tentacles cascading about her shoulders. Wet! a voice said in her head. Her hair was wet from being in the tub after rescuing Harry! Harry! Nell! What if Nell returned now with her gown? By all the saints in heaven, what was she doing in Edmund's arms without a stitch on? The thought caused heat to sear her body, even as Edmund's mouth found hers again. Dear God, why did she want him so? Her lips clung to his before she withdrew her arms hurriedly and wrenched herself out of his grasp.

Edmund's breath came unevenly, and he reached out a hand for her again. She made a hasty grab for the towel, which had slipped to the floor. Her face was aflame, and she looked anywhere but at him as she wrapped the cloth round her nakedness.

'Felicia!' His harsh voice contained a

note of entreaty as he stepped forward.

'No! Don't touch me!' She gazed up into his burning eyes and was frightened of her own responding wave of yearning. 'Go! Please go.' She backed away from him, pressing against the wooden tub, her eyes wide and apprehensive.

'What?' He stared at her dully, running a hand repeatedly through his hair. 'You can say that, after ...'

'You should not have stayed. Go now. If Dickon ... or Nell ...' The words faltered on her lips at the expression on his face. She turned from him and went over to the fire, staring unseeingly into its golden heart.

'Damn you, for the cold-hearted wanton you must be!' Edmund exclaimed in a seething voice before turning on his heel and going from her.

The shock of his words caused her head to shoot up, and an anguished cry rose to her lips. She wanted to call him back, to deny his accusation, to explain her fears and to hold him in her arms again, but her affronted pride caused the words to die even as the door opened and shut behind him. Tears pricked her eyes, and a sense of utter desolation overshadowed the wonder of what had gone before.

She bent to pick up the other towel that had fallen, and sank on a stool to rub her hair again, holding her head near the fire, trying not to think. It seemed a long time before the quick patter of Nell's feet came into the hall.

'I beg your pardon for being so long,' she said, slightly breathless. 'Harry was not in his bed, but looking out of the window. Then I met Edmund and Dickon in the garden, so I paused to have word with them.' She handed a gown to Felicia, who took it with a murmur of thanks. It had white daisies worked at the hem and neck, and its long yellow sleeves were tight fitting. Felicia shrugged herself into it, shivering slightly.

Nell frowned. 'I do hope you haven't caught a chill? Edmund said he must be on his way in the morning.' She looked pensive. 'Dickon offered to take you to Meriet, if Edmund wanted to go on ahead and you were not fit in the morning, but Edmund said in such a strange angry voice that he had charge of you and would see you safely to your manor.' She glanced at Felicia, and smiled. 'I think he is cross with you because you did not let him know that you had improved so much, and he could have been away earlier. It is not very flattering to me, but then I suppose he has much on his mind with what happened to his mother.'

'I suppose so,' murmured Felicia, feeling

cold at the thought of what Nell would have felt and said if she had come into the hall earlier. She fastened the riband about her throat with stiff fingers.

'I shall take these towels to Mary,' said Nell with a slightly worried frown. 'Do not wait for me, but go up to bed if you wish. Mary shall bring us both a goblet of wine, and we shall drink each other's health.' She disappeared behind the screens with a whisper of cotton.

Felicia sat down again and combed out her hair. It was still damp, but it would have to do. She braided it and then slipped her feet into the pair of soft leather slippers Nell had left by the fire. Her own shoes she had left at the river bank, and Sam had not thought to pick them up. She rose to her feet and, feeling slightly apprehensive, walked to the back of the hall, hoping that Edmund was not still in the garden. She felt unbearably weary.

Dickon came towards her as soon as she stepped outside. He took both her hands and squeezed them tightly. 'How are you feeling, Felicia? You look as fresh and pretty as the daisies on your gown. Who would have believed, Edmund, that she has been through so much?' He turned his head slightly towards his friend.

'Who, indeed?' said Edmund sardonically, approaching them slowly. Felicia could not help glancing at him. Their eyes caught but briefly, and the chill in his caused her to look away at once.

'Harry said you must have swum like a fish to save him,' said Dickon, still holding Felicia's hands. 'You must be the veriest mermaid. Don't you agree, Edmund? It is unusual in a woman.'

'Of course I agree,' responded Edmund in a smooth voice. 'But then Mistress Meriet is full of surprises.' He snapped off a rosebud and held it to his nose. 'I just pray she will continue to surprise me by being ready to ride in the morning.'

'I shall be ready,' she said with determination.

'Good!' Edmund tossed her the rose. 'Best you go to bed; we don't want you fainting on the way.' He turned away and took Dickon's arm. 'Now, my friend. I think a game of chess?'

'Ay!' Dickon's voice was slightly grim, and his eyes went from Felicia's pale face to Edmund's set one. 'Good night to you, Mistress Felicia.'

'And to you, sirs,' murmured Felicia.

They both bowed slightly and went on into the hall. Felicia stared after them. There was an unfamiliar ache inside her. She sniffed the rose, and then dropped it angrily before turning and climbing the stairs to bed.

CHAPTER SIX

'Are you certain you feel well enough to ride?' insisted Nell, as Edmund was lifting Felicia on to the pillion seat he had managed to purchase.

Felicia's mouth was set firmly, despite her trepidation. She had been going to suggest that she rode with Dickon, but one look at Edmund's stern face had caused the words to remain unspoken.

'I am certain.' Felicia's lips eased into a smile. 'Thank you for your concern, Nell. I shall always remember you with much gratitude.'

'It is kind of you to say so, although our debt is the greater.' A shadow flickered across Nell's face. 'You speak as if we shall never meet again, but surely you come into town on occasions? If you can, come for the fair in July and stay with me.'

'Thank you. And if you are ever in need of a rest from town life, come to Meriet. You will find my direction from the abbot.'

Briefly the two women clasped hands before Nell stepped back. She turned to Dickon, and kissed him on the cheek.

'Take care, brother! I do not quite trust to your common sense if you are to be in Edmund's company.' She smiled mischievously at Edmund and held out both hands to him. 'Take care of him for me. And yourself.'

'I shall, never fear.' Edmund squeezed her hands briefly. 'Do not forget to ask one of Sam's brothers to teach Harry to swim. Even Paul will not be able to keep his eye on him all the time, Nell.'

Nell nodded. 'It is not easy to bring a boy up without a husband.' She sighed, and gazed into Edmund's face.

'You do your best, and that is all you can do,' he responded quietly. 'I shall return your brother to you safely.' He released Nell's hands and turned away.

Felicia scrutinised his features for any sign of the despondent lover, but his expression was an enigma as he climbed into the saddle. She could only be glad that he had not whispered words of love to Nell, and was instantly ashamed of herself. She gripped the back of his belt, and then she had time only to lift a hand in farewell before the horses began to move. The next time she looked back towards the house, Nell had gone. For a moment she experienced a sense of regret and loss. Never having had a older sister, she would have liked a closer relationship, as close as the tie between herself and her cousin Joan. Perhaps her own awareness of Edmund and his long acquaintance with Nell had made that impossible. Why had he started to make love to her as he had last night if he did truly care for Nell? Or did he think to treat herself in any way he desired? At the beginning, did he already think of her as the wanton he had several times accused her of being? Her throat tightened. She should never have let him touch her. She raised her head and gazed at his straight back, feeling its strength and warmth beneath her fingertips. No! She must not think of how it had been—that way lay weakness. Best to put him out of her mind utterly. The sooner she parted from him, the better. But heart-searching could wait until another day, and her spirits rose as she looked about her. It was a lovely morning. When she took a deep breath, the scent of baking teased her nostrils. She smiled to herself determinedly. It was good to be alive!

They halted at the bridge, where Edmund dismounted, to Felicia's surprise, and went over to a small boy. Several beggars huddled at his approach. Edmund sat back on his haunches, so that his face was almost level with the boy's. He could not have been more than ten years old, and he moved himself along on a wheeled trolley by pushing two wooden plattens beneath his hands. Edmund seemed to speak very earnestly to him before ruffling the mop of matted hair. The lad grinned, and he smiled back before dropping several coins into his pouch. She felt a stir of admiration as Edmund rose to his feet and mounted again. It was a Christian duty to give to the poor and disabled, but there were not many who would go to the length of actually touching such a dirty urchin.

'Is he the one?' asked Dickon, as they moved on to the bridge.

'Ay. You will do as I ask when the conflict is over, and give him a chance?'

'If you think him worth it, my friend.' Dickon shrugged his shoulders. 'Are you sure he is as clever as you think?'

'He is,' replied Edmund.

'What is wrong with the boy?' Felicia looped her fingers through Edmund's belt again. 'And what a lovely smile he has, despite the dirt.'

'He has withered legs—and he would say that his dirt kept him warm. He has been unable to walk since birth.' His voice was matter of fact.

'Was he damaged at birth? I have seen a maid thus in our village,' persisted Felicia, interested.

'Ay, his mother died after his birth. His

grandmother takes care of him—but there is little money.'

'Is that why you were arranging matters with Dickon so that there might be more money?' Felicia was discovering a different side to Edmund. He nodded. 'Can you do nothing for him?' Her voice was soft with concern. 'My nurse used to say that demons caused sickness, and that deformity was a punishment from God. Yet sometimes I think it is a lack of care and the dreadful food these poor people have to eat. So often it is rotten.'

'I consider that food and filth have much to do with sickness,' responded Edmund. 'But not John's. I helped in the infirmary at Huppingescumbe, the monastery where my uncle Walter is abbot. A boy there had lost both parents and had been living off scraps until he was brought to our attention, thin as a reed and always sickly. We thought he would die, but it was like a miracle. Some good plain food, warm clean clothes—and Brother Thomas was a great believer in the healing properties of spring water! The boy was scrubbed thoroughly.'

Felicia could hear the smile in his voice. She had accepted him as a physician without really thinking of it being such a part of his life, and an important part.

'What is it like to be a physician—do you

151

find pleasure in it?' she asked in doubtless tones.

'Pleasure!' He gave a mirthless laugh. 'Sometimes I hate it. My patients often die, despite the cures I learnt at Oxford. I study the stars in their courses, as I was taught. I know about the humours of the body and of potions from the East. I patch up wounds and give advice, but often the remedies I learnt from my mother are the ones that work. I make a living, and sometimes I can help those who cannot help themselves. I can always watch and learn. Sometimes I find to my surprise that I have cured someone of an ailment that I had no luck with before. Then I find pleasure. And I thank God for it!' He fell silent, and Felicia, moved by his words, could not think of anything to say.

She considered him unusual in her experience of physicians. The majority of those whom she had encountered were charlatans—out to make the most of their life and death calling, but he seemed to care. She felt the sun on her face, and banished her gloomy thoughts. To their left lay the abbey buildings. Her ears caught the song of a lark as it hovered high above the fields of pease and corn. Blossom, pink and creamy, covered the fruit trees ahead. Her spirits rose further.

For a while they rode abreast. Edmund and Dickon chatting desultorily about the town and the passing scene. The road was busy with people going to and fro. Monks were on their way to the abbey, either on foot or on muleback. Richly dressed merchants sat astride fine horses, while their servants walked, leading the pack-animals laden with goods. A peasant passed, driving his pig before him, his stout wife panting to keep up, at the same time trying not to spill the eggs in her basket. Gradually the road became less populated, and unexpectedly they heard thundering hooves and the jingling of harnesses.

Swiftly the two men dragged their horses off the road, only just in time to avoid being trampled by a company of armed and mailed men. They swept by, banners flying, their faces determined and grim. Felicia stared after them, noting the colours and markings on the trappings, surcotes and shields. For a fearful moment she had thought it was her cousin in pursuit of her, although she knew she was being foolish. Surely he would be well ahead of them on the road to the south? Never would he have delayed as long as this in obeying Earl Simon de Montfort. He was well gone. She dismissed him from her mind, and instead concentrated on the way ahead. Soon they would need to turn and go east.

Another mile, and she pointed out to Edmund a barely discernible path that twisted snakelike between two gently sloping hills. Eventually it led them to rough moorland, thick with bracken and yellow gorse, which gave off a sweet nutty fragrance. Overhead a sparrow-hawk soared, and instantly she was reminded of her cousin again. She was angry with herself. She should be feeling happy now: not far to Meriet. Why did she keep on thinking of Philip now that home was so near? He would be far away, and her thoughts should be on what lay ahead: Joan, her cousin—Sir William, her steward—Ralph, the bailiff. She would gaze on her own manor. It was a long year since she had called it home. The house amid the gardens; the river where she had learnt to swim purely to annoy Sir William's son; the forest, where she had killed her first boar. Oh, it would be good to be home again!

Yet, even as her spirits lifted, they drooped again. Soon she would be parting from Edmund, and from Dickon. Edmund had done as she had begged, and was taking her home. Her mind touched lightly on what it would feel like when he left and went out of her life. She barely knew him, yet it felt as though she had known him for a long time. What power was it that made her feel like that—and to want him to touch her, and she, him? Surely it would pass once he was gone. It must. Within the hour they topped a hill and began the descent into the valley wherein Meriet lay.

'There is the copse where my father took me on my first hunt!' cried Felicia, her fingers curling and uncurling on Edmund's back. 'Soon we shall come to the mill and the river. Then we shall see the village, and not far from there is my manor house.'

'You are glad to be coming home.' Edmund's voice was rough, his words a statement more than a question. He surveyed the scene, interested despite the irrational sense of gloom that suddenly descended upon him. 'It is fertile soil here?'

'Fertile enough. But, like all land, it requires much work and a fair share of serfs. My father and brother desired to buy more land, to cut down trees and put the land to the plough—but the war came, and—and I do not know yet what I shall do about such matters.' Her voice tailed off.

'What of this steward of yours, Sir William? Will he not advise you?' said Edmund impatiently. His fingers tightened on the reins.

'Either he—or Ralph, the bailiff,' she answered.

Suddenly Edmund wanted the parting to be over. Her voice had contained a note of loneliness and sadness that he did not want to think about. He had his own life to get on with and would rid himself of the effect of this woman on him. He urged his horse forward.

They clattered over a stone bridge, and Felicia was suddenly aware of a sense of urgency. Perhaps the horse had caught both their moods, because now it began to quicken its pace. She clung tightly, as her veil and braids flew out behind her, bumping with the rhythm of the lengthening stride. The village was in sight, as were the walls of the demesne land. Above those walls rose the fat finger of the stone keep, and the roof of the house should also have been visible. She stared incredulously. There was no roof to speak of—and the walls of the keep were darkened, not only with creeper, but with the effects of smoke.

'Dear God,' she whispered, clutching Edmund's sleeve. 'Something is terribly wrong!'

She yelled for him to stop as they came to the village. Swiftly he tugged on the reins and brought his mount to a plunging halt. Dickon, who had galloped on, realised that they had stopped. He wheeled about and came cantering back.

A woman working in a garden looked up swiftly, showing them a face that was both relieved and frightened at the same time. A white linen bandage peeked from beneath her head veil. The hoe she held clattered to the ground, as Felicia slid from the horse without waiting for Edmund to help her down.

'Agnes!' cried Felicia, clinging to the stirrup for a moment, before stumbling over to where the woman stood. 'Tell me quickly—what has happened here?'

'My lady! My lady!' Agnes squawked, pausing to grip and kiss Felicia's hand before curtsying. 'Your cousin! He has been here!' The weatherbeaten face creased into innumerable wrinkles as she gazed up with faded blue eyes. They darted swiftly towards Edmund and Dickon—then back to Felicia.

'He—He is still here?' Felicia whispered.

The old woman shook her head. 'As wild as if a thousand devils possessed him, he was! But it is three days since he has gone, thank God.' She crossed herself swiftly. 'Not before he did much damage.' She paused, and bent to pick up her fallen hoe. 'You will discover for yourself just how much when you go in search of your house.' She rammed the hoe suddenly hard into the ground. 'He called me a witch, the whelp of Satan. And he killed my cat! He beat me around the head with his sword when I cursed him, and thought he killed me. It will take more than his sort to kill Agnes Fletcher!'

'What of my cousin Joan? Where is she? Is she safe? And Sir William—why did he not prevent this happening?'

'She is hiding somewhere, the poor child. We have not seen her in the village since he went, but Ralph caught sight of her walking in the forest.'

'I see.' Felicia attempted to clear her throat of the obstruction that seemed wedged there. Why should Joan be hiding if Philip had departed? Surely it would have been more sensible for her to shelter in the village? Unless some shameful deed caused her to hide herself away from people? No! She would not believe that! She was aware with part of her mind that Edmund had dismounted and stood behind her.

'What of Sir William?'

'The steward? Aaah!' Agnes shrugged bony shoulders. 'A message came. He went to Ludlow and has not returned yet.' She rammed her hoe into the soil again. 'You should not have gone away, my lady. Why have you been gone so long?'

'It was not my doing, Agnes.' Felicia's voice was quiet. 'But tell me, is my home completely destroyed?'

'Let it burn, your cousin said. The bitch shall have no kennel to hide in. If she comes here, tell her I will find her where'er she goes.'

Felicia gave a gasp and her fists clenched tightly. 'God! If I were a man, I would kill him with my own hands!'

Agnes stared at her. 'But you are not, my lady. Best let one of these fine gentlemen, or Sir William, deal with him—if he can be destroyed, the devil!'

A quiver raced through Felicia's body, and she shut her eyes briefly until she felt Edmund's hand on her shoulder. 'He is only a man,' she muttered. 'I have seen him bleed, and shall do so again. I am not an animal that he should hound me.'

'Perhaps we should ride on and take a look at your house ourselves,' said Edmund in a rough voice. 'And we should surely seek out your cousin, Mistress Meriet.'

Felicia glanced sidelong at his hard face. 'There is no need for you to delay your journey, Master Edmund,' she declared, tilting her chin. 'You have done what you have promised, and I am home.'

'Home? It is a sorry homecoming if you have no roof over your head,' he cried harshly, the grey eyes fierce. 'And you forget that I have an interest in seeing your cousin meet his fate—at the point of my sword, preferably. Besides, I would make sure that Mistress Joan is safe. I fear ...' He did not finish, but from his expression she guessed he was thinking along line similar to hers.

'Almost we agree, it seems, Master Edmund.' She gave a small bitter laugh. 'Take me up, then, and I shall show you the way.'

'You can go before me.' His eyes glinted as he swung her off her feet and lifted her up on his horse. He mounted behind her.

Felicia barely noticed the looks of the women working in the gardens. The cold dread that had her in its grip caused her to stare ahead between the horse's ears in a controlled concentration. Philip was a devil! The words beat into her brain. Had she escaped him, only for Joan to become his victim? She did not want to believe it could be so. But why hide away if it was not to lick her wounds like a terrified animal?

There was no one on watch at the gatehouse, and they passed its torn off gates and under the stone arch without being challenged. Some of the villeins worked on the demesne land, weeding the corn. Felicia thought she caught her name as the men murmured among themselves, but she made no response. They rode slowly up the path, and her fingers suddenly clenched on Edmund's sleeve. Now she could see the charred beams of the roof. Part of one wall still stood, but the main structure of the house had fallen in. Icy desolation clamped her heart.

Edmund dismounted, his eyes fixed upon her set, white face. She came down from the horse, not seeing the hand he held up to her, and she walked from him to the husk of what had once been her home.

'At least you can be thankful that your cousin was not inside!' Edmund exclaimed, poking the black ashen remains of a bench with the toe of his shoe.

'Can I?' Felicia lifted her eyes to the forest that crowded the skyline beyond the house. Was Joan there, still lurking, frightened and alone?

'You will be able to rebuild,' Dickon muttered, coming to stand next to them. 'It will take time, of course.'

'Do I not know it!' Felicia said bitterly. 'And, in the meantime, I am defenceless.'

'There is the keep,' said Dickon. 'That, at least, seems intact.' The three of them turned slowly and looked towards the stone tower. It was clad in newly burgeoning creeper, which curled crisp and brown in places, scorched by the heat of the fire.

'Perhaps you will be able to make it habitable until you can rebuild the house?'

Dickon leapt over a pile of stones and walked on towards the keep.

'It would be spartan,' said Edmund, his eyes narrowed thoughtfully, 'but maybe Dickon is right.' He glanced into Felicia's drawn face. 'What did it contain?'

'Some stores, most likely. It is a year since I was last here.' She drew a shaky breath, remembering how her cousin had come then in the guise of a helper. What did they say about the devil? Once he had been an angel! 'The door is on the other side. It might be locked, but Ralph, my bailiff, would have the key.'

Felicia began to walk slowly behind Dickon, who had already disappeared round the corner. Edmund set his pace to hers and walked by her side, looking grim. Barely had they skirted the corner than they heard a piercing scream—then another, and another. Felicia's startled eyes flew to Edmund's, and they both broke into a run up the steps. The door, like the gate, had been battered down and hung tipsily on broken hinges. Sacks near the doorway had been slashed, and grain flooded the floor in gold gleaming hummocks. They crossed the threshold out of the sunlight and into the dimness of the tower's interior.

Dickon turned to face them. His long face was taut and concerned. They could hear a girl sobbing uncontrollably.

162

'I keep telling her that she has nothing to fear from me,' he said. 'That I know you, Mistress Felicia; but she does not seem to heed me.'

Edmund and Felicia looked towards the wall furthest from the door. A girl was huddled there on the floor. Her face was hidden by a tangle of hair that showed barley-white, even in the shadow.

'Joan?' The name came out in a barely whispered breath. 'Joan!' Felicia repeated in a loud cry. All her forebodings were crowding into her mind. There was no pause in the girl's weeping. She darted across the room and knelt in the dust, putting an arm about the quivering shoulders. 'Joan! 'Tis I, Flissie, sweeting! I have come home. Do stop crying, I beg you. I can't bear it.'

There came a break in the sobbing, and the girl lifted her head. She pushed aside her long fair tresses with a trembling hand, and stared intently into Felicia's face. Tears formed furrows in the dirt on her cheeks, and a mouth that normally tilted prettily upwards was dragged down by the weight of her private sorrow.

'It—It is you, Flissie!' she muttered in an unsteady voice. 'But you have come several days too late. Why did you run from him? Why—Why could you not have ... agreed ... to marry Philip?' A sob escaped her, and

163

set her mouth quivering. 'Then he would not have come seeking you here and found me!' She banged her fist against her breast. 'I feel dirty. Do you know that, Flissie? Dirty! I have heard of such acts performed by beasts like Philip. But never ... never ... never did I think it would happen to me!' Her voice broke suddenly. 'Do you understand what I am saying, Flissie?'

The two girls stared at each other and Dickon made a move forward, but Edmund held him back. They both watched the horror explode in Felicia's face, and she gave a choking sound.

'Ay! But I don't want to believe it! I did not want it to happen to you, Joan!' Then her voice broke, and she flung her arms about her cousin and began to weep.

Edmund stared at her, his face dark, and then he turned and walked out of the keep.

CHAPTER SEVEN

'If only I had stabbed him in the heart with my scissors instead of in the arm!'

Felicia leaned back against the stone wall and stared across the room. Her eyes were a hard cerulean blue. Edmund drew in a sharp breath at the expression on her face. She seemed to have aged since he returned to the keep during the last emotional stormy hour.

'Well, you did not, so there is no use in saying it!' groaned Joan. 'There is no use in anything now.' She closed her eyes and rested her head on her hand.

'There is revenge,' murmured Dickon in a dreamy voice. 'A swift slash of a sword-blade, and that's the end!' He gazed at Joan from his perch on a collapsed sack of grain.

Joan lifted her head and considered him dispassionately. He hardly seemed her idea of a fighting man, dressed like a merchant in cool blue. 'It is all right for you to say that! How can you, a man, know how I feel?' She pushed aside a great handful of hair and sat up straighter. 'Who are you, anyway? You have sat here an age, witnessing my distress, without speaking a word. And now you speak of revenge—which you look unable to carry out!'

A flicker of annoyance creased Dickon's face, and he rose to his feet. He bowed. 'I am Richard Mortimer, a wool-merchant from Shrewsbury. Unlikely champion I might look—but appearances can deceive. I have often had to fight my way out of difficulties.'

Felicia regarded him in surprise, and could not resist glancing at Edmund. She saw his lips twitch, and suddenly remembered his saying that Dickon knew exactly how to woo a lady. Had he perhaps tried to woo where he should not?

'Be that as it may, sir,' her cousin interrupted her thoughts, 'you are hardly a match for Philip Meriet. He is trained in bearing arms and used to slaughtering any who cross his path. Unless they be women, of course. He deflowers them!' she said bitterly.

'You have my sympathy, Mistress,' interpolated Edmund, rising and stretching. 'But sympathy, bitterness—senseless regret, will not help you. Count yourself fortunate that you are still alive.'

'Flissie! Who is *this* man?' Joan asked in a furious voice. 'How can you let him speak to me like that? If it were not for you, I would not be suffering now!' She scrambled to her feet and glared at both men.

'Your words are unjust,' Edmund said sharply, seeing pain flash in Felicia's eyes. 'Do not blame your cousin for escaping Philip's attentions. I took her from him. Or, if you wish to be really just, blame Philip Meriet.'

Felicia stared at him in amazement; she had not expected him to champion her!

'Who are you, sir?' retorted Joan, her face flushing beneath the dirt. 'Are you the lover that Philip raged about?'

Felicia felt warmth flood her cheeks as the words seemed to vibrate in the silence. 'Don't be foolish, Joan!' Her voice was sharp. 'I have no lover ... It was all in Philip's mind.' She was aware of Edmund's gaze. Surely he did not believe that she had a lover? An angry despair surged within her.

It was Dickon who answered Joan's first question. 'Edmund is a physician,' he said quietly. 'Philip Meriet raped his mother. She died. He also killed ...'

'That's enough, Dickon,' interrupted Edmund in a rough voice. 'All this talk is of little use. Let us agree that it is time justice caught up with Philip Meriet. I have experienced Mistress Joan's anger, and maybe I spoke unthinkingly.' He grimaced. 'Now I suggest we go outside.'

'You are leaving?' Felicia stood up. 'I regret that I can offer you little hospitality.' She tried to smile. 'Unless ...'

'Food, Flissie? Beds for the night?' Joan gave a harsh laugh.

'I could go in search of my bailiff.' Her eyes questioned Edmund and Dickon.

'It does not matter,' said Edmund. 'Anyway—if I am not mistaken in my judgment of villagers—the news of your coming will have reached him.'

'Then you are going?' Felicia looked at her feet, attempting to hide her sudden dismay.

Edmund hesitated. He was strangely reluctant to be parted from her, but Dickon spoke first.

'I'm hungry if you are not, my friend. Perhaps we could go hunting? And surely we could light a fire to cook our supper?' The two men exchanged looks, and Edmund gave a shrug.

'Why not? If it is agreeable to Mistress Felicia.'

Felicia nodded. She was glad he was not leaving yet but did not delve into the heart of that gladness, only reasoning that it was good to have a man's strength to lean on at such a time. She went with him from the keep, Joan following sulkily, with Dickon bringing up the rear.

The wood crackled, sending sparks flying high against the blue sky of evening. The heat of the fire was welcome, as was the smell of roasting meat pervading the air. Felicia gazed into the flames, wondering what she was to do. When she stole a glance at Edmund, they highlighted the grooves in his cheeks, altering the shape of his face, so that he appeared almost a stranger. She had thought he might make a move to leave, despite his earlier words, but he seemed in no hurry as he turned the boar. As though sensing that she watched him, he lifted his head and their glances met. Her breathing seemed to be suspended.

'It won't be long now. I hope you are hungry. It is a large boar.'

'We did well catching it.' She cleared her throat. 'I thought that Ralph might have come by now. Perhaps I should go to the village?' Her brow creased.

'I would wait a little longer. He could be out on the hills. It is a busy time for a bailiff: soon it will be haymaking, and then sheep-shearing.'

'You seem to know much about manor life—for a physician.'

'I was reared on the manor, and—Sir Gervaise made sure I was of some use to him before I became a physician.' He prodded the meat again, this time with his fingers. He blew on them hastily and drew back. 'I think it is done.' Quickly he removed the boar.

Felicia turned and called Dickon. He rose swiftly from the broken wall he had been sitting on, strumming his lute.

'It smells good,' he murmured, coming to the fire. He placed himself not too near Joan, who deliberately hunched a shoulder and looked away. He gave an exasperated sigh, and smiled at Felicia. 'It is a pity we have no bread or ale.'

'Do not give up hope yet,' said Edmund, taking his knife from his girdle. 'The bailiff might still come.'

'You might have to wait for a long time,' muttered Joan. 'He is lazy, that one.'

'You are unfair, Joan!' Felicia gave her a startled glance. 'Admittedly Ralph used to be late at times for the manor court, but he has much to do. And a large family to see to.'

'His wife cares for the children!' Joan tossed her head defiantly. 'While you were away, he never took any notice of my orders.'

Felicia made no answer. She was trying to be as patient as she knew how with her, guessing how she must be suffering. Despite Edmund's words earlier, she did not feel entirely blameless for what Philip had done.

Edmund, who had not spoken during their exchange, nudged her elbow and offered a slice of meat. She smiled her thanks, taking it from his fingers. At that moment a rumbling sound broke the evening calm, and the four of them glanced at each other before looking towards the gatehouse. Felicia scrambled to her feet.

A few moments later three figures came into view. Two were only lads, pushing

170

a small cart laden with goods, who were being encouraged to strain a little harder by the man who walked with majestic ease by their side. They all came to a halt in front of Felicia.

'Milady,' gasped Ralph, breathing heavily, his pendulous jowls flushed. ' 'Tis good to see you home.' He doffed his cap and bowed, showing a bald pate. 'Alas! It is a sad homecoming for you.' He appeared distressed and discomfited as he met Felicia's appraising look. 'We did what we could but that was not much, I grant you. We were unprepared—and your cousin had many men, all armed.'

'I do not blame you, Ralph,' she said quietly.

Relief brightened his plump face. 'God bless you, milady.' He fell on his knees and kissed the hem of Felicia's skirt before bumbling to his feet again. 'In all the years I was your father's bailiff, such a thing never happened.'

'Pray God, it will not happen again. But tell me, what was the message that took Sir William away to Ludlow?'

Ralph scratched his nose and shifted from one foot to the other. 'It concerned the uprising. The Lord Edward was said to be there and calling on those who had aided his father's cause last year. Sir William went off like an arrow, not knowing what was to happen here. We have heard nothing since you went away, but often we wondered what happened to the messages he sent to you.'

'Messages?' Felicia gave a startled glance. 'I received no messages—and it seems you did not receive mine.' She continued, with a bitter laugh, 'How foolisih of me to think that Philip would send them on. Sir William's, he must have read and destroyed.'

Ralph growled angrily. 'And the money, milady. You did not receive that, either? Sir William entrusted it to two of our most reliable men, and they said they delivered it.'

Felicia shook her head, and her eyes blazed with fury.

'God's bones, my lady, I do not know what to comfort you with. Your cousin took all that there was in the chest in the hall, too, smashing the lock. There is no money to keep you until the sheep are sheared and the wool sold.' He lowered his voice. 'It could be that your cousin has left spies in the vicinity. Strangers have been seen, and I was fair worried about Mistress Joan wandering in the woods.' He nodded his head several times.

A chill shivered along Felicia's spine. 'They could be common outlaws,' she murmured, glancing towards Edmund, who was close enough to hear the conversation.

'It might be best if you left here,' he suggested, 'if you really wish to escape your cousin's watch.'

'Do you still doubt it?' asked Felicia vehemently.

Edmund raised a brow. 'Did I say so?' He turned to Ralph. 'What about a decent roof for your lady that would suffice her and her cousin? The keep is hardly suitable.'

Ralph scratched his head. 'Perhaps I can think on the matter, sir, while we unload the food. I shall have these scamps of mine set to it. My wife has sent some bread, and the priest gave me eggs for you, milady. There are a few pots and platters, cups and spoons, and a couple of pallets and several blankets ... Oh! Agnes sent you some of the ale she has been brewing.'

'That is good of them, Ralph.' Felicia half smiled, but his words had made her anxious, and she glanced at Edmund, who had begun to help the boys to unpack the cart.

Ralph was standing still, his lips pursed. Suddenly he gave a cry. 'What about Chipbury, milady?'

'Chipbury! Of course!' she exclaimed. Then, with a frustrated groan, 'But how shall we get there? Sir William and the rest of the men have gone, and it is some distance. You will have to stay here, Ralph, because there is so much to do on the manor at this time of year.'

'Where is Chipbury?' demanded Edmund, taking a rolled pallet from the cart and tossing it into Dickon's outstretched hands.

'It is in Gloucestershire. Chipbury is my other manor, much smaller than Meriet. We grow vines, apples, pears and plums, mainly.' Felicia fell silent.

Edmund and Dickon exchanged glances.

'We could ...' began Dickon hesitantly. 'Or I could.'

'Perhaps *we* could—if the ladies wished it,' murmured Edmund, watching Felicia.

'If we wished what?'

'If you wish to go to Chipbury, Dickon and I could escort you.'

'But what of your search for the Lord Edward? If he is in Ludlow ...?'

Edmund shrugged his shoulders. 'He might not be there now. Besides, I intended to visit my uncle first. He is a man who keeps his ear firmly to the earth and might know something more about the conflict.'

They stared at each other. 'Well?' grunted Edmund. 'Do you wish us to accompany you or not?'

'Ay!' Felicia decided, slightly breathless. 'Why not? I thank you ... and Dickon.'

She turned her head and smiled at him.

'It is settled, then,' muttered Joan, who had been listening avidly despite an appearance to the contrary. 'I cannot deny that I shall be glad to leave here for a while. And if Felicia trusts you two, I suppose I must also,' she added ungraciously.

Dickon stared at her, not quite able to hide his irritation. 'I presume you will be spending the night in the keep, Felicia?' he called, lifting a pallet on to his shoulder. 'Edmund and I shall take the ground out here.'

'I suppose so.' Felicia smiled her relief. 'Are you certain we shall not be taking you out of your way? I do remember that Edmund said his uncle's monastery was in Worcestershire.'

'It will be of little consequence.' Edmund gave a polite smile. 'Pour out some ale while we take the pallets in, if you would, there's a good girl.' He followed in Dickon's wake, the other pallet balanced on his shoulder, and a couple of blankets slung over his arm. Felicia stared after him, her mouth twisted ruefully. Then she proceeded to pour out four horns of ale.

Darkness came slowly. The light was just fading when they finished eating, and the scent of honeysuckle sweetened the air. Although there was a chill in the breeze, Felicia was reluctant to move. She felt again that surge of guilt as she looked at Joan. What if there was a child from Philip's raping? Now that she knew he had taken all that she had hoped would be here, she was ill equipped to help Joan in the way she would have thought best. Yet she would do all she could to support her. She sighed, and pillowed her chin on her hunched-up knees, gazing into the slumbering fire.

'More ale?' Edmund held out a horn, which she took, watching the liquid gleam in the firelight as he poured it. 'We shall have to make an early start in the morning.' He put down the pitcher of ale. 'Best you do not ride too long at a stretch, for it is only just over a week since you hurt your back. Did you feel any discomfort from the journey today?' He picked up his own horn and saluted her with it.

She responded with a murmur of good wishes and took a sip of the ale. It was refreshing. 'I have had no time to think of it,' she murmured, looking down and feeling strangely shy of him. 'But, Edmund, one thing bothers me. If we are to stay at the monastery where your uncle is abbot ...' she paused, moistened her lips. 'I have little money, only a few pence, and ...' Her voice tailed off, and she flushed. She could hear the popping of a flame as

Dickon threw on more wood.

'I think we shall be able to make a small recompense for their trouble. We shall stay only one night, and then be on our way to Chipbury.' The corners of his eyes creased attractively. They had discussed earlier just where Chipbury was in relation to his uncle Walter's monastery. 'I have enjoyed your hospitality. We have had food and drink, and we have a place to lay our heads—so do not let us talk of money.'

'The ground is a hard pillow for your head.' She fiddled with the hem of her gown. He had understood, and his words were reassuring. She felt glad that it could be so between them, and sat on in silent contentment as the light slowly died from the sky and the stars appeared one by one. She caught Joan's eyes upon her. Her cousin sat silent, seeming to brood like some great night-bird, and Felicia felt her peace evaporate.

'I want to go to bed, now, Flissie. Are you coming?' Joan uncurled herself and stood up. She stared sullenly at the figures about the fire. She felt an outsider.

'Of course.' Felicia placed the horn on the grass and scrambled to her feet. 'You must be tired. Where have you slept the last few nights, love?'

'Slept! I have not slept!' Joan gave a mirthless laugh. 'I have spent the nights in the keep. It is not so bad, if you do not mind the vermin scrabbling in the grain.'

'Vermin?' Felicia's voice shock slightly. Her fingers curled tightly in her palms.

'They will not bother you, cousin.' Joan smiled unexpectedly. 'They are interested only in food.' She put her hand through Felicia's arm. 'Come, let us go to the keep. Perhaps with you to keep me company, I might sleep this night.'

Felicia placed a hand over Joan's. 'Of course, Joan. How brave you are to have stayed there alone. Much braver than I.'

'Or I,' interrupted Dickon, with a quiver of humour in his voice. 'I don't mind rats, but I can't abide spiders.' He twinkled up at Joan. Her smile vanished and she stared at him stonily.

Felicia swallowed a groan of exasperation. Why could not Joan at least be polite! Her cousin tugged at her arm.

'God grant you both a good night!' Felicia called, as Joan dragged her towards the keep.

'And to you.' The men lifted a hand. Reaching for their blankets, they stretched themselves out on the ground and talked for a while about what might happen in the next couple of days. Then gradually Dickon's voice slurred, and soon there was nothing to be heard but their steady breathing.

The keep seemed dark. Felicia peered nervously about her before giving a resigned 'tut'. It was a far cry from the solar that had graced Meriet's manor house.

'It doesn't get any darker in this place,' said Joan. She shook out a blanket and wrapped it about her slender figure before lying down. 'In truth,' she added, 'once your eyes become accustomed, it seems as if some light always penetrates the doorway.' She flicked a nervous glance towards the hanging door and lowered her voice. 'I suppose we are safe in here, Flissie?'

'Safe?'

'The men,' she whispered furiously.

'You are safer with them than without them, I should think!' Felicia picked up her blanket. 'I feel safer, anyway, with them outside.' She pulled the blanket about her shoulders and lay thankfully on the pallet. The blanket smelt of goodness knows what—but she was not going to let it keep her awake. Shutting her eyes, she murmured a prayer beneath her breath. Never would she have admitted to Joan that she could not abide mice or rats! She jumped when Joan spoke out of the darkness.

'Is he your lover?'

Felicia's heart seemed to stop.

'Philip said you had a lover who helped you to escape. That Edmund is the one, isn't he?' Her voice was petulant. 'I have seen the way he looks at you.'

Felicia did not answer at first, taken aback by Joan's words. 'The lover Philip spoke about was a figment of his imagination.' Her voice was weary. 'Philip kept me a prisoner. He killed his wife, I am certain, so that he could wed me. He wants Meriet—for some reason that I find hard to comprehend, when he has so much of his own.' She paused, wondering what to say about Edmund and Dickon, for the truth would not serve. If she told Joan that Edmund had abducted her, it might cause her to fear instead of to trust. They needed the men if they were to reach Chipbury.

'I met Edmund on the manor that Philip had taken. He slaughtered its lord and his sons. When—When Edmund realised that I was my cousin's prisoner, he saw it as a way of hitting at Philip when he helped me to escape. I fell off the horse and hurt my back. That is how I met Dickon. We stayed with him and Nell in Shrewsbury. Otherwise I would have come here sooner.'

'Oh! So that is how it was.' Joan's voice

held a note of doubtful acceptance, and she yawned. 'I think I might be able to sleep now.'

Felicia gave a relieved sigh, and listened to Joan's movements until at last she lay still. Now that she herself could rest, she discovered that sleep eluded her. When she remembered Ralph's words about strangers, her body shifted nervously. Philip! Was he a devil who could not be destroyed? She had often thought so. How he must hate her—and want Meriet. Yet he had burned her house to the ground. She tried to think of something else. Chipbury and the journey tomorrow. It was good in Edmund—and Dickon—to go with them. Her heart seemed to swell and warm at the thought of Edmund.

There came a scrabbling sound, and then a squeaking. For a while she lay listening, but when something brushed her leg she could bear it no longer. Scrambling up, she shot across the floor and fled down the steps, her bare feet making hardly any sound. She sank to the ground, her breath coming fast, and huddled into the woollen blanket about her shoulders. She lay, staring into the glowing embers of the fire, trying to steady her heartbeats. Then a humped shape a few feet from her moved.

181

CHAPTER EIGHT

Edmund rolled over swiftly, and Felicia caught the gleam of a knife.

'What is it? What is wrong?' He lowered the knife.

'N-Nothing.' Felicia's teeth chattered uncontrollably as she pulled the blanket tightly about her.

Edmund repeated, 'Nothing?'

She nodded and closed her eyes tight, trying to shut out his probing glance. He would think her an utter dolt. There was a short silence.

'That cousin of yours hasn't been upsetting you again, has she?' He spoke with a vehemence that caused Felicia's eyelids to fly up.

'It is nothing like that!' She flushed beneath his scrutiny. From the expression on his face, he would not be fobbed off with a lie.

'It—It is mice ... I cannot abide them. The thought of their little scratching feet scrabbling ... and the sight of their long naked tails!' She shuddered.

'Mice!' There was the barest hint of a quiver in his voice.

'I knew you would laugh!' she said indignantly, moving slightly away.

'I am not laughing.' The grooves in his cheeks deepened, and a muscle twitched in the bare column of his throat.

'You are! Or you would like to. You do not know how utterly demoralising it is to confess to a fear of mice.'

His smile grew. 'We are all afraid of something.'

'Afraid! You? I don't believe you fear anything.'

'Don't you?' Startled, he leaned up on an elbow and returned her gaze. 'I'm afraid of you,' he said in a serious voice.

'You're jesting!' She flushed, lowering her eyes, veiling their loveliness with a sweep of long dark lashes.

'Don't you believe me?' He reached out and took one of her hands, feeling her fingers still trembling. 'I think you're a witch.'

Felicia peered at him from beneath her lashes. 'That is even more foolish than my fear of mice,' she said in a low voice. 'You called me a wanton yesterday.'

'A wanton witch who has set an enchantment about me. I want you, and it hurts here.' He placed her hand over his heart.

Her pulse had begun to race. 'This is a foolishness, Edmund. It is the ale and the starlight; they have gone to your head,' she said unsteadily. 'I—I had best get back to Joan.' She tried to pull her hand out of his grasp, but he held it tightly.

'Haven't you a remedy to break the spell, beautiful witch?' He gazed into her face, and she could see the glint of his eyes catching the starlight. 'A kiss might do it,' he said, a slight tremor in his voice. 'A kiss from a witch, who knows what might happen.'

'You're laughing at me again. You cannot be trusted, Master Abductor,' she said with a touch of anger, as she experienced a trembling in her limbs. She wanted to kiss him! She tried to pull away from him again, when an owl screeched. Instinctively she shrank towards him and he put an arm about her. They both looked up at the noise of the bird's flapping wings. It swooped, then swung up again with its prey dangling from its talons.

'One down,' he said softly, turning his head and looking at her, amusement creasing his face.

She murmured, 'Poor creature,' and chuckled suddenly. A delightful sound, thought Edmund. 'Now you will believe me completely foolish,' she continued in a smiling voice.

'Perhaps. Maybe it's the starlight, as you say—it makes fools of us both.' His arm tightened about her, and the smile stiffened on her face as his searching mouth found hers with barely any effort or protest.

A peacefulness rippled slowly over her as his mouth brushed hers, feather-light, in a sensuous joining before hardening, lifting, demanding, then hungrily seizing with a kiss that seemed to have had no beginning and would never end. She thought she would float away as he lowered her against the turf. Then he lifted his head and she drew breath, her breasts rising and falling hurriedly as she stared up into his shadowy face against the star-sprinkled sky.

'Witch,' he muttered, his hand running slowly up her body and coming to rest beneath her breast.

Felicia blinked up at him, confused by the sensations he had aroused. 'No—No witch or wanton, Edmund,' she stammered. 'Just a maid. You must not do this.'

'Must not—cannot, Felicia,' he whispered fiercely. 'But you want me to kiss you and touch you, don't you, my little wanton?' He caught her to him, moulding her body against his with urgent hands, and covered her face with gentle biting kisses.

She gave a sob. 'Ay, but it is a madness! Please let me go.' She was suddenly aware that Dickon was stirring a few feet away.

Edmund was still. His mouth had caught the taste of salt on her cheeks. He had the most ridiculous desire to shield her from aught that would hurt her. Dear God, he wanted her, but in this moment it was himself she needed protection from. He suddenly felt like laughing. How had he got himself into this tangle?

Felicia felt herself released abruptly, and at once moved away, scrambling to her feet before reaching down to grab her blanket.

'Best go quickly,' he whispered, leaning on an elbow and following her with his eyes. 'Watch for mice,' he added wickedly.

'Beast!' she muttered, before running swiftly across the grass and up the steps. When she paused, listening for sounds of the mice, they seemed to have left the keep.

Joan, who had lain wide-eyed in the darkness, shut her eyes quickly. She had slept only fitfully since Philip Meriet had raped her, trembling each time a sound disturbed the stillness of the night. It was the owl that had disturbed her. After the first heart-stopping moment she had begun to relax again, then she had caught the murmur of voices outside—one softly feminine. Instantly she had peered through the dimness to where Felicia had lain. When her eyes had become adjusted, she saw what she already suspected: her cousin was not there.

Anger, hot and uncontrolled, surged through her slender frame. He was her lover! Flissie had lied to her. Tears, painful and burning, stung her eyes. Why was life so unjust? She had no one to care for her, and it was unlikely that any man would want her now. She lay, trying to shut out the terrifying pictures that immediately rose up for attention when she thought like that. It was weird, frighteningly so, how the tiniest detail of her raping took on horrifying form. She could feel the bite of Philip's nails as he tore her gown apart, feel the painful wrench at the roots of her hair as he forced her backwards and down. She could even smell his odorous breath and sickly perfume.

It was not fair! Tears oozed from her eyes. It was Flissie's fault—Flissie's! Even as Philip had almost suffocated her to force her into submission, he had muttered Felicia's name against her throat. Bitterness and fury burned white hot in Joan's mind as she listened to Felicia settling herself once more on the pallet. That man outside would not want Flissie if she had been soiled by Philip. Felicia had what should be hers. Admiration—attention—purity! Even that lute-player merchant smiled upon her! Angry tears rolled down her cheeks again and she wished she could forget, but she could not. She dozed for only minutes at a time, until at last the dawn greyed the room and there came the sound of movement outside.

Felicia woke to the sun slanting on her face. She sat up slowly, her eyes still closed, wondering what had woken her. Blinking them open, she saw that Joan had gone out. She rose, and stumbled to the doorway. The stunted outline of her house showed stark against the morning sky, in which rays of splintered light forced their way through splodgy fingers of cream and silver, apricot- and gold-edged clouds. She had slept well, despite her tumultuous thoughts. There was no sign of Edmund and Dickon. Swiftly she cast a glance to where their horses cropped the grass and felt relief that they had not gone far. But where were they—and Joan? Joan! The thought of her caused her spirits to sink. Philip seemed to have destroyed all her cousin's former vivaciousness and warmth, and it was difficult to imagine that she would ever be her old self again. Felicia walked back into the keep, found her brown surcote and put it on, realising in that moment that she had nothing else to wear—neither did Joan, she presumed. All their clothing must have been destroyed in the fire, and the rest of her own garments she had had to leave behind when she had fled from Philip. At least she could wash. She ran down the steps out into the sunshine again and walked through the ruins of her house to the garden. There was the well. Good! The pail was still intact. Swiftly she turned the handle and ran the bucket down until she heard the splash of water. She let the pail run a little further, then brought it up.

It was after Felicia had cupped her hands and had taken a drink of the water that she felt as though she were being watched, but a slow glance about her revealed nobody. It was very quiet except for the wind stropping the leaves on the trees. She put her hands into the pail again and rinsed her face with the cold clear water, her nerves taut, her ears pricked for the sound of footsteps, but none came. Yet still she had an eerie sense of not being alone. She dabbed her face swiftly with the end of her veil and then turned and ran through the herb garden and the remains of the house until breathlessly she came to the foot of the steps leading to the tower. Barely had she reached the bottom step when Joan appeared in the doorway, staring down at her with sullen, cornflower-blue eyes. 'Is there anything to eat? I am hungry.' She had braided her barley-white hair, and her face was washed clean of tears and dirt.

'I should think so. There was plenty of meat left. I wrapped it in a napkin and put it in a crock.' Felicia smiled, swallowing her apprehension as her cousin continued to stare unblinkingly down into her face.

'The men might have eaten it.' Joan's voice was sharp with resentment.

'And they might not have.' Her voice rose slightly and then softened again. 'Joan, we need the men and their horses. Philip took ours. I understand your anxiety, but do not let us quarrel.' She knelt in front of Joan and took one of her hands, stroking the back of it soothingly. 'Love, you do not want to stay here—you said so. Besides, I do not think it is safe.'

Joan did not look at her but shook her head. 'I have been thinking of going into a nunnery,' she said in a queer, high voice. 'There is nothing for me now. No man would have me.'

'Such a life would not suit you! You have never been the least bit religious,' said Felicia vehemently.

Joan laughed hysterically. 'I did at least believe there was a God of justice once. If I bear a child to that devil, I shall kill myself,' she cried, flinging her arms about Felicia. 'You will not leave me, will you? Or cast me off if it is so?' She buried her head in Felicia's lap.

'Of course not.' She smoothed a curl

from Joan's forehead. 'Only do not talk of killing yourself, for I cannot bear it.'

'Even if you marry, Flissie?' insisted Joan. 'Promise me.'

'Who said anything about marriage?'

'Philip—even though it is wrong for cousins to marry.' Joan's voice sank. 'He said he would kill you if you do not wed him. He is evil, Flissie! Maybe he is in league with the devil himself. What chance would your fine lover or that lute-player have then?' She stared at Felicia with wild eyes.

Some of Joan's fear seemed to transport itself to Felicia, and her mind seemed to freeze on all rational thought. Dear God, what if it were true, and Philip had spies out—if he would not give up his plans for her? An irrational terror had her by the throat, so that she did not hear Edmund's, or Dickon's footsteps. Only when Edmund spoke did she turn to him.

'What is it? What is wrong?' he demanded. 'Has anyone been here in our absence?'

Felicia's throat moved as she looked into his face, and slowly the fear ebbed from her eyes. 'What is the matter? Why do you stare at me so?' Her mouth shivered into a smile. 'Cannot a woman grieve over the loss of her home, and worse?' Philip was miles away and unlikely to be able to seek her out for an age. The conflict might continue for months and months. He could even be slain in a battle. The men in the forest could be outlaws. Her spirits lifted.

Edmund scanned Joan's face, then he squeezed Felicia's shoulder and got to his feet. 'Of course ... I have brought some newly-baked bread from Ralph's wife. I thought we might need more on our journey.'

'Good.' Felicia stumbled to her feet as Joan uncurled abruptly.

'You will be ready to go soon?' Dickon asked Joan.

She laughed scornfully. 'We are ready now, Master Lute-player. We have no clothes to pack and little food.'

'Have you two broken your fast?' said Felicia to the men.

Dickon shook his head. 'We have been down to the river and had a dip.' He shivered, and rolled his eyes expressively. 'It was Edmund's idea ... He has this liking for water. We also managed to obtain a few handfuls of dried fruit from your miller—at a price.'

'Bartholomew! Did you not say you were friends of mine?'

'Ay, but he said how was he to know we spoke the truth, and we thought it easier to pay what he asked. Let us eat now, and be on our way before the sun rises much higher.'

They ate in silence, and it was but a quarter of an hour before they set off, up through the wooded hills. The air had lost its coolness and the sun was already climbing the sky. A bird soared high above them scouring the grassy hills scattered with sheep. Felicia prayed that it would not seize a lamb, since she could ill afford to lose even one. They travelled for some miles, busy with their own thoughts.

'It is not much further to the monastery at Huppingescumbe now.' Edmund turned to Felicia as they paused to rest. 'You are not too tired? Another hour, and we should reach the Malvern hills.'

'I am not too tired, but I think Joan is finding the journey arduous.' She glanced at her cousin, who sat a few feet away, her arms clasped about the hunched-up knees. Dickon sat a few yards away from her, his feet dangling over an outcrop of rock into thin air. Every now and again Felicia had noticed that, while they ate, his eyes would go to Joan's tragic face.

She sighed inwardly and turned back to Edmund. 'Huppingescumbe? It is a strange name for a monastery.'

'It means the place of the stepping-stones. They are not far from the monastery gates.' He pulled a blade of grass through

193

his fingers as he looked out into the distance. Then he said, 'Time we were on our way.'

They travelled on, and Felicia was beginning to feel weary when Edmund at last pointed ahead to a huddle of buildings. The horses quickened their pace as though they, too, knew that the journey's end was in sight for that day. Within a short time they were splashing through the ford near the stepping-stones and came to the gatehouse. A porter emerged as they approached, his hands tucked into the wide sleeves of his black habit. He had a small round head with greying hair about his tonsure. As he saw Edmund, his expression lightened.

'Well met, Master Edmund! It is good to see you.'

'And I you, Brother Thomas, and looking as healthy as ever. The lord abbot, how is he?'

'As well as can be expected when the cellarer is ill. He finds the burden of responsibility lying a little heavier on his shoulders.' Brother Thomas cast a swift glance at the women before averting his gaze.

'It seems I have come at an inconvenient time?'

The monk shook his head. 'It will do him good to see you. And the infirmarer will be glad of your advice over what ails the cellarer.'

'Then I must make time to visit him. First, I shall take the ladies to the guest hall. You know Dickon?'

Brother Thomas nodded and gave Dickon a brief, long-suffering look, and Dickon grinned back. He had had fun with Brother Thomas all those long years ago when he had first learnt his music and letters here.

The monk stepped back to make room for the horses to pass beneath the stone archway that led to the great court. They left them in the hands of one of the brothers, and made their way to the lodging-house.

Edmund had word with the hospitaller before turning to the others. 'The brother will show you the way to your chambers. I shall join you after I have spoken with my uncle.'

Felicia gave him a tired smile. She would be glad to wash herself and then lie down. 'You will return before supper?'

He nodded before turning away and making his way through the doorway and out into the sunlit court. He crossed the great court and entered a passage that led to the cloisters. The time for the monks' rest hour was over, and most of them would be at their studies at this time of day. His uncle Walter was most likely in the scriptorium, translating the scriptures or a book of learning, one of his favourite occupations. After pausing at the gate to speak to the monk there, he was allowed through, having had his guess confirmed. His feet rang loudly on the stone tiles of the slype, which led to several doors, and he listened intently before selecting the second one on the right.

Walter looked up as he entered. His gentle, intelligent brow eased as he recognised him. 'My boy, what brings you here?' He clapped a hand on his arm, and his thin, rather austere face lit with pleasure.

'I have matters of importance to discuss with you.' Edmund cast a glance towards the brother who was writing down the translation.

Walter's snowy brows drew together. 'Let us walk in the garden,' he said.

Edmund nodded and followed him from the room, walking silently by his side until they came at last to the fish-ponds. It had been a favoured place all those years ago. He gazed down at the grey-green shadowy shapes gliding through the waters.

'What is it, Edmund?'

Edmund caught the note of concern in the gentle voice, and ceased his contemplation of the water to look at his uncle. 'Mother is dead,' he murmured, only a slight blurring of the words betraying his emotion. 'So are my father, Sir Gervaise, and my half-brothers.'

Walter's eyes dilated with shocked amazement. 'Sweet Jesu! What pestilence took them off?' He took a hand from his sleeve and placed it through Edmund's arm. 'I grieve for you, my son.'

'It was no plague or fever,' muttered Edmund. 'Unless you rightly call Philip Meriet such.' His mouth twisted into an ugly grimace. Then, slowly at first and then more rapidly, he began to tell his uncle how he had come from Chester to visit his mother on his father's manor. How he had met the peasants, who had told him of his father's and brother's deaths, and of what Philip Meriet was doing in the village.

'I did not stop to think of the stupidity or danger of my actions because I feared for my mother.' His fists curled uncontrollably. 'He raped her before my eyes. I managed to wound one of the men with my dagger, but I was hit over the head. My cap saved me.' He paused, and now his eyes were the cold charcoal that Felicia had seen that first day. 'I came to with the thatch descending in flames about my head. Whether Philip Meriet knew of my mother's relationship with my father and who I was, I do not know—but he intended to kill us both.

Mother died a couple of days later—but before she did so, she told me to come to you. So I have come.' He fell silent, rubbing a hand wearily across his forehead. 'I am late in the coming, I know, and have a confession to make before you and God concerning that!' His voice was hard.

His uncle stared at him with compassion in his grey eyes. They had been walking across the shaven lawns all the time Edmund had been talking, but now they paused as they came to the fish-ponds again.

'You sought revenge? That is natural, my son. Although it would be best to leave it to God. Tell me—do you know why your mother sent you to me?'

Edmund hesitated. 'No. She was not lucid enough in those last days. I have a hope—I am Sir Gervaise's bastard, and his only remaining kin, after all. So tell me, Uncle Walter, am I right to hope?'

'Your birth was a well-kept secret.' Walter brushed back a strand of white hair before placing his hand on Edmund's arm. 'But it is possible that Philip Meriet might have known who you are. You are very like your father in appearance.'

'He made no sign of recognition when I played the part of a serving-man, but I was careful to stay in the background.'

'What is this?' Walter asked thoughtfully.

'But later; you can tell me later. I have not answered your question yet. Let us go back to my lodgings. I presume your mother sent you to me for the document I have kept these last twenty-seven years?'

Edmund nodded. 'If it is what I hope—ay!'

They retraced their steps to the abbot's lodgings, which overlooked the great court. There Walter poured out some wine made from the monastery's own vines and took a sip before turning to the great carved chest that stood in the corner of the shady room. It took some time to find what he was seeking, but at last he straightened and came over to Edmund with the scroll in his hand. There was a painful smile upon his thin lips.

Edmund took the document, turning it over before fingering the seal that closed it. With the knife from his girdle he prised off the seal, conscious of his uncle's watchful eyes upon his face as he scanned the Latin swiftly. Then he perused the words again, more slowly. When he had finished, he picked up his goblet of wine and drank it down thirstily. His eyes gleamed with a relieved satisfaction. He was heir to all his father's lands, as he had hoped!

'What are you going to do?' Abbot Walter filled their goblets again.

Edmund did not speak at first, but

walked over to the window and gazed out at the great court. He took a sip of wine before turning back. 'It is unlikely that I could gain my lands without help, so I mean to seek out the Lord Edward.' He tapped his fingers against the silver goblet's rim. 'You have heard the news?'

'Of his escape while a prisoner at Hereford? Ay. It is rumoured that the young Earl of Gloucester, Gilbert of Clare, was behind it. His brother Thomas was one of Edward's guards.'

Edmund's eyes blazed, and he grasped the edge of the table. 'But he was on Earl Simon's side a year ago! If he has gone over to the prince, he will take many more with him.'

'The Mortimers are with him. It was to their castle at Wigmore that the Lord Edward went first. Then to Matilda de Braose's castle at Ludlow.'

'Do you know if he is still there? Mistress Felicia's steward, Sir William, is said to have gone seeking him out at Ludlow.'

'Mistress Felicia?' His uncle lifted a delicate brow, and Edmund's mouth eased into a slight smile.

'I shall explain later. But tell me, is he still there?'

'I do not think so.' Walter sat down at the table. 'Yet, if he is in league with the Earl of Gloucester, it might be to Gloucester they go. Albeit I think it still in the hands of his enemies.'

Edmund's fingers curled about the scroll. His mouth was set firmly. 'Then it is to Gloucester that I shall go after I escort Mistress Felicia to Chipbury.' He picked up the scroll. 'This I would have you keep. It will be safer with you than with me, I think.'

'It would be wiser.' The abbot took it and put it back in the chest. 'How long do you mean to stay here?' He closed the lid.

'This night only. I would have liked to have stayed longer, but there is Mistress Felicia ...' His voice faded, and he fiddled with the stem of his goblet.

'Tell me more, nephew, about this Mistress Felicia.'

Edmund hesitated. Then he sat down and began to tell his uncle all that had happened since his mother's death.

CHAPTER NINE

Felicia stretched languidly.

'You are awake at last! Perhaps you did not sleep so well last night that you fell into such a deep slumber!'

Felicia blinked and sat up. 'The journey was tiring.' She stared at Joan, who was standing by the window, and her heart sank. It seemed that she was about to be difficult again.

'Ay!' Her cousin dragged the ends of the cord about the waist of her blue surcote through quivering fingers. 'Why have we come here? It is tiresome sitting in this room with nothing to do, while you sleep.'

'Edmund's uncle Walter is the abbot here,' she murmured patiently, getting down from the bed and walking slowly over to the window. 'He has come to inform him about his mother's death. She was the abbot's sister.'

Joan turned as she drew near. 'Did Philip really kill her? Did he do it with his own hands?' There was a strange gleam in her eyes.

Felicia's heart gave a jerk. 'No! He set fire to her house, and she died later, despite all Edmund's attempts to save her.' She leaned against the stone wall and stared out of the lancet window opening. 'But it was because of what Philip did to her that she died.'

Joan looked askance at her. 'It seems providential that he should be at hand to help you to escape. How did he know you were an unwilling guest of Philip? It

202

sounds as if you barely know him—yet now you are lovers.'

'We are not lovers!' Felicia exclaimed as calmly as she could. 'I told you that he helped me because he saw it as a way of injuring Philip.' She held her face up to the sun's rays. 'Tell me. While you wandered the forest after Philip had gone, did you see any strangers—or men that you would recognise as Philip's followers?'

'What? I—I don't know.' Joan put a hand to her head, and appeared disconcerted. 'What does it matter? You spent the night with him. In his arms! Yet you say you are not lovers.'

She replied angrily. 'Then is it you who are spying on me? How dare you! I ran out of the keep because I do not like mice. I came back again after I had calmed down.' Her voice was tinged with ice. 'I suppose it was you that followed me this morning?'

'Why should I follow you?' A nerve twitched Joan's cheek. 'It is that man who is your follower. He lusts after you.'

She flushed, not answering. She did not want to listen to her cousin any more. Perhaps she was spy for Philip now!

'Perhaps he has already had you, and done ...'

'Done what?' Her voice was suddenly steely.

Joan hitched a shoulder high and turned

away. 'What—What Philip did to me. Men are all the same, if you are thinking that this Edmund is different. Do not tell me that he has never kissed you,' she sneered.

Felicia felt the remnants of her patience deserting her. 'So? Edmund has kissed me, I do not deny it, but it has nothing to do with you! He is not my lover. What Philip did to you has turned your mind—perhaps he has even turned you against me. But he is to blame for what happened, not I. It is not my fault!'

'He would not want you if he thought you were Philip's whore,' panted Joan.

Felicia cried, white-faced, 'Do not even think that! Or say it! It is not true!'

'It—It was you that Philip wanted!' Joan choked. 'Even as he ... It should have been you ... you ... you!' She turned and ran across the room before Felicia could make a move, dragged the door open and slammed it behind her.

Felicia made to go after her, but stopped. Her cousin's words had shocked and hurt, and tears were near. Best wait, seeing the mood she was in. She moved back to the window, trying to calm her jangled nerves, and became aware of voices rising from the court.

'I have followed this far,' said one man gruffly. 'You may take over now. It has gone well. How goes the conflict and the Earl?'

'I have tired of it all. Matters were different when I first followed his star. I am glad of this new task. Perhaps I shall come out of it with some gold in my pocket for a change! But I am still to see her.' The voice was harsh.

Felicia pushed herself up, leaning on the sill in an attempt to see the owners of the voices. She dislodged a lump of mortar that bounced on the head of one of the men, and he looked up. For a moment their glances held, and then she slipped back down into the room, her face hot.

'That was fortunate!' She caught the muffled sound of the first voice, and realised that the men were moving away.

'Ay, chance is a strange lady,' laughed the man she had instantly thought of as handsome. 'Love passed me a dud coin. Perhaps now this gamble will pay off!'

Rubbing her sore elbows, she leaned on the sill again. Who was the owner of the second voice? Never had she seen a man so fair: his hair was the colour of newly-minted gold as it had glinted in the sun, and by any lights he was the handsomest man she had ever seen. He reminded her of someone, and she would be interested to see him again. There was no sign of him or his companion in the court now.

She heard a door open on the other side of it and saw Edmund, who seemed deep in thought as he went across, and did not notice her. She remembered in that moment, as she watched him, who had described just such a fair man to her. Her elbows began to ache excruciatingly and she dropped down from the sill. She smoothed her skirts, dismissing the men from her mind, and turned from the window. Where had Joan gone?

Joan sped along the stone-flagged corridor as if her life depended on it. She felt sick, and a panic-stricken horror had her by the throat. She must get out—out into the open air where she could breathe properly. Her chest was wheezing as she came to a great oaken door. She wrenched it open with shaking fingers and stumbled through, only to collide with a tall figure who put forth a steadying hand. She looked up at him with great wild eyes.

'Do not touch me!' she gasped, tugging herself out of his grasp and slumping against the wall, realising that several disapproving faces were turned towards her. A sob burst in her throat.

'Joan! What is it? What has frightened you?'

The voice was filled with such gentle compassion that it caused tears to rise. She looked up, and shook her head wordlessly. Concern shadowed Dickon's face, and she suddenly recognised it for such. She allowed him to help her up—even to take her hand and pull it through his arm with a firmness that brooked no argument.

'Let us walk,' he murmured. 'We shall go into the gardens, away from this place. There you shall tell me what it is that has alarmed you.'

Joan did not answer, but she went with him, her feet dragging slightly. It was a relief not to have to think for herself.

Felicia came down into the hall. Outwardly she was composed, but inwardly she was still disturbed by the exchange with Joan. She could not stop thinking of the look in her face when she had asked if Philip had himself killed Edmund's mother. From there it was but a short step to remembering Philip's threat to kill her. Would he think of sending his men to Chipbury? Maybe they had been there already and set it, too, alight. The thought numbed her.

'Felicia!'

She lifted her head and saw Edmund coming towards her. Relief flooded her before she remembered that this was the first time they had been alone without Joan or Dickon since the night before. She went to withdraw her outstretched hand, but already he had it in his grip.

'What is it?' He looked down into her face and held her hand more tightly. 'You shall tell me!'

She hesitated, and then spoke only half the truth. 'It is Joan. She left the chamber in a hurry, and I do not know where to find her.'

'Do not worry.' His brow lightened. 'She is with Dickon. They were crossing the hall when I came in, but they did not see me.'

'That is good, I think. She was in such a mood!'

Edmund glanced down at her but did not ask questions. 'Would you like a stroll round the herbarium? It lacks an hour to supper, and I think you would find pleasure in the garden.'

'That is just what I would like.' Felicia smiled up into his face as he pulled her hand through his arm.

'I would also like you to meet my uncle Walter later. He has expressed a wish to make your acquaintance.'

'You have spoken with him? Could he tell you anything concerning the Lord Edward? Or the whereabouts of Earl Simon?'

Edmund began to tell Felicia what the abbot had said on the matter as they strolled across the court. Eventually they came to the herbarium, having seen no sign of Joan or Dickon.

Felicia glanced about her as they passed through the gate set between a hedge of hawthorn. She drew a deep breath, laden with fragrance. Many of the plants she recognised: pennyroyal, mint, thyme, fennel and many more. Away down the garden she spotted a bed of lavender.

'It is beautiful,' she murmured, 'and so peaceful.' A flicker of sadness crossed her face.

'What is it?' Edmund turned to her. 'And do not say it is nothing,' he teased.

'I shall not, then.' A smile replaced the sadness. 'I was thinking of the herb garden I had at Meriet—and how it was trampled down by my cousin and his men.'

'But you will be safe at Chipbury?' His tone demanded an answer. 'You do not think Philip will come seeking you there?'

Was now the time to speak of her fears? Or had she imagined being watched—or had it been Joan? 'There is nowhere else I can go,' she said at last. 'I have no other male kin—and perhaps it is as people say: that my cousin is a devil who would find me wherever I went.' Her voice shook slightly.

'If you were already wed, you would not need to fear him. He could not force you into doing anything,' said Edmund. 'All this talk about his being a devil! You said yourself that he bleeds, so he is a man! And it is as a man you fear him. But if you were wed?'

Felicia stilled. What was he trying to say?

'A marriage of convenience is the usual way, is it not? I would suggest such—not for my gain, but for your protection.' Edmund forced the words out, finding them more difficult to say than he would have believed. 'I would offer you my name, Felicia, if it would serve you.'

'Your name?' Felicia's heart was beginning to pound. He had taken her completely unawares. A slight breeze wafted a strand of hair across her face, and she eased it away with unsteady fingers. 'What do you mean?'

'Marriage, of course! I am Sir Gervaise's bastard. I came here to my uncle to discover if I was heir to his lands, as I had hoped.'

'What? Why did you not tell me the truth? Or was it that you did not trust me, thinking still that I might be Philip's whore and give you away to him?' Her voice had risen and her eyes sparkled. 'I trusted you, despite what you did to me.' Her tone was tart as she turned from him and began to walk away.

He grabbed her arm and jerked her to

a halt. 'Trust me a little more, then,' he demanded harshly. 'I told you no lies! I told you I was kin to him.' He watched the anger die on her profile. 'You say you hate and fear your cousin. It is for that reason that I am bold to suggest a way of escape. De Vert blood runs in my veins. In most men's eyes that would make me your equal, despite my being a bastard. I need a wife now! So what say you, Felicia Meriet—will you wed me and confound that cousin of yours?'

Felicia put a hand to her head. She felt dizzy. The idea of marrying him filled her with a strange blend of excitement and trepidation. She must think! She twisted in his grasp and ran down the garden.

She did not get far. Edmund brought her to a swinging halt in front of a bed of poppies and spun her round. His eyes were hot and angry as they raked her face.

'In God's name, why do you run from me? I am not your cousin that I would force you into wedlock! Let us forget that I ever spoke. I shall escort you to Chipbury and leave you there, perhaps never to see you again, if you find my presence so distasteful. Come, I shall take you back to the lodging-house.' He pulled her hard.

'I do not want to go back yet.' Felicia dug in her heels, trying to release herself from his remorseless grip. 'I—I have not finished looking at the plants.' She glared at him. 'I have never thought you the least bit like my cousin, except in that you and he are like all men, overbearing. You never give a maid time to consider—if you think we consider at all!' She averted her face and presented him with a view of her stormy profile.

He let go of her, and threw up his arms. 'Consider, then,' he said in exasperated tones. 'I swear I shall never understand women if I live to be a thousand years!'

'That is unlikely!' She bent and pulled one of the poppies out by its stem, twisting it between her fingers. He made it all sound so calculating, and while she knew that was how most marriages were arranged, she realised that she wanted more than a convenient arrangement from Edmund de Vert.

'Well! Have you had time to consider?' he muttered impatiently, scuffing up dust with the toe of his shoe. 'Do not say that you are indifferent to me—or that we barely know each other. I consider that we know each other better than do many a couple that wed after being betrothed from the cradle.' He came behind her and slid his arms about her waist, easing her back against his chest. As she stiffened, he kissed the side of her neck. 'Do not pretend that you find my touch abhorrent, Felicia.' He

212

bit the lobe of her ear gently. 'I would not believe you.'

She gave a gasp of outrage. 'Do you not have any sense of ... of ...'

'Decency?' He laughed, squeezing her waist. 'You forget that I abducted you.' He kissed her flushed cheek. 'You must know I want you. Last night I wanted you. Ever since I saw you in the tub, I cannot get you out of my mind.'

'Are you sure it is a wife you want? You have called me a witch and a wanton!' She attempted to pull away, but he turned her about ruthlessly and kissed her full on the mouth, forcing her stubborn lips apart with his tongue. A delicious melting spread through her body, and she was trembling by the time they drew apart.

'Well?' he demanded huskily, holding both her hands firmly. 'You will marry me?'

Felicia nodded wordlessly, unable to deny her own tumultuous emotions. 'But who will wed us without my cousin's consent? What about banns?' she whispered.

Edmund frowned. 'I don't give a fig for your cousin's consent!' He pressed her hand. 'I think I can persuade my uncle to do the deed without banns.' He tilted her chin and kissed her hard.

'But ...' she began, pulling herself out

of his embrace and gazing up at him seriously, 'why so soon?' She clenched her hands tightly together, suddenly frightened of the feelings he roused within her. 'Could we not wait a little longer?'

'Wait?' His brow darkened. 'Wait for what? You would wait for your cousin to return from the conflict, perhaps?'

Felicia shook her head, feeling slightly worried. She wanted him, but what did she know of him, after all? She suddenly felt young and vulnerable.

Edmund sensed her indecision. 'You do hate your cousin, don't you?'

Felicia nodded.

'Then see our marriage as a body-blow to him. You cannot fight him with the sword, but to find you wed will injure him perhaps even more.' He smiled.

Felicia's lips began to smile, also. 'Perhaps you are right.'

'I am!' He grinned. 'Let us go now and seek out Uncle Walter. Afterwards, we shall break the news to Dickon and Joan.' He began to lead her down the path.

'Joan!' She came to an abrupt halt, and Edmund stopped, a question in his eyes. 'Joan will not like it,' she added.

'Then she will just have to bear it,' he said softly. 'Joan has my sympathy, but you cannot let her rule our lives. Besides, she should be glad that you will be safe from your cousin. She surely hates him as much as you do.'

'I think she does, but I think she hates me as well.' Felicia intently studied a bed of purpling lavender.

'She will get over it. I think she hates me, and so you think she will cause a storm because we are to wed?'

'You do understand!'

He nodded. 'But that does not mean that I think you should give in to your cousin's moods. Leave her to mope—or to Dickon! He has a way with women. Perhaps it comes from having a sister.'

'Nell!' Dismay clouded Felicia's brow. 'She thinks that ...'

'Nell thinks what? That I was going to marry her? Is that what she told you?' He gave an exasperated grunt.

'No, she did not, but I thought ...'

'Perhaps you would be better if you thought less. It was always Steven for Nell. She will shed no tears for me.'

'Steven?' She was perplexed until she remembered. 'Is he the lover as fair as an angel whom she told me about—the man her father would not let her marry?'

Edmund grinned suddenly. 'Is that what Nell called him? He would not like that: he hated his good looks! Did she talk much about him?'

Felicia's concern was assuaged. 'No, but

I think she still cares for him. It is a pity he does not know she is a widow. Nell said that he followed the Montfort. Have you ever had word from him?'

'No. We had an almighty disagreement—he and I, and Dickon.' He shrugged. 'But it is no use our being concerned about it. We can do nothing for either of them.' He paused at a wooden bench set against a wall. 'I shall go and fetch my uncle. This is the infirmary, and I know he is within. Do not despair if I am more than a few minutes. It will be because my opinion is sought.' He kissed her cheek, and then was gone, leaving her to her thoughts. She wondered what would happen to Meriet if her cousin survived the conflict and fought in the courts over its possession. Or if he would overset her marriage. Was she doing the right thing? How would Joan react to her news? She could only pray that she would not go into a fury.

Joan stared down at the fish swimming like lazy shadows in the pond. Dickon watched her expressive face, guessing that her private grief had her in its hold, but he doubted she would give in to it in front of him.

'Should we be here?' She looked up at Dickon.

He shrugged. 'I used to come here often

when I was a boy. Edmund and I used to try and catch the fish in our early days—before the monks caught us.'

'Why did you try and catch them?' She spoke in a listless drone. 'Were you hungry? I am hungry, yet I don't feel like eating. It makes me sick.'

'We did it for sport,' he explained politely. He put a foot on the stone wall round the pond and rested his arm on his knee. 'You should eat. If you were any thinner, you would go through the eye of a needle.' He smiled inwardly at the flicker of annoyance that showed in Joan's eyes. That had roused her!

'You prefer my cousin?' She flung the words at him, turning from him and walking across the lawn. 'If you had not eaten for a week, you would be as thin as I,' she called angrily over her shoulder.

'Why did you not eat?' Dickon drew alongside her. 'Was it because you lacked courage to go into the village and ask for food?'

A dull red stained Joan's cheeks. 'They would have looked down on me. They did not like me being in Flissie's place,' she muttered vehemently. 'They would be glad of what happened to me.'

'Why should they be? Agnes called you "that poor child". You would have found an ally, and a sympathetic one, there.

Philip Meriet tried to kill her by hitting her over the head. She would have helped you.'

'What! Accept help from a serf?' Joan turned as she replied disdainfully. 'It is a wonder you do not follow the Montfort! Did he not want to help them?'

'I did, once,' he said calmly. 'You would say that Philip Meriet follows the Montfort to help the serfs?' He came to a wicket gate at the far end of the garden and unlatched it, standing aside to let Joan go through before him. But she just stood there, staring at him.

'He wanted her,' she said in a hard voice, her eyes flashing. 'Just like you and your friend do. I have seen the way you look at her. And Edmund ... He kisses and cuddles her, but she does not know or believe that all men are like Philip. He will use her and toss her aside, as Philip did me.'

'You're wrong.' Dickon felt slightly sick at her vehemence. 'I have no designs on Felicia. As for Edmund, he is not in the least like Philip Meriet. He's not a man for picking up folk and tossing them aside.'

'He wants her.' Joan's voice was suddenly uncertain. Feeling Dickon's disapproval, she lowered her eyes and fiddled with a ring on her finger. 'Philip would kill him if he knew that he had laid a finger on Felicia.

He is mad with jealously over her lover.'

'How will he get to know?' he asked matter-of-factly. 'Unless the birds are his spies. Besides, Edmund is not her lover.' He took her by the arm and urged her through the gate. The conversation seemed to be set in a groove.

She shrugged his hand off as soon as they were through into the herbarium. They did not speak as they walked slowly between the banks of plants, and every now and then Joan would pause and finger one. Almost lovingly, thought Dickon. Was it among plants that her cure lay? A garden was a restful place for the spirit, although its healing often lay in hard work. Perhaps that was what Joan needed. It sounded as though she had tried too hard to play the lady of the manor in Felicia's place, and had been rejected. Maybe at Chipbury, with Felicia's help, she would in time find her rightful place. There came a murmur of voices, and when Dickon looked up he realised that they had reached the infirmary. Sitting outside on a bench in the late sun were Felicia, Edmund and the lord abbot.

Felicia got to her feet, a mixture of relief and anxiety on her face. She came towards them and slipped a hand through Joan's arm. 'You are feeling all right now?' she whispered.

Joan nodded as Dickon moved away towards Edmund and the abbot.

'Well met,' said Dickon, making a reverence towards the abbot.

'How are you, Richard? And how is the business?' Abbot Walter's face relaxed into a smile. 'Could we interest you in some of the finest wool in the realm?'

'Perhaps, my lord abbot. But Edmund has told you what we are about?'

He nodded. 'And I think he has more news for you. Good news, in my opinion. But now I must leave you.'

'My lord abbot, I would make my cousin Joan known to you,' said Felicia, swiftly pulling her forward, 'and ask your prayers for us both.'

Joan made a reluctant reverence, but as she rose her eyes went almost involuntarily to the abbot's face. She felt a tremor in her limbs at his look of warm understanding. He knew, but he did not scorn or blame her as some churchmen would have. She was reminded of her own father and how he had always been ready to comfort her after some misdemeanour, unlike her mother, who had always despised her for being a girl. She smiled at the abbot and kissed his ring fervently, without understanding why. Briefly she forgot about her grievances.

The abbot held up his hands in a

blessing, then turned and went into the infirmary.

Dickon turned to Edmund. 'What is this good news that the abbot spoke about? Is it what you hoped?'

Edmund opened his mouth to answer, then realised that Felicia was looking at him warningly. Her eyes flicked briefly towards Joan.

'In part,' he murmured, 'but let us go ahead of Felicia and Joan. I need to wash some of the dust from me, having had no chance before. I shall tell you on the way.'

Dickon nodded and fell in step beside him. Their heads came close together as they talked.

Felicia felt Joan tug her sleeve, as she said, 'I think they have already forgotten us.'

Felicia smiled at her. 'Most likely.' She was relieved that her cousin seemed to have thrown off her mad mood. 'What do you think of this garden? Is it not beautiful?' She put her hand through Joan's arm again. 'Perhaps, at Chipbury, after Edmund and Dickon have gone to Gloucester, we can see what can be done to the garden. It is two years since I have been there, and I know not its state, although Thomas, my bailiff, and Emma have been entrusted with overseeing it.'

'I would like that.' A smile of pure pleasure lit Joan's face. 'It will be good to be together again, just the two of us.' Felicia nodded. 'Will the men be staying long? Did you say it is to Gloucester they go? That is not so far from Chipbury. Do you think they will perhaps come back and see how we fare?' Her brow puckered, and for a moment there was a look in her eyes that caused Felicia's heart to sink. Then it went, and she began to talk about herbs.

Felicia wondered if it had really penetrated her thoughts that the men were going off to war and might possibly never return. Her throat tightened, remembering the awfulness when the news had come that her father and brother were dead. God willing, she would not have to go through that again!

'I wonder what there will be for supper,' Joan murmured as they came to the gate. She paused, a hand on the wicket. 'Do you know, Flissie, that lute-player said I was thin!' Her voice was indignant.

'Well, we can soon remedy that!' Felicia chuckled. 'If I remember one good thing about Chipbury, it is that Emma, the bailiff's wife, is a paragon of a cook who enjoyed nothing better than trying to fatten me.' She gave her cousin a push that sent her flying through the gateway. Joan began to run, laughing as she did so, with Felicia in hot pursuit. For a moment they were girls again.

They crossed the great court with most of the other travellers staying at the lodging-house, and partook of the sacrament. Felicia had been surprised at how willingly Joan had come with them. She had thought she would protest after her comments the night before about no longer believing in God. After Mass they went to supper. It was good. There were eels in a rich creamy herb sauce, mutton with onions and barley, and small wood strawberries topped with cream.

At the end of supper Edmund drew Felicia aside, leaving Joan and Dickon walking ahead. 'I would speak with you a moment.' He led her into the shadow of a towering buttress of pale stone. He touched her cheek and she lowered her eyes. 'If you are willing still, shall we be married in the morning before we leave for Chipbury?'

Felicia could not see his face clearly, but she thought she heard a tender note. It made her heart melt strangely. 'I am willing,' she whispered. 'Rather you than Philip,' she added, in case he might think her too willing.

'Not much choice,' he said drily. 'Were you never betrothed, Felicia? I would have thought some knight would have asked for your hand before now.'

'Once,' she said, her lips twitching. 'I was five years old, and he died of a fever. You have no idea how cross I was with the poor boy!'

Edmund did not touch her, yet she felt almost as though he was holding her. If not by strength of arms, then by a strange singing magnetism that seemed to stretch between them. It snapped suddenly in a chilly breeze that rose, and she felt cool air at her ankles, as if a door had been opened and shut.

'We must go,' she whispered.

He nodded, and they parted in the hall. Nerves twisted in her stomach as she neared her apartment. She must tell Joan tonight. The door opened before she touched it, and Joan stood framed there, with the glow of candlelight behind her.

'Flissie, I thought you would never come!' she exclaimed in a querulous voice. Her face was screwed up with weariness. 'I could not settle to sleep without you—and in the morning we shall be leaving for Chipbury.' She pulled Felicia into the room.

'In the morning,' Felicia began, clearing her throat, as she moved over to the bed, unfastening her surcote. 'In the morning, I am marrying Edmund de Vert.'

She sank on the bed, realising in that moment the meaning of the words. She was committing herself to a man who had once abducted her. A physician, born on the wrong side of the blanket, who had not yet gained his inheritance. Suddenly she felt like laughing.

'You are jesting, Flissie. Say you are jesting!'

Felicia saw that Joan's mouth was working as tears filled her eyes.

'You said that you were not lovers. You lied! What will happen to me?' Joan beat her breast.

'I did not lie. And you will still be with me, of course.' Felicia took off her surcote and placed it on the bottom of the bed.

'I don't understand.' Joan placed a hand to her head and rubbed it slowly. 'How can you be marrying this man if you barely know him? And you say that he is not your lover.' She sat on the bed, staring wide-eyed at Felicia, pleating and unpleating a fold of pink undergown. 'Philip said you had a lover. Is there someone else in love with you, then?' Her mouth trembled. 'It seems that everyone is in love with you, and nobody loves me. Even the lute-player looks fondly on you.'

Her tone was so pitiful that Felicia was moved to slide along the bed and put an arm about her shoulders. 'Joan, forget what

Philip said. There was no lover. Philip thought there was only because ...' Felicia paused and gnawed her lower lip. Should she tell?

Joan looked at her. 'Because ...?' She lowered her head on Felicia's shoulder.

'Because he could not understand how I escaped from the castle. But I did not escape the first time—I was abducted. Edmund abducted me. He did it as an act of revenge. Philip had killed his father and half-brothers. You see, he is Sir Gervaise de Vert's bastard. That is why we came here. His uncle has a document verifying the fact, and saying that Edmund is heir if Sir Gervaise and his sons die before him, with no further issue.'

Joan lifted her head and looked at Felicia. 'You say the first time? Did you escape twice?'

Felicia shook her head patiently. 'The first time I was abducted—and I escaped Edmund. I was recaptured by Philip's men. The second time when Philip tried to bed me, I escaped with Edmund's help. He was going south, so he brought me to Meriet.'

'It sounds unbelievable! But—But why do you wed a man who abducted you? How could you hate and love someone at the same time. Can he be any better than Philip?'

'He is!' Felicia nearly shouted the words. Her cousin scanned her face with round, incredulous eyes. 'The marks on my cheek are nearly gone now,' she said, lowering her voice. 'Philip hit me—and I am certain he killed his wife, as I told you. He certainly slew Edmund's family. Edmund has never treated me so—so unkindly ... roughly, maybe.' She blushed.

Joan pulled away. 'He has bewitched you,' she said slowly. 'Or perhaps this physician has given you a love potion. That is why you wed him. And what of him? He might be like Philip and want your lands.'

'No! It is not like that!' Felicia rose to her feet. 'He thinks to protect me from Philip by giving me his name.' She walked slowly over to the window, and thought she saw a man move into the shadows.

'It is not that. He wants you.'

Felicia did not answer. She knew he did, and she delighted in the thought while she yearned for something more from him.

'He does, Flissie. He does!' Joan slid off the bed and came over to her. 'Why is it that men want you and not me? Am I so plain?' Her voice was dull and dreary. 'Philip wanted you, too.'

Felicia turned swiftly. 'It was Meriet he wanted—not me.'

Joan shook her head. There was a

strained expression on her face. 'He loved you. He told me so. I was in love with him, Flissie. He is a handsome devil, don't you think?'

There was pity in Felicia's face. 'I thought I loved him once, but that was a long time ago, before I knew him. He is, as you say, a devil.' She paused. 'I think it best if we do not talk about him. You will distress yourself.' She put out a hand and would have led her cousin to bed, but Joan shook it off.

'He was pleasant, at first. Then a day and a night passed, and you did not come. He began to drink, but that did not bother me.' Her voice had taken on that strange high note. Felicia felt a shudder pass through her.

'Joan!' she pleaded. 'Come to bed.'

Joan moved away from her. 'He kissed me and fondled me, and called me "my love".' Her fingers twisted convulsively. 'And I returned his kisses! I let him touch me ... Then—Then he said he loved you and meant to have you. But ... if you were not there, I would do instead.' She pressed her lips together, and her face was so blank that Felicia wondered if she saw her at all. 'I fought him then,' said Joan softly. 'I scratched and kicked. But he would have choked the life out of me if I had not submitted.

I was even in the house when he fired your bed.'

'Joan, please! You do not have to tell me. I know what he is!' Felicia stepped forward and held out a hand beseechingly. 'Let us go to bed. You must try to forget. At Chipbury there will be much to do to occupy our minds and hands.'

'Forget?' Joan stared at her. 'I shall never be able to forget. It is with me night and day. And it is your fault. Perhaps I shall forgive you. I don't know yet.' She walked past Felicia, and pulling back the covers, she climbed into bed and shut her eyes.

Felicia realised that her cousin was shutting her out. She rubbed her arms. How cold she felt! She shivered, trying to ignore the sick feeling in her stomach, and went over to the bed and slid beneath the covers, snuffing the candle as she lay down. But it was a long time before she slept.

It was still cool when Felicia woke. Light filtered through the shutters, turning the shadows in the corners of the room pale lavender. Gradually it pearled and creamed as she lay there, watching and thinking.

Joan shifted in the bed, pulling the covers from her. Felicia grimaced but made no effort to retrieve them. She rose and went over to the pitcher of water on a stand beside the metal basin. She poured the water into the basin and dragged her undergown down to her waist. If she had nothing fresh to wear for her wedding, at least she could be clean underneath. She shuddered as she began to wash. By the time Felicia had finished and was fastening her gown once more, Joan had woken.

'Will he still be leaving you, now that you are marrying him?' Felicia turned and went over to the bed, picking up her surcote. Joan looked at her. 'You would rather he stayed, wouldn't you?'

'He will not.' Felicia slid her arms into the brown linen sleeves. 'Do you not understand? Edmund and Dickon are going to join the Lord Edward. Not only because Edmund wants the help of the Prince, but to fight in the conflict and seek out Philip.'

'But they are not knights.' Joan's brow creased in bewilderment.

'Not all men who fight are knights.' Felicia gave a sigh of exasperation. 'War is not a tournament—a game in the art of combat. It is a deadly struggle for power and passionate ideals. Dickon and Edmund are both skilled in the use of sword and dagger. Dickon is a burgess of the town, having a say in its government. He would be a leader in times of its defence—or if there are riots in the streets.'

'I did not realise,' said Joan slowly.

'These matters were never spoken of in front of me at home. How is it you know so much, Flissie? You are a woman, and have no part in such matters.' Joan slid off the bed.

'You forget ... Mark and Father spoke often in front of me, and they were fighting men.' Felicia began to unbraid her hair. 'I used to listen to them often when at my sewing in the hall.'

'I'm sorry about Mark and your father. You went so quickly after the news came of their deaths.' Joan touched Felicia's arm and pressed it. 'Would you like me to comb your hair out for you? Are you going to wear it loose?' Her voice suddenly contained a note of animation. 'Would you like me to seek out some flowers? I could form them into a garland.'

Felicia smiled at her, pleased at the change. 'I would like that! It would make me feel a little more ... festive.'

'I shall get dressed and go, then,' said Joan eagerly, reaching out a hand for her surcote. 'I shall not be long. I know just where to find some cowslips and heartsease.'

She soon returned, clasping the yellow and purple flowers in her fist. 'Are they not pretty?' she murmured, holding them out. 'I think I almost prefer meadow flowers to those that grow in gardens.'

231

'Yet still I like working in a garden,' said Felicia.

'So do I.' Joan sat down on a stool and began to twist and weave the stems of the flowers. 'You have combed your hair out yourself. It is a pretty colour.'

'Not as pretty as yours,' responded Felicia, peering through a strand of her dark hair. 'I don't think I have ever seen hair the colour of yours. Yesterday I saw a man whose locks were the shade of minted gold. But yours is the colour of barley in the ear. It is truly your crowning beauty.'

'Thank you.' Joan blushed with pleasure. 'It is the same shade as Father's when he was young, so Mother told me. She did not really like it. She preferred dark men.'

A shadow crossed her face and her fingers faltered. For an instant, Felicia thought she was going to toss the flowers aside as her hands tightened and crushed several of the heads. Then, after a few moments without saying another word, Joan began to work busily again until she had finished the garland. She bade Felicia sit, and carefully placed the garland over her hair.

'The dew was melting in the sun when I gathered the flowers. I think that perhaps you will need to go soon.' Joan stepped back and gazed carefully at Felicia. 'You will do.' She turned away and went over

232

to the window. 'I shall stay here until we are ready to leave for Chipbury.' Her voice was strained.

'But I want you with me.' Felicia hurried across and put a hand on Joan's arm. 'I need you at such a time. You are my only kinswoman. Do this for me, Joan. Look!' She held out her hands in front of Joan's face. 'See how I shake. Let me comb out your hair. See—there are still some flowers.' She pointed to the tumble of blossoms on the bed. 'I want you for my maid. It will not be an affair of grandeur, my wedding—but let us make it as grand as we can?'

Joan's face lightened, and she grasped Felicia's hands. 'We shall have to make haste, or it will be noon before we are ready! That will never do.'

Edmund and Dickon were waiting in the hall by the time they arrived. Edmund had changed, and now wore a surcote of blue linen with wide sleeves edged with fur. His hair was neatly combed, and he had shaved. Felicia's eyes went to his face in an attempt to find some reassurance there. He smiled.

Some of her misgivings fled. 'I have nothing else to wear,' she whispered, placing her trembling fingers on his proffered arm.

'It is of no matter. You are ready?'

Felicia nodded. She had to trust him; she had no one else.

Edmund pressed her hand. 'Let us go, then.'

They went together.

CHAPTER TEN

'I Edmund take thee Felicia to my wedded wife, to have and to hold, for fairer, for fouler, for better for worse, for richer for poorer, in sickness and in health, for this time forward, till death us do part, if holy church will it order; and thereto I plight thee my troth.'

His words sounded loud in the shaded porch of the church, and so binding. Trepidation surfaced within Felicia, and for a moment, knowing Edmund watched her, she could not speak. Then Abbot Walter murmured something, and she raised her head and began to repeat hesitantly. 'I Felicia take thee Edmund to my wedded husband, to have and to hold, for fairer, for fouler, for better ... for worse, for richer for poorer, in sickness and in health, to ... to be meek and obedient in bed and at board, for this time forward, till death us do part, if holy church will it order; and thereto I plight thee my troth.'

It was done! She experienced a moment of unexpected relief. Edmund tugged a gold ring from his little finger, and for a moment he balanced it on the palm of his hand. 'It was given in love by my father to my mother—despite his not being able to wed her. He had been betrothed from the cradle, and could not break it off without great dishonour to his name. I think she would have liked you to wear it.' He took her hand. 'With his ring I thee wed ...' Felicia listened to the familiar words. She had been to many a marriage ceremony, but never had she paid such attention to the solemnity of the occasion '... and with my body I thee worship, and ...' Her fingers trembled beneath his firm hold. So many promises and words tying her to him. He held the ring over the tip of her thumb—'In the name of the Father'; over her index finger—'in the name of the Son'; over her middle finger—'in the name of the Holy Ghost'; and finally he said 'Amen' as he slipped it on her third finger. It felt heavy! She touched it lightly with her thumb as he kissed her cool lips before leading her inside the church for the nuptial Mass.

As she waited for the Host, her shoulder touching his, Felicia thought how some might call their wedding clandestine, with no banns read and no father to give her away. There were no gifts from family or friends—and there would be no banquet afterwards, such as her father would have had prepared—but she could have fared much worse, she decided.

Afterwards they went to the abbot's lodgings and partook of wine and oatcakes, but they did not linger. The morning was getting on, and the journey was before them. As they rode beneath the arched gatehouse, Felicia placed her hand in Edmund's belt. She had put herself under his rule now by becoming his wife; nothing could be the same again, and only time would tell if she had acted wisely. For an instant, as her eyes caught Joan's, she remembered her cousin Philip and his threats. Could Edmund's name protect her from his fury? He would be doubly angry when he discovered that a de Vert still lived who would challenge him in the courts as well as on the battlefield.

The shadows were lengthening by the time they came to Chipbury. Edmund and Dickon dismounted before helping the women down. Felicia swayed as her feet touched ground. She was stiffer and sorer by far than she had been the previous day, and Edmund steadied her before turning to look at the small manor house.

Here there were no outer walls of

defence, only a ditch and an earthen bank sloping up to the house gave some little protection. It was quiet, and there seemed to be no one about. They walked up to the door, which was closed but yielded to Felicia's hand.

She led the way into the hall, pulling off her gloves as she did so, and sniffing. The place stank, and a bone crunched beneath her foot as she walked further into the room. Her heart sank. The walls had not been whitewashed that year, nor had the hangings been taken down and beaten to rid them of dust. God only knew when the rushes had last been changed! Annoyance and embarrassment showed on her face as she rested her weight on the back of an oaken chair.

'A case of while the cat's away the mice will play, do you think?' Edmund's eyes met her frown. 'It is unlikely that even a visit from your cousin would create this neglect already.' He dusted the seat of the chair with his sleeve, and ushered Felicia to it.

'No. This is not my cousin's doing,' she said with a sigh of relief. 'But something is amiss. Emma would not allow the hall to become so neglected, otherwise.'

'Well, I hope you do not expect us to start tidying up, Flissie,' Joan yawned. 'I am far too tired.' She subsided on to a stool and gazed about her with sullen eyes.

'I do not expect you to do anything this day, Joan,' she replied quietly. 'But we shall need food, so I must go in search of Emma and Thomas.'

'I shall come with you,' murmured Edmund, casting Joan an impatient glance.

'We must stable the horses too,' drawled Dickon, straightening up from the table he leaned against. 'I suggest we leave Mistress Joan to her solitary rest if she is as weary as she says.' He smiled at Felicia. 'I presume the stables are to the rear of the house?'

She nodded and rose to her feet wearily. 'Yes, that is so, and the buttery and storeroom are also in that direction.'

Joan darted a glance from Dickon's pleasant face to Felicia's weary one, and then to Edmund's concerned profile as he opened the door to the rear of the hall and bade Felicia go before him. She sprang to her feet. 'I might as well come with you,' she said in a long-suffering voice. 'There is little to do here while I wait.'

'You could always fetch a broom and start to sweep up,' murmured Dickon, politely holding the door open. 'But I suppose you would say that was serfs' work and beneath your dignity.'

Joan gave him an angry look and flounced out. Dickon shut the door

238

behind her, a slight smile on his face, and went back through the hall to fetch the horses.

Felicia stood by Edmund's side for a moment, listening, identifying sounds. The clucking of a hen, the wind in the trees, the clop of a horse's hoof, and a noise reminiscent of the buzzing of several swarms of bees. She exchanged a smiling glance with Edmund before they began to walk through beds of cabbages and beans planted in straight rows, although they needed weeding. A field planted with vines sloped down to the river, which gleamed between the trees in the distance. To the left stood an orchard, the trees nearly stripped of their blossom. At their right hand loomed a huddle of buildings, and it was from them that the sound of snoring came.

She put her hand to the buttery door and pushed it wide. Several barrels and a couple of sacks stood on the floor. On the shelves were numerous stoneware jars. Onions hung from the rafters, as well as herbs and a haunch of salted beef. There was even a large round cheese set on the table, and within just a few inches of it, turned away from her, was the face of the snorer.

'Thomas,' breathed Felicia.

'He's drunk,' Joan muttered, peering

239

round Felicia's shoulder.

'So it seems.' Felicia frowned. She had some experience of men in their cups, and was glad that Edmund was with her. Together they approached the slumbering figure. Joan slowly wandered out of the buttery towards the stables.

Edmund shook Thomas's shoulder roughly. There was barely a break in his snoring. 'Wake up, man!' he shouted in his ear, before shaking him hard again.

Thomas groaned, muttering a curse under his breath.

'That's better,' said Felicia grimly. 'Again, Edmund.'

After further prodding, Thomas at last opened his eyes, lifted his head, and blinked into her scornful face.

'M-Mistress Meriet?' He groaned and pushed himself up from the table.

'You know it is I, Thomas. Go and duck your head in a pail of water, then come back here. I have much to say to you.' Felicia leaned back against the table and folded her arms across her chest in a determined manner.

With an amused gleam in his eyes, Edmund put a hand on Thomas's arm and hauled him out of the buttery before the man could speak. They were back speedily. Thomas's black hair glistened with droplets of water, and he slouched in front of her, running a hand nervously across the dark stubble on his chin, looking at a point somewhere over her shoulder.

'Are you going to remove me, Mistress?' His voice was low, almost ashamed. 'I can't blame you if you do.'

'You admit I have reason, Thomas,' she said sternly.

When he lifted his head, his eyes were heavy and dazed, but he seemed to be in control of his wits. 'Ay, Mistress,' he mumbled. 'But without Emma, things have been hard.'

'Emma? What has happened to Emma? I have noticed the lack of her presence in the house.'

'Dead, Mistress.' Thomas coughed and cleared his throat, a pulse beating in his temple. 'Of the cough. More than ten deaths. Several babies have died, and naught seems to stop it. Now my Godric has it.'

'The cough?' She glanced at Edmund. 'Oh no! I am so sorry, Thomas. Emma will be sadly missed. No wonder you have been drinking! But it will not do, you know. I have need of you—as does your son. Where is he?'

'With Beatrice in the village. Fair worried I am, Mistress.'

'Then we must see what we can do.' Felicia was aware of Edmund's hand on her shoulder, warm and reassuring, and she turned to him. 'Can you ...?' she began.

'There is no cure that I know of,' he interrupted, 'but I do have a recipe for a mixture that will ease the cough. If you wish, we could try it on the children of the village.'

'Would you?' she impulsively reached up and covered his fingers with her own. 'Thank you.'

'I cannot promise a cure, Felicia. You do understand that?' He raised her hand to his lips. 'Yet I shall do my best. You will show me the village later?'

'Of course.' Felicia lowered her eyes, trying to hide the glow in them. She had not expected him to be so forthcoming.

Thomas gave Edmund a furtive glance, and suddenly noticed the gold ring on his lady's finger. He instantly understood the stranger's familiarity with her, although their talk about cures for the cough puzzled him. He had never known any lords to know about such. 'Is—Is this your new lord, Mistress?' he asked eagerly. 'Your cousin did say that we would be having one soon.'

'My cousin!' Felicia's head shot up, and Edmund's hand tightened on hers. 'When was he here?'

'Maybe three days ago.' Thomas scratched his head. 'I, perhaps, says it as I shouldn't,

Mistress—but he has an eye to your land. And I did think for a moment it was himself he meant—asked me that many questions that my head spun. Yet he did not seem to care about the state of the hall, but rather seemed pleased.'

'He did not hurt anyone, Thomas?' Felicia's voice was hesitant.

He shook his head and looked at Edmund. 'Barely here for more than an hour, sir. Said he was late for a meeting, or he would have stayed longer, hoping to see you.'

Felicia paled, seeing in the words a threat. 'Did he leave any men behind?'

'Not that I've noticed—and I would have heard if there were any in the village.'

'Any strangers?' Edmund asked sternly.

Thomas shook his head, then uncertainty flashed in his eyes. 'Only a pedlar, but he came and went in the same day.'

Edmund and Felicia exchanged glances, and Edmund smiled reassuringly. 'He has gone,' he said softly. 'His words are idle—meant to frighten you if you did come here.'

Felicia tried to smile, glad of his words. Yet she was not so sure as he concerning her cousin's motives. For all that Edmund had suffered at his hands, he did not know, as she did, his cruelty or his determination to have what he wanted.

243

'It is probably as you say. But now we have other matters to think on,' she added firmly. 'Thomas! Bring in some of that cheese, some dried fruit, barley and several onions—as well as some of the salted beef. Enough for four. Oh! And a flagon of cider.'

'Ay, Mistress! Master!' He eagerly set to work.

Felicia turned away with Edmund. She would cut a cabbage. They were not fully grown, but that did not matter. She began to wonder where Joan and Dickon were, but did not go looking for them. Instead, she went with Edmund towards the house. There was a meal to prepare, and it would take some time to cook.

Joan stood leaning against the wall watching Dickon's straight back as he lifted the saddle from the horse. He irritated her, this merchant. How dared he judge her behaviour! Yet on the tail of the thought was the remembrance of how he had spoken kindly to her at the monastery of Huppingescumbe.

A hen walked sedately into the stable, pausing when her beady eyes spotted Dickon, but when he made no threatening move, she strutted over to some straw on the other side of a wooden partition and out of sight of Joan.

'Do you think we would find eggs in here?' Joan moved away from the wall and towards Dickon.

'Perhaps.' He turned his head slightly, and his brown eyes washed over Joan. 'Look for some, if you wish.'

He did not sound surprised, and she guessed that he had known she was there watching him all the time. She felt annoyed that he had made no sign of it. 'Will you not help me?' she demanded petulantly.

Dickon moved to the other horse before replying. Joan's face was pale and thin, set in the frame of the almost white hair. 'I have a task,' he said slowly, his brows puckering. 'Surely the finding of a few eggs is not beyond your powers?'

'No, but ...' She paused. Why had she asked him to help her? She did not need his help, willing or no. He did not care about her, despite his kind words. Her skirts swept the earth floor as she moved beyond the partition and began to search in nooks and crannies, wherever she thought she might find an egg. She was successful. She laid the five eggs carefully on the wall before she looked for more.

Dickon, having finished with the horses, idly walked over and picked an egg up. 'Eggs in cheese sauce garnished with a little parsley or fennel is a dish worth eating,' he murmured, throwing it up a little way and catching it.

'Don't do that!' Joan stared at him crossly. 'You will break it. Give it to me!' she demanded, as he threw it into the air again.

'Come and get it!' There was a challenging note in Dickon's voice.

Joan eyed him. Her cheeks were flushed and her cornflower eyes sparkled. She jumped, attempting to snatch the egg from Dickon's upstretched hand. He smiled, and raised himself further on his toes.

'You are a beast!' panted Joan, falling back again to the ground. She put her hands on her hips and glared at him.

'You do give up easily!' Dickon cocked an eyebrow, and winked. 'Try again. Perhaps if you stand on that cask you might do it.'

She gave an exasperated groan. She would have told him to keep the egg and stalked out, but there was such an infuriating look on his face that she was determined not to give in and admit defeat. She walked over to the cask, kicking wisps of straw out of her path, and put her arms about it, trying to lift it. It was much heavier than she would have thought. After a struggle, she managed to raise it a few inches, and with her back bent she stumbled across the floor and dropped it with a thud in front of Dickon.

'You could have rolled it, you know.' His voice was smoothly helpful.

'Why did you not say that before I lifted it?' she gasped, her breasts heaving. She sank on to the cask, clasping her hands on her lap. 'Now I am too tired to climb on it.' She dragged back a heavy braid from her face and looked up. There was a smut on her cheek.

Suddenly Dickon realised that the game was no longer funny. She looked so defenceless that he experienced a strange sensation in his stomach. He sank to his knees, and taking one of her hands from her lap, he placed the egg in it. She gazed at him as her fingers curled protectively about it. Their faces were only inches apart, and for a moment they stayed looking at one another.

Joan could feel her heart thudding uncomfortably. She waited, expecting him to kiss her, not knowing if she wanted him to or not. Abruptly he got up, and without one word, moved away from her and out of the stable. Joan sat on, the egg still held in her hand. Then she crushed it so that the yolk and white squelched between her fingers and the shell bit into her palm. Then she flung the shattered remains against the stable wall and rose to her feet. She swept the remaining eggs from their perch, then stalked out.

At that moment Thomas came out of the buttery, loaded with food; swinging from one finger was a flagon of cider. Joan saw Dickon step forward and deftly remove the flagon. She heard the musical tones of his voice as he spoke, and he took a bowl of dried fruit from beneath Thomas's arm; then he began to help himself from the bowl as he strolled towards the house without even a backward glance. She stared after him, her face twisted with annoyance. Already it seemed he had forgotten her, and like most men was thinking of his belly above all other matters. How she despised him—and his friend, who had helped Felicia to escape from Philip. She stood thinking a moment longer, the familiar black despair shadowing her thoughts, then she began to walk towards the house, having made a decision.

'Is the supper almost ready?' Dickon peered over Felicia's shoulder into the cooking-pot. 'It smells good.'

'It is not nearly ready,' laughed Felicia, looking up at him with a smile. Her gaze shifted from his face to Edmund's, who was cutting some of the salted beef into small chunks. What a strange match she had made! Never had she seen her father do such mundane tasks, or any other lord, for that matter. Yet in so doing Edmund did not lose an ounce of his manliness. He looked up and grimaced ruefully.

'Are you ready for the meat?' He put down the knife and came over with the platter of beef, thinking that she looked tired. 'If you wish, Thomas can take me to the village. It might be best for you if you rested. How is your back?'

She wiped her damp brow with the back of her hand, and pulled a face. 'Aching—but it could be worse.' She took the platter from him and swept the meat into the cooking-pot.

'Joan could help you more.' He glanced, frowning, at the girl who was slumped on a settle, regardless of its unpolished state or the activities in the hall.

'She is tired,' put in Felicia speedily. 'Her shock was greater than mine.'

'Perhaps.' Edmund's tone was bitingly derisive.

'Why do you speak so? You saw the condition she was in when we reached Meriet.'

'Ay! And it seemed to me she was more furious about your escaping Philip than upset by her raping,' he said grimly.

'No! That isn't true!' Felicia dropped the spoon on the table with a clatter, and lowered her voice. 'How can you understand a maid's feelings in such a situation? Or are you like so many men and think that women are a snare to men, put on earth and used by the devil to bring about their downfall?' Her tone was intense. 'Men are the stronger. What chance did Joan have against Philip? I—I find the matter very disturbing, and cannot blame Joan for her resentment towards me. So let us not speak of the matter again, Edmund. With God's help, time will heal her pain.' She looked up at him, unaware that Joan watched them carefully from beneath lowered lashes.

Edmund hesitated before speaking. 'You think I forced you by strength of arms to wed me?'

'I did not say that!' she flushed.

'No! But perhaps you are thinking it! I did take you into my arms, but your protestations were not noticeable.' There was a gleam in his eyes.

Felicia experienced a spurt of anger. Why did he always make her feel a wanton because she had desires similar to his? 'A marriage of convenience, you said—and I agreed.' Her tone was cool. 'We both desire revenge—is that not so, Edmund?'

'Ay,' he murmured, frowning. 'My original aim for revenge still stands, but we need not discuss it now because you already know that.' He turned, and began to pour cider into cups.

For a second Felicia stared at his broad back. His words made her feel suddenly uneasy, unhappy even. Then she picked up her spoon and carried on with the preparations for supper, thinking over their conversation as she did so.

The meal was good, and they all, even Joan, ate with relish. Dickon said that Felicia's cooking even excelled Nell's, a compliment she laughingly denied. Edmund made no comment, which hurt her, causing her to talk more animatedly to Dickon than she would otherwise had done.

Joan's fingers curled about the cup of cider set by her platter and she drank deeply, her blue eyes gazing at Dickon's long, lively face. Was it because she was another man's leavings that he had not kissed her in the stable—or was he in love with Flissie? There was no hiding the warmth in his eyes when he looked upon her. Did the physician husband see it?

Thomas stood at her shoulder, so Joan lifted her hand and bade him fill her cup, looking towards Edmund and Felicia. It was a wedding feast—why should she not drink her fill? Felicia was wed to that man, who frowned on her. She felt an unexpected tremor of apprehension. Now that he was Felicia's husband, it would be he who would give the orders.

Would he try to get rid of her? It was a frightening thought ... She would have to be more circumspect. She lifted the brimming cup, regardless of her decision, and drank deeply.

Felicia watched her anxiously, not guessing the mood she was in. She sipped her own cider cautiously, knowing its potency and wanting a clear head. Even so, it made her drowsy.

The meal finished, Edmund rose from the table. 'I shall go now and see the children.' He called Thomas to him. 'Will you accompany me? What has so far been tried with your son?'

'I have passed him nine times under and over the priest's donkey—and he's drunk some of the beast's milk with three hairs from its back and three hairs from its belly placed in it. But it doesn't seem to have done him much good. Beatrice made him some mouse tea also.' Thomas sounded sombre.

Edmund smiled slightly. 'I see. We shall try another way.' He picked up the saddlebag from the chest against the wall, and turned to his wife. 'I hope I shall not be long.'

She got to her feet to go out with him and Thomas, watching them until they were out of sight among the trees. It was likely that, when Edmund returned, he would claim her as his wife. Her pulses jumped, and the trepidation and excitement that were becoming familiar when she thought of him were suddenly strong. Suddenly she resented his hold over her emotions. Perhaps she should play the part of shy reluctant maid instead of yielding to his touch so easily? She tilted her chin, and went back into the hall.

Felicia began to collect the dishes. Tomorrow she would see about getting some maids from the village to help, but tonight she would wash the crocks and make up the bed herself. Dickon, perched on the settle with his lute, was plucking the strings discordantly. Joan was slumped at the table, her elbows on its wooden top. Her chin was in her hands and she was staring at some spot high on the dirty walls.

'Joan!' Felicia was aware of a sense of helplessness as she turned to her cousin, who reluctantly returned her gaze. 'Will you help me?' She could barely control her voice.

'If—If you wish.' Joan pushed herself up from the table and stood swaying. One hand clutched her head, the other hung grimly to the table edge. Dickon cast a glance at her and then looked away.

Felicia gave a murmur of exasperation.

'You should not have drunk so much cider, love,' she whispered, helping Joan to sit down again. 'You stay here.' She sighed. 'I can manage alone.'

It did not take her long to deal with the dishes, or to place pallets in front of the fire to air for Joan and Dickon to sleep on. Only as she delved into the large chest of linen and blankets did she realise that she might have difficulty in persuading Joan to sleep in the hall, even if she put screens between her and Dickon. For a moment she stood still, gnawing her lower lip, her arms filled with blankets and sheets, before shrugging and going up the ladder leading to the bedchamber.

With some difficulty Felicia managed to lift the trapdoor, wedging the linen under her chin, and a groan escaped her. The bedchamber, too, was in need of a thorough cleaning. She went over to the narrow window opening and flung wide the shutters to let in the scent of the fields as the cool air wafted in. She dragged into a corner the dirty bedding that Thomas seemed not to have changed since Sir William, her steward, had last visited. Then she set to making up the bed, spreading lavender-scented linen over the feather mattress, trying not to dwell on what would take place that night.

She had almost finished when feet came

treading, up the ladder. For an instant her heart seemed to suspend its beating, then she realised that the hands gripping the edge of the opening were Joan's. The next moment her cousin had heaved herself up and into the bedchamber. She stayed kneeling on the floor, swaying slightly and giggling. 'So ... So ... you are ... pre-preparing the ... marit ... al bed!' She hiccuped. 'Pardon!' She stumbled to her feet and half ran, half fell across the room and slid on to the bed. For a moment she lay there unmoving, gasping.

Felicia stared down at her, angry and exasperated. 'Joan ...' she began.

'Shhh!' Joan held up a finger and pressed it to her lips. 'I ... I don't want them ... hearing us. Them men.' She winked. 'I've been thinking about ... your Edmund.' She yawned, before pulling herself further over on the bed by grasping the scarlet coverlet. She blinked several times and smiled brightly at Felicia, who had moved forward and was just in time to prevent Joan from sliding off the far edge.

'I don't think I wish to hear what you have to say about Edmund while you are in this state. God only knows how you managed to get up the ladder! What was Dickon thinking of to let you?' hissed Felicia angrily, heaving her back on the bed.

'Oh, the minstrel's gone ... Don't think he likes me, Flissie. Said he was going to che-check the horses.' Joan gave another yawn and gazed up with drowned cornflower eyes. Tears slowly oozed down her cheeks. 'Likes you, though ... But he—he can't have you. You're Edmund's. Clever fellow that husband of yours, Flissie. Have—Have you thought that if—if he kills Philip he will have his land as well as yours. You are Philip's only kin, aren't you?' Suddenly her eyes were hard and cold, maliciously so. 'Revenge? What a perfect jape to play on you—and Philip. Tricked by a—a bastard physician! Well, they do say most of them are charlatans, don't they? And—And you love him, don't you, Flissie?' Joan's eyelids began to droop. 'You—You are more to be pitied than ... I.' Her head fell on to the cover and she was still.

Felicia stood staring down at Joan and in that moment she hated her. Resentment and fury mingled with a chill desolation. Could it be true? Could it? Was Edmund so cold-blooded a planner? She sank to her knees by the bed, resting her head on her hands. Her throat was uncomfortably tight as she remembered the first time she had set eyes on Edmund. How he had hated her and Philip! He had said later that to possess that which your enemy most wanted was the perfect revenge—or something like that. And she had played into his hands by marrying him! What had he said earlier that evening? That his original aims for revenge were still the same! Dear God! What had she done? Joan's words kept repeating themselves in her head, intermingled with images of Edmund's face ... harsh, cold, gentle, angry, soft with tenderness, hot with desire. Which one was Edmund? her heart cried. She wished she knew. Then—Then she would know what to do, perhaps. Time ... She needed time! She slowly rose and stumbled across to the trapdoor, hesitating as her fingers curled over its edge. Then she carefully let it drop into place and slid the bolt shut before going back to the bed.

CHAPTER ELEVEN

Edmund ran a hand wearily over his face as he came to the hall, yet his step was light as he opened the door and went in. He had spent more time than he had intended with the villagers. At first they had been suspicious of him, despite Thomas's words, not understanding his interest in their troubles. They were accustomed to the lady of the manor giving food and potions in times of need when she was there on her few visits, but a lord ... He must be after something! More work on the strips and among the vines and fruits, most likely. But Edmund had persisted, and maybe it was his tone of authority that had made them listen to his words on how the mixture of marjoram, thyme, lavender and vervain had served well to ease the cough in the past. They would rather he had done something more dramatic. He grinned as he thought of the muslin bag one woman had shown him. It had contained six large dead spiders for a six-year-old lad—it had been held in the boy's mouth before being hung over his bed. Dear God, he was tired—but not too tired!

Dickon looked up at him, and cleared his throat uncomfortably. 'Thomas not with you?' he asked casually.

Edmund shook his head and dropped his pack on the settle. He looked about the hall and then poured himself a drink from the flagon of cider on the table. 'Where are they?' he said quietly.

Dickon hesitated, then motioned upwards with his head. 'I presume they are both in the bedchamber. Joan was a little the worse for drink, so I left her. Felicia had already gone up the ladder with linen.

When I came back from the stables, there was no sign of either of them.'

'I ... see.' Edmund's voice barely hid his anger. There was a strange sensation in the pit of his stomach, and he drank off the cider and refilled his cup. What should he do? If he and Felicia had been alone in the house, he would have battered the trapdoor in and claimed his wife. He gulped the cider and poured himself another cup. Damn! He wanted her, yet he could hardly charge up the ladder and demand Joan's removal. What was Felicia thinking of to let her up there, and to stay? He barely tasted the cider. Or was Joan's presence there deliberate? It was hard to believe that Felicia was frightened of him. Naturally she would be apprehensive, but she had agreed to this marriage. Had she expected him to woo her? No! She was a woman of surprisingly good sense, and she knew there had been no time for such pleasantries.

Dickon could guess some of Edmund's thoughts from the set of his mouth. Would they still leave on the morrow for Gloucester, as planned? At that moment Edmund lifted his eyes, and gave a bark of laughter.

'Not the first pickle we have shared, Dickon!' There was a strange note in his voice.

'No,' murmured Dickon, studying him. 'But this one is yours alone to sort out, my friend. However, they say love always finds a way.'

'Love?' Edmund frowned, his anger and frustration simmering beneath his outward calm. 'What has love to do with this?' He yawned. 'You talk like a man who has sung too many tales of chivalry and romance!'

'Perhaps.' Dickon grinned and rose to his feet. 'I'm for bed. Gloucester tomorrow, isn't it?'

'Thanks for reminding me. But we do not have to go with the dawn.' Edmund got up and stretched. Tomorrow ... He would have to settle matters tomorrow.

Felicia stood staring unhappily across the field of vines towards the distant gleam of water. She dropped the smelly rushes, her gaze suddenly arrested. A man was coming towards her, but even as she began to move she realised that it was not Edmund, but Dickon.

'Well met, Felicia.' Dickon noted how she immediately attempted to mask her disappointment with a smile. 'It will not be long before we leave for Gloucester.'

'Gloucester? I had forgotten. I did not think you and Edmund would go so swiftly.' Her fingers rested momentarily on his blue sleeve. 'Where is he?'

'Down by the river. I think he intended having a word with you before we left.' He smiled slightly.

'A word?' blurted out Felicia, anger replacing her unhappiness. 'Just a word for his wife!'

'Perhaps he wants more than a word,' he replied evasively. 'Where is Joan?'

She hesitated, a slight flush on her cheeks. 'Still lying down, with a compress on her head. Is he angry?'

'Too much cider,' grunted Dickon. 'It will not do her much good to try to forget in that way.'

'No!' She toyed with the keys hanging from her girdle. 'Is he *angry*, Dickon?'

'Do you think he has cause? He did not force you to marry him, did he?'

'No.' Her flush deepened, and she pressed a key hard into the palm of her hand. 'Perhaps a walk round the herb garden might do Joan some good.'

Dickon gave a twisted grin. 'You think it would make her more amenable?'

'I don't know,' said Felicia frankly, 'but she would not be trying my patience for a while! That sounds ...' She bit her lip guiltily.

Dickon gave a shrug. 'I shall go and seek her out.' He blew her a kiss and left her, going towards the house.

For a moment Felicia stood there, a

frown knitting her forehead, then she began to walk away. She caught the sound of splashing as she neared the river, which ran deep and slow there beyond the trees. She strode forward, her skirts sending pollen flying. Beneath the trees it was cooler, and she was thankful for the shade that dappled down from leaf and branch. Halting on the bank, she saw that Edmund was swimming. She could almost feel the warm touch of the sun on the glistening shoulders, and apprehension quivered in her stomach as he looked up. Their glances held, and he began to approach the bank.

'It won't be long before dinner.' Her voice quivered as he came within range. She felt the need of an excuse for seeking him, now that he was so close. Why had she come? Was what Joan had said about him true? Uncertainty shadowed her eyes as Edmund looked up at her.

'I've got more things on my mind than dinner,' he growled.

Felicia's heart gave a jump. He *was* angry! 'I thought you might not have broken your fast—and you are going to Gloucester today, aren't you?' He was just beneath her feet now.

'Ay. Will you be glad to see me depart, wife?' She made no answer, and his eyes were glistening charcoal. 'I needed a swim. I drank too much cider last night after I returned from the village.'

'It—It is potent, the Chipbury cider.' Felicia was nervous, extremely nervous, as she looked down at him.

'So your cousin found out, I hear.' He leaned his elbows on the bank, treading water. His tawny hair was sleek and darkened, making him look almost a stranger. She stepped back, but before she could go any further he put out a hand swiftly, grabbing her ankle, then pulled hard.

Felicia let out a scream, teetered on the edge, then overbalanced and fell in with an almighty splash. She came gasping to the surface, her veil covering her face with cold clammy folds, and she groped at it with shaking fingers. After the warmth of the sun, the water seemed extremely cold. Edmund's fingers were before hers, wrenching off her veil and throwing it on to the bank. She shouted angrily, 'How dare you! This is my only gown!'

'And extremely flattering it is too, when wet. I had not forgotten!' Edmund's eyes danced suddenly. 'Don't look so furious, Felicia. It will dry in this sun.'

'That is beside the point,' she retorted, resisting the charm he now exuded. She turned from him and began to swim towards the bank, only to feel his hand instantly on her shoulder, then her head.

He ducked her, letting her go after a couple of seconds. She popped back up like a cork. 'That was not very chivalrous,' she spluttered.

'I don't feel chivalrous,' Edmund mocked. 'I feel savage.' He gave a growl, making her shriek, and strike away from him. He chased her across the river and back. Every now and then she would pause and splash him. She was determined not to let him catch her, yet he did, and then he dragged her backwards by her braids until she begged for mercy. At last, with an unspoken understanding, they both swam for the bank.

Edmund was out first. Quickly Felicia looked down as he pulled himself on to a rock. She waited, watching his feet, but they did not move away. Slowly she raised her eyes, her teeth chattering. His eyes twinkled down at her as he held out a hand, having wrapped a linen cloth about his waist. 'Come, wife. You will take a chill.' He grasped her wrist, dragged her up, and kept hold of her as she stood shivering on the rock, her wet toes curling on its warmth as he stared down at her with eyes that suddenly darkened.

Felicia lowered her gaze. When he was close like this she could not think him false. His arms slid about her, bringing her close to him—so close that even the edge of a blade could not have gone between them. Neither of them spoke. Her heart began to pound, and she could feel water dripping from her braids down her neck and back.

'Sweeting,' he whispered, touching her neck with his lips. 'You will not escape me this time.'

'I am your captive, then?' She hardly recognised her own voice. The shivering ceased as the heat of his body penetrated the silk of her gown.

'Captive? I would not have you think that.' He stopped her mouth with his own, rocking her slightly to and fro as he held her.

'Then—Then why speak of my escaping you?' she demanded tremulously when at last she had breath to speak again.

'Last night.' Edmund held her a little away from him, his grey eyes searching her face as he traced the curve of her breast with the tip of a finger through the thin material.

'Last night?' She drew a shaky breath, not wanting to think of last night, but the thought darkened her eyes. She grasped his hand and pressed it against her breast, stilling the tantalising caress. 'Let us talk.'

Edmund sensed her fear. 'Talk ... *now*, sweeting? You must not fear me, for I will not hurt you,' he said gently, stroking the nape of her neck with unsteady fingers, mistaking the cause of her fear.

'Hurt me?' He was already hurting her ... Her longing to respond to him was intense, but the commonsense that had kept her from losing control when in Philip's charge held her still in Edmund's arms.

'I would not force you, Felicia.' He rubbed his unshaven chin slowly against her cheek. 'Is that what you feared last night when you had Joan share your bed?'

'I did not have Joan share my bed,' she whispered, beginning to tremble as the corner of his mouth touched hers. 'She—She fell asleep on it.' He kissed her full on the mouth with a passion that caused her mind to empty of all rational thought and her arms to go round his waist. His taut skin was still damp from the river, and she rubbed it dry with gentle fingers that caressed, wanting to go on touching and holding close this man she had never feared as she had Philip.

Edmund whispered endearments in a barely recognisable voice as he eased her down among the meadowsweet, scattering its perfume and sending insects scurrying away. A thin ribbon of sound escaped her lips as a sudden uncertainty surfaced in her mind, and she would have fought him.

'No, love!' he insisted, lifting his head a moment and looking down into her clouded eyes. 'I will have you.'

Felicia shook her head wordlessly, her eyes bright with tears. Then he kissed her eyelids and tasted the tears on her cheeks and against her nose, but this time it did not make him turn away and release her as it did at Meriet. She was his wife now, bound to him with words that were stronger than any rope of iron. Relentlessly he kissed her mouth, her throat, her breasts, his desire mounting. He would have her! The thought was a desperate bid to shut out the feel of the sobs that shook her body beneath him, and he longed for her to stop.

'Damn! Why do you cry? I have not hurt you!' Edmund's words tore the air savagely as he rolled away. He sat up, his bare chest heaving. 'You're my wife, and I'm off to war. Do you understand that, woman?' He ran a hand through his wet hair.

The wind stirred the trees, cooling and drying the tears of Felicia's cheeks. 'I—I understand,' she said in a low voice, sitting up a foot or so from him. A shudder shook her body. 'I'm sorry.' Her teeth chattered unexpectedly.

'You're sorry,' he said bitingly.

She nodded, not understanding herself.

'I need time,' she whispered in a miserable voice.

'Time? Time is something we do not have!' he exclaimed, desperate to make her understand. 'I am leaving today for Gloucester.'

'I know.' Her throat moved convulsively. 'I know, and I don't want you to go.' She lifted dark blue eyes to his face. 'I have no wish for you to kill Philip. I don't want you to go!' Her voice was vehement.

'Philip? So it is Philip who is behind all this!' His face twisted and his eyes were suddenly cold. 'You still have feelings for him, despite all he has done to you? Dear God, I shall never understand women!'

'No!' She sprang to her feet. 'You are wrong. I despise him,' she said desperately. 'I just do not want you to fight with him.'

'What it it, then? Do you think I fear your cousin's blade?'

'No! I ...' Felicia held a hand to her head, which seemed to be whirling. How had she got herself into this tangle? Joan! It was because of Joan's words. 'Why did you marry me, Edmund?' Her voice broke.

Edmund stared at her, his eyes narrowed. 'You know why I married you. I told you, to give you the protection of my name.'

'Naught else?' she demanded, a flush on her face.

He rose to his feet with great deliberation and stood facing her. 'What else were you thinking about? I wanted you ... But you knew that, didn't you—and did not seem to mind?' He regarded her keenly and the scarlet in her cheeks deepened. 'Or did I read the signs wrong? Do you want me to stay here so that Philip can find me more easily?'

'That would be foolish! How can he know of your existence?' Felicia was shocked by his words.

'You could have sent him a message.' Edmund was suddenly mad with jealousy.

'How? Saying what? He thinks he killed all the de Verts! And why should I? He destroyed my home and threatened my life!'

'So he did—but they say love is akin to hate. How do I know that anything you have told me is the truth?' He flung the hurtful words at her in frustration.

Felicia paled, and stepped back. 'And how do I know that you have not used me as a tool in your search for revenge? It would not be the first time, Edmund de Vert!' She stormed away from him and began to run through the trees in a desperate bid to escape his words and his fury.

He immediately leapt across the space between them, furious with himself and with her. He caught her and pulled her hard against his chest.

'What did you mean by that? I have told you the truth about why I wed you,' he rasped. 'And did you not in part wed me to infuriate Philip? Are you any better than I?' He held her tightly, as she struggled to be free.

'I have never pretended to be better—but you insist on treating me like Philip's whore!' seethed Felicia, glaring at him.

'Perhaps I would not, if you let me treat you like a wife!' Edmund ran a finger swiftly down the smooth curve of her cheek, tracing the outline of her mouth before turning her face up to his and kissing her with a barely controlled angry passion.

Felicia tried to drag her mouth from his, to shut off the feelings he was rousing in her, to let her mind rule her passions, but he would not allow her to do so. He kissed her so long and so hard that she had no strength to resist. He swung her off her feet and stood for a moment, searching her features.

'What does it matter *now* why we wed? We have made promises to each other—for fairer for fouler—and you promised to be meek and obedient in bed till death us depart, wife.'

'You would worship me then, Edmund?'

she demanded in haughty tones, unexpectedly affected by his words but attempting to hide the fact.

'Ay,' he chuckled suddenly. 'I would worship you with my body.'

When he kissed her, it was as though he had set his seal on her. He lowered her to the grass, and within moments their bodies seemed to merge into one flesh. She let out a moan, which he stopped with another kiss, turning it into a whispering sigh mingling with his own breath.

He was gentle at first, lulling her trepidation, for she did not know what he expected of her. Meekness? His lovemaking did not make her feel meek. It was a storm of unexperienced sensations he roused within her, sweeping away her preconceived ideas of how she should behave. She wanted him—his soul—his body—to be his heart, his love. She moved tentatively in response to his rhythm, surprised that the act was pleasurable; not at all like she expected from what her mother had told her years before.

Edmund bit her bare shoulders and groaned her name. Immediately she faltered, her movements became discordant. Was she behaving wrongly, unmaidenly? The turbulence of his lovemaking was now her pain. An ache welled up within her, a great ache of regret, but she resisted the cry that demanded utterance, not realising she tensed her whole body. The consuming moment came and passed, and when she felt tears on her cheeks, she dashed them away furiously. She would not have him think her a milksop, although her spirit was hurt more than her body.

'Don't cry, Felicia—or if you must, save your tears until I have gone.' Edmund's voice was low and harsh. He moved off her and lay beside her, pillowing his head on his arms.

'Gone?' She felt as though he had already abandoned her. 'You would still go?'

'I must gain my own inheritance—and face my enemy. See the Prince, beg his help. I cannot do that by staying here.' He moved away over to the river and picked up his linen tunic, pulling it over his head swiftly, his eyes not on her but on the water. He did not want to leave her. Having thought that making love to her would have eased his desire, he was surprised, and a little angry, at how difficult it was to leave her. 'You must understand that marrying you changed a lot of things.' He turned then, and looked down at her.

Felicia gazed up at him, not seeing how taut were the lines about his mouth and jaw. Only his seeming lack of emotion spoke to her, and her heart ached so that she wanted to hurt him.

'Of course,' she said swiftly. 'You are lord of a manor now. No—two manors! No bad situation for a physician.'

Edmund stilled in the act of scooping up the rest of his clothes, and a muscle tightened in his cheek. 'You are now saying that I married you for your manors?'

She shrugged, her heart beating uncomfortably fast. 'You said that marrying me changed a lot of things. What am I to think, but of your changed position in life?'

'There are other things, but perhaps you need time to find them, Felicia.' Before she could speak again, he had disappeared among the trees.

She scrambled to her feet, realising, with part of her mind as a twig scratched her sole, that she had lost her shoes in the river. 'Edmund—wait!' She winced as she put her foot down. Then she knew it was too late. She stood irresolutely, wondering what he had meant, then went over to the river bank and picked up her sodden veil. Slowly she limped back to the house.

Joan, considering the straggling clumps of herbs, decided that this part of the garden badly needed attention. Nettles and groundsel were already crowding out the thyme and sage. Her fingertips twitched, and she bent down to pull up a nettle, which she threw to one side and brushed soil from her glove.

'Well, do you have any chamomile or pennyroyal?' Dickon muttered in a patient voice, staring down at her.

'I told you chamomile does not normally grow in gardens. It can be found on the waste, in the meadows, anywhere. As for pennyroyal, I think there has been some here once.' Joan scratched in the dry soil about the stem of a withered plant reminiscent of mint. 'It has been trampled on. Why did you say the physician wanted it? Perhaps, if I watered it ... But I can't understand why he should want it. Are you not leaving soon for Gloucester?'

Dickon avoided answering her question. 'I shall fetch some water from the well, if you wish,' he suggested.

'It can wait,' she said brusquely, confused, and suspicious of his willingness to help. 'I wonder where Felicia has gone?'

'Probably still cleaning up the hall with the maids from the village. There were two of them in there when last I looked. And two lads are taking down the hangings from the wall,' he said hastily, not wanting her to go in search of Felicia, hoping that she and Edmund had resolved their differences.

'Have—Have you any lavender in this garden? They had some in the herbarium, and Nell has it in her garden in Shrewsbury —she puts it in the water when she washes her hair.'

'Nell?' Joan looked at Dickon sharply. She had heard that name before, she realised. 'Who is Nell?'

'Nell? I live with Nell and young Harry,' he said, deliberately obtuse.

Joan stared at him, wondering if his words meant what she inferred. She flushed slightly, at a loss for once. He cocked an eyebrow and stared back. He sat down on a wall. He was beginning to enjoy himself.

'Has Felicia met this Nell?' Joan asked at last, her voice stiff. She lowered her eyes.

'Ay. At first they were somewhat suspicious of each other, but they parted the best of friends.'

'You like Felicia, don't you?' Joan's voice trembled slightly. 'Everybody likes Felicia—but you can't have her, can you? She's your friend's wife. Well, not quite his wife. I saw to that!'

'You ...' Dickon moved away from the wall swiftly and grabbed hold of Joan's shoulder. 'So you were not as drunk as you made out last night! Why did you do it? Come between them?'

'Let go!' Joan wriggled beneath his hand, her eyes hard and furious. 'Why should

275

I answer you? We don't need you or the physician round here. Felicia belongs to Philip. If—If she had not run away ... If—If she had not run away,' she stammered. She held a hand to her head and moaned. 'He will—will make her love him instead of that physician. Then I shall be free of him.'

Dickon stared at her, pity and exasperation in his face. 'You've got everything in a tangle, you poor bitch.' He touched her cheek lightly, but she shook his hand off.

'You only say that because you want her yourself!' Joan shouted. 'But neither of you will have her. I shall see to that! She is Philip's.'

'You're mad!' Dickon's face had gone red with anger. 'I've had enough of listening to you.' He turned away. 'I would not speak to Felicia of this if I were you,' he called over his shoulder. 'You might just wear her patience thin!'

Joan's heart jumped erratically and seemed to miss a beat. She did not care what he said. She didn't care! She screwed up her eyes, not seeing the garden. Felicia was Philip's. Somehow she would see that Felicia was returned to him intact. The physician would be leaving soon. Only then would she be free of the black demon that had possessed her since Philip raped her. Only then would she be free!

Edmund had almost reached the stables when Dickon came striding towards him. Each sensed that the other was disturbed, but asked no questions.

'Time to go?' Dickon's voice was terse, his eyes still angry.

'Ay! I would have no farewells,' Edmund stated brusquely.

'Some women cry,' muttered Dickon. Then he wondered what had happened to cause the sudden whiteness round his friend's mouth.

'Exactly.' Edmund pushed open the stable door and went inside. The horses were swiftly saddled. Swords sheathed. Saddlebags filled and fixed.

They were already mounted when Felicia reached the front door. She went into the hall, but it was empty save for Thomas and a lad whitewashing a wall. She did not pause, but ran limping to the rear of the house. She heard the clatter of hoofs but could see no horses. Frantically she stumbled round the side of the house through the dust they had raised.

'Edmund!' The word rasped in her throat.

They had reached the trees, were under their leafy cover, out of her sight. Still

Felicia limped on, her foot sore where she had stood on the twig. When she came to the trees, she knew she had come too late again.

Slowly she slid to the ground, shut her eyes and rested her head against the bark. She could hear a blackbird somewhere overhead and concentrated on the sound of its call, not wanting to think. Bees hummed in the grass, and from the house she could catch the rise and fall of voices. Maids' voices talking with one of the lads from the village. They were supposed to be beating the hangings. Felicia stayed on, remembering, experiencing, regretting, despite not wanting to think. The pictures in her head were a reminder that she was indeed Edmund's wife, and nothing could alter that. All that was left to her now was to wait for his return.

She got to her feet. Despondency would not serve her. There was much to do in the house ... cleaning, cooking, mending. She had noticed that there was some woollen cloth in the chest, a deep green. Summer would pass and she would need warmer clothes. There was the garden—and there was Joan.

Joan! If it were not for Joan's words ... She should not have heeded her. Or was it that Joan's words had only voiced her own inner fears? Yet what had she to fear? It was natural for a man to desire land of his own. Most marriages were arranged for the most advantageous gain. As she began to walk back towards the house, she slowly realised the truth of some of Joan's words. 'You love him! So you are more to be pitied than I am.' Was she to be pitied because she was in love with her own husband? There was pain in the act—that was true. But there was also joy. She glowed slightly at the thought of how Edmund had kissed and held her. If he were not killed—God willing he would not be—there could be many more moments. If—If! What had he meant by 'there are other things in life', and that she needed time to find them?

Land and power! They were the two goals sought by most men she had known—even by her father and brother. Honour—another! She frowned, trying to think. Love! Men did not rate love high—did not expect it in marriage. Coupling was for begetting. Children! Was it an heir he wanted? A child? The thought frightened her for a moment, then she remembered Harry. A son would be no bad achievement.

Reaching the house, she walked in and her eyes immediately met Joan's. Her heart sank.

CHAPTER TWELVE

'Where have you been, Flissie? He said that you were in the hall, but you were not.' Joan's voice held that strange note that caused Felicia to experience a chill down her spine.

'Down by the river. I went to call Edmund for dinner.' Felicia was suddenly conscious of her damp hair.

'They've gone.' Joan gave a slight smile, and ran a finger along the dusty edge of the table, made so by the maids' sweeping.

'I know. I heard them go.' Suddenly Felicia did not want to carry on the conversation. 'Are you hungry, Joan? I am,' she lied. 'There is some of the beef and barley stew left.'

'Hungry?' Joan's smile widened. 'I believe I am.' She rose, following Felicia to where the cooking-pot hung over the fire. 'I think this afternoon I would like to go for a walk, Flissie, to see the extent of Chipbury and the village.'

Felicia turned round in surprise, a ladle in her hand. 'You are feeling that much better?'

'Ay!' Then she noticed that Felicia's hair

was damp. 'Why is your hair wet? Have you been for a swim?' She shuddered slightly. 'I don't know how you can bear going in the water.'

'I like it,' she replied briefly, filling a bowl with stew. 'But I'm afraid that if you want to walk, you will have to go without me. I have hurt my foot.'

'Oh!' Joan took the bowl from her and shrugged narrow shoulders. 'I'm sorry. But I do not mind going alone. I shall try not to get lost.'

'I doubt you could,' said Felicia drily. 'Chipbury is not so large—unless you wander into the forest, of course. But you will not, will you?'

Joan shivered. 'Not here. There might be outlaws or—or evil spirits, demons or wolves.' She took a mouthful of her stew, as Felicia sat down opposite her. She swallowed. 'Where do you think Philip is now?'

'Philip?' Some stew dripped from Felicia's spoon as it tilted. 'He will—will be with the Montfont. Why do you ask?' Her eyes wore a wary expression.

'I just wondered. Do you think he will come here?' Joan tore a lump from the loaf on the table. Her eyes were sparkling with an unexpected brilliance.

'No,' said Felicia, forcing herself to be calm. 'He has already been here. He will not come again, I think, having more important matters on his mind. There is a conflict, a struggle for power, taking place, Joan, and that is of more importance to most men than aught else.'

'Philip is already powerful.' For a second fear flickered in Joan's eyes. 'More powerful than the minstrel and the physician.'

'He is powerful only while the Montfont rules. If he falls, Philip will fall also,' she said vehemently. 'And why do you insist on calling Edmund and Dickon the physician and the minstrel? Edmund is kin to you, now that we are wed.'

'He is no kin of mine. You are not really wed to him ... It can be annulled,' said Joan in a staccato voice, a shadow crossing her face. 'The minstrel ... He is nothing to me.'

'Edmund is my husband,' insisted Felicia, feeling exhausted beyond measure. She had barely slept the night before, and the emotional content of her morning had laid her nerves exposed so that she felt she could not cope any longer with Joan that afternoon.

'If you had not run from Philip, I could have had a husband!' Joan's face was sullen. 'Now no man will want me. I have no lands or fortune—what will become of me?' She dropped her spoon on the table.

'There is no need for you to be anxious,' said Felicia in a weary tone. 'I would not cast you out.'

'He would—that abductor!' Joan's eyes flashed. 'He has all that was yours now he has wed you. Keeping it, of course, is another matter! When Philip ...'

'Philip can do nothing!' Felicia rose abruptly to her feet. 'I think I shall go and lie down, and shall see you anon, Joan.' Before her cousin could protest, she left the table and limped over to the ladder, mounting it, awkwardly.

She lay fully clothed on the bed, pulling just the coverlet over her. Joan's words had once more raised those feelings of fear and doubt. She had sensed that Edmund had not told her the whole truth when he had given his reasons for marrying her. How she wanted to trust him—to believe in a future together; companionship, working side by side. Yet, now he had gone, she was aware more than ever that he had vowed vengeance. Was she just a tool? And Philip? For all her own words to Joan, she was not heedless of her cousin's power. Men could change sides at the last moment in a conflict. If Philip threw in his lot with the Lord Edward and was accepted, his power could be as great as Joan had said—and what chance would Edmund, a bastard physician, have then against a knight of the realm and a mighty landowner? It was not unknown for a marriage to be dissolved whether it had been consummated or not. Philip could still win.

Her heart suddenly seemed to be gripped by an iron gauntlet, and she slid off the bed, unable to lie thinking any longer, and went over to the window, the coverlet still about her. The sun shone in and she held her face up to its warmth, and slowly she began to feel less cold. She could see Joan walking, and guilt smote her. Joan would still be a maid had she herself not fled from Philip—she would not speak in that strange high voice or be so bitter. Perhaps the uncertainty and fear that she was now experiencing was a punishment from God? Perhaps never again would she be utterly free from guilt or doubt. She turned away from the sight of her cousin and climbed down into the hall, no longer able to bear her own company. She began to talk to the maids from the village, asking about the cough, and gradually her own troubles were pushed to the back of her mind.

Joan shook her head, but the buzzing did not cease. The voice had terrified her when first it had begun to speak. Some of its suggestions were quite horrible. Momentarily, almost without knowing she did so, she fingered the knife at her girdle. A picture flashed into her mind of a bare white throat stretched and exposed. At first she had answered the voice, rejected the picture. She still rejected the picture; only when she saw Felicia and the physician together did it persist. The voice frightened her still but she had come to accept it, believing that she could not get rid of the demon on her own.

Felicia's words came back as she approached the edge of the forest, and for an instant her eyes were wide and frightened, and she hesitated. Then the voice spoke again and she obeyed, believing that with the help of the spirits who, everybody knew, dwelt in the forest, she would be able to find Philip. She wandered among the trees, almost in a trance, unsure of just what she was expecting. Her long hair flowed about her shoulders and her thin white face was devoid of expression; only her blue eyes gleamed with colour and light.

The grazing boar took her utterly by surprise at first, then she remembered one of the holy stories told by the priest in church. Had not some demons once been commanded to enter a herd of swine? She went up to the animal and spoke to it. The beast grunted, and moved away uneasily. Joan persisted, touching its rough hairy back and asking it to speak to her. The boar shifted, beginning to peer at her unpleasantly from small piggy eyes, tossing its head in a threatening manner. She was suddenly unsure, and an instinctive sense of self-preservation caused her to back away. But now the boar was roused, and it began to trot slowly towards her. There came a hissing in the air and a spear thudded into the animal. It faltered—tottered—and then slowly sank to the ground.

Joan looked at it, and then raised her head as the undergrowth rustled. The next moment a man appeared. Or was it a man? She stared at him in a dazed fashion. His golden hair shone like a nimbus about his face. A face that was so fair and nobly sculptured, despite its anger, that she could not take her eyes from its beauty. His light green eyes touched her face in a chilling fashion, and she felt fear.

He gave the boar a prod with his foot, and then pulled out his spear before he turned and gazed at her. 'You should not be tarrying here,' he said in a strangely harsh voice. 'It is dangerous to you, wench.' He fingered the end of his spear, still staring at her. She gave a strangled cry and slowly crumpled to the ground.

Something was touching Joan's face, wetting it, lashing her cheek gently with flurried strokes.

'Are you all right, Mistress?' The words seemed to be coming from far away.

Joan's eyelids slowly lifted and she looked up into Thomas's face. For a moment she could not remember where she was or what she was doing there. She pushed the dog's head away with an unsteady hand, and attempted to sit up.

Thomas seized the fur at the back of the dog's head. 'Give the lady air,' he muttered, staring at Joan still with a worried air. 'Would you accept my arm, Mistress?'

Because her head was still feeling light and strange, she accepted his hand to rise. She stood swaying a moment, clutching Thomas's arm, staring into the trees, and her eyes slid over the flattened grass. A sense of fear gripped her—of the boar and the angel there was no sign: they had vanished like spirits surely could. It had been a warning—surely a warning for her wicked thoughts. She was fortunate that she had not been struck dead! A shudder sent a ripple trembling through all her limbs, and her face paled.

'I shall take you back to the house, Mistress. That would be best.' Thomas patted Joan's hand roughly. 'You must have tripped over a root, perhaps, and banged your head. Mistress de Vert will see to it for you.'

Joan nodded slowly. She would say nothing of what she had seen. Felicia would only ask questions that she did not want to answer. It would be her secret. She half smiled, certain that Felicia had never seen such a terrible messenger.

A hand pressed her arm, and she looked up at Thomas. How ugly he was in comparison with the angel! But she would go with him.

Felicia looked up from the green fabric spread on the trestle table as the hall door opened. Surprise replaced the pucker of concentration between her dark brows as Thomas entered, Joan clutching his arm.

'I found the lady in the forest, Mistress,' said Thomas softly as he approached the table.

'The forest?' Felicia's eyes went to Joan's face. How pale and strange she looked. 'What happened, Thomas?' She dropped the shears on the table and went over to take Joan from Thomas.

'I don't rightly know, Mistress.' Thomas helped Felicia to seat Joan on the settle. 'I found her in a swoon on the ground. She came round right enough, but she is so quiet that I think she must have banged her head when she fell.'

'Perhaps.' Felicia looked up at Thomas with a puzzled frown. 'You did right in bringing her home. But why did she go in the forest? Earlier, the thought seemed to frighten her, and I warned her not to.'

He shrugged. 'Maybe she was tempted by the flowers. The forest can be right pretty at times.'

'Perhaps.' Felicia placed a cushion behind Joan's head. She still sat unmoving on the settle, her eyes strangely fixed on a point somewhere over Felicia's left shoulder. 'You may go about your affairs, Thomas, now,' she murmured.

'Thank you, Mistress de Vert.' Thomas twisted his cap straight. 'I was thinking that I might set the men to cutting the grass in the Long Meadow soon. June is well in now, and the grass is lush and thick.'

'Of course. You do what you think best, Thomas.' Felicia gave him a preoccupied smile, which caused his expression to lighten. He went from the hall with a carefully soft tread.

Felicia turned to Joan. Except for a graze on her cheek, there did not seem to be any sign of injury. Had she fallen? Perhaps some woodland creature had startled her and caused her to flee, and by so doing she had tripped and been stunned.

'Joan,' she said softly. 'Does your head

hurt, love?' Joan made no answer, so she repeated her name a little louder—and her question.

'Hurt?' Joan's eyes moved and she took a deep breath, and slowly she shook her head.

'Did you trip?'

'No.' Joan smiled slightly. 'I feel perfectly well.' She got up from the settle. 'Is there aught I can do for you, Flissie? Perhaps I can help you to prepare supper. I am hungry!'

'You're hungry?' Felicia stared at her cousin's suddenly animated face. Perhaps she did not remember falling? Perhaps the fall had only been slight and she did not think it worth mentioning. No. That was not like Joan. But perhaps it might be best just to accept her words at the moment. At least she seemed to have rid herself of her previous bad mood. She would just keep her eye on her, and perhaps make certain that she stayed quiet and calm.

Over the next few days Felicia tried to make Joan rest, but her cousin did not seem to wish to do so. To Felicia's relief, her previous moodiness seemed to have evaporated and she was willing not only to help to sew and work in the garden, but she also accompanied her into the village to visit the sick, taking some lavender she had found hidden away behind a bush in the garden.

Yet Joan had changed in another way. She now seemed to want to go on more solitary walks, and when Felicia tried to insist on accompanying her, her cornflower eyes would glint strangely and her voice would change so that Felicia feared a recurrence of her awful moodiness. She could only think that the solitary walks were in some way partially responsible for Joan's changed manner. Solitude was a state that Felicia found herself seeking more and more as the days passed and there came no word from Edmund.

After being in Edmund's company almost continuously for days, she missed him. Not only did she long for the sight of his face, his smile, but for the teasing gleam in his eyes and the amused note in his voice. She yearned for the feel of his arms holding her safe. Only in his reassuring presence did she feel that Philip would never be allowed to harm her. Yet it was not only to feel safe that Felicia wanted to have Edmund's arms about her. Somehow she felt that when they both came willingly together, the doubts and questions between them could be resolved. But as the days passed he did not come, and no word was heard of the conflict.

The grass was cut and Midsummer's

Day came. There was always a feast when haymaking was done and the longest day of the year came round. Felicia would provide the food and the ale for the villeins. There would be games, and at the end of the day, a great fire would be lit. Several maids from the village had come up to the hall to help with the preparations. They set to work willingly at Felicia's bidding, looking forward to the merriment and games, and the good food. There would be mutton and chicken, plenty of white bread for a change, and the thought of such luxuries made their mouths water and their hands work the swifter.

'You are coming to the feast, Mistress?' One of the girls looked up at Felicia as she passed the end of the table on which they were setting platters, outside on the grass.

'Ay, Beatrice. I am coming. How is young Godric?'

'Improving, Mistress. That mixture seems to be doing its task. He isn't coughing so much.' Beatrice smiled happily, and gave Felicia a shy glance. ' 'Tis a pity your lord isn't here for the feast, Mistress. These nights are made ...' Beatrice flushed, and fell silent.

'I know, Beatrice.' Felicia's eyes were suddenly moist. 'But it cannot be helped.' She paused, taking in Beatrice's round pleasant face and the soft mass of dark hair beneath her veil. 'I would have you know that I think it time Thomas took a wife again. The boy could do with a mother, and Thomas a good helpmeet like yourself.'

'I could tell him that, Mistress?' Beatrice's eyes shone, and Felicia knew that her guess had not been wrong. Emma's closest friend would make her bailiff a good wife. Life was too arduous and short to cope with alone.

Felicia nodded and walked from the table, the familiar ache within her breast. Beatrice was right, of course. These nights were made for lovers. She looked about her for a sign of Joan, but could not see her. Off on one of her solitary walks again, she supposed.

The feast was a merry affair, as was anticipated. The men drank freely and Felicia expected that there would be many sore heads in the morning. Joan had returned, but seemed reluctant to join in with the festivities, being persuaded to come and enjoy herself only when the evening was softening to a pale grey and silver and the bonfire was lit.

The wood crackled, and soon flames were blazing against the sky, casting a glow over the faces of those gathered about its liveliness. When it began to die down, some of the women were persuaded by their sweethearts or husbands to leap over its embers. It was an old custom, and several of her villeins looked towards her to see if she would leap, but Felicia did not have the heart when Edmund was not by her side. Thinking of a child could wait for another time.

She wandered away a little from the glow of the fire, her eyes scanning faces. Joan had gone indoors, and soon she would follow. The hour was getting late. An unfamiliar figure was standing well away from the crowd gathered near the fire. Some folk had wandered away, but they had been in twos, looking for a soft bed to lie on. It was a man. Her heart gave a lurch. He was dressed in a dark surcote, and his coif was pulled back to reveal a mass of hair that seemed to shine in the twilight. She could not see his face, but there was something familiar about him so that for a moment her heart misgave her and she called out to him. She began to move, a smile lighting her face. Then, before she could speak again or get a closer look, he turned swiftly and vanished amongst the apple trees. Disappointment brought tears to her eyes and she slowed her steps, peering towards the place where he had disappeared. Then she turned back towards the fire, realising how deep her loss would be if Edmund did not return from Gloucester. She was seeing his face now in every stranger.

Not until past midnight did Felicia get to bed, and wondered for the first time whether the stranger might be one of Philip's men. Of course he could be an outlaw drawn by the sight of the fire, good food and company. Why must she see danger in every lurking shadow? Still, she must be on her guard. She slid in next to the slumbering Joan, but it was some time before she slept.

The days passed slowly and July came in, blooming with a rampant fertility that somehow hurt. Felicia sought to keep Edmund's face fixed in her mind's eye. Would he seem a stranger when he did return—if he returned?

No news came from Gloucester, but rumours started to flit about. Gloucester was besieged—it had fallen! No, it had been relieved by the Montfort and there had been a battle with hundreds, even thousands, slaughtered. Bands of fugitives were roaming the countryside in search of food and clothing.

Felicia tried to ignore the rumours, believing that if there had been a battle she would have surely heard about it. There was one thing she could not ignore, though:

the villagers spoke of food missing—a loaf of bread, a jug of ale, onions pulled up from gardens, even a chicken or two. She warned Joan again about the dangers of wandering about alone, but she barely heeded her words and did as she pleased. Joan hardly referred to Edmund or Dickon. Nor did she mention Philip, something that Felicia was thankful about.

One morning Felicia woke to the sun pouring through the window. It painted an oblong of gold on the wooden floor, and her heart lifted with unexpected pleasure. There was no sign of Joan in the bedchamber, and Felicia realised that she had slept late. She lay there a moment, her hands behind her head, pondering on her cousin's behaviour in going off alone. It was almost as though she looked for someone. She had also noticed that Joan, like herself, had fallen into the habit of scanning faces in the fields and orchards.

She dressed swiftly in the new gown of green she had made, which fitted snugly about her breasts and hips. Joan had worked red flowers in silk at its hem and neck, pleasing her with the results. After rebraiding her hair, she went down the ladder into the hall, relieved to find that Beatrice had already been at work and made some fresh bread. Felicia cut herself a hunk, and taking a slice of cheese to go with it, went out into the garden. The air was just warming up, and the grass was drying beneath her feet. She opened the wicket and turned in the direction of the river. There by the bank she paused, gazing down at the water's satin stillness, remembering. She was roused from her contemplation by the sound of hoofbeats, and her heart began to thud. She was just deciding whether to run, when the horses broke cover and splashed into the ford.

She stared and stared, then, picking up her skirts, ran towards the horsemen. She first saw Edmund's grim, weary face, then Dickon, swaying in the saddle. His face was ashen but for two burning spots of colour high on his cheekbones. His eyes were closed, and for a moment she thought he would surely fall from the horse.

'What has happened?' For a brief luxurious moment Felicia allowed her eyes to rest upon her husband's face; greedily she consumed its strange but familiar appearance, aware that he, too, was looking her over.

'An arrow in the shoulder. I dealt with it as best I could, but I think the wound has become infected. I shall explain later.' The severity of his expression had eased slightly. 'Will you ride my mount for me? I think Dickon has ridden as far as he can, but I had to bring him.'

'Has there been a battle?' Felicia had paled, but she did as Edmund bade.

'The city of Gloucester has fallen.' Edmund seized her about the waist and lifted her up on his horse. For an instant their hands touched and their fingers clung. 'Very becoming—the gown.' The corner of his mouth lifted a fraction before he turned to Dickon.

By the time they reached the house, Dickon was in a swoon. Felicia dismounted swiftly and ran into the hall. She fetched a pallet and put it on the table. Beatrice looked at her in astonishment, but fled when told to go and build up the fire. Felicia went over to the chest as Edmund came in with Dickon in his arms. By the time she had found an old sheet and was tearing it into bandages, he had removed Dickon's surcote and under-tunic. He was covered by a blanket to the chest, leaving his shoulders bare.

She gasped at the angry red circle and the discoloured swelling with the arrow-puncture at its centre. Her throat tightened, but she did not move away. Edmund looked at her as Beatrice came running once more.

'I need water, Felicia—and if you have

some of the herb elecampane in your garden, fetch me a handful, there's a good girl.'

'I'll fetch the water, sir,' gasped Beatrice, her face concerned as she looked upon Dickon. She gave a tut of dismay.

Edmund nodded, merely glancing at her, but Beatrice did not seem to mind and went to bring the water.

'The elecampane—it has yellow flowers and a hairy stem?' asked Felicia swiftly.

Edmund gave her a twisted smile. 'You're learning! Go quickly!'

Her heart missed a beat as she sped from the hall, not knowing that Edmund stared after her before turning to the fire that now burnt brightly. He took a long thin blade from a fold of linen he had taken from his pack and plunged it into the heart of the fire.

Felicia soon came back into the hall carrying a bunch of herbs, and went over to Edmund by the fire. His brow was furrowed, and his hair lank and untidy. An overwhelming urge to smooth back his hair and kiss his worry away filled her, but she did neither.

'He is still in a swoon,' she murmured in a worried voice.

'Not for long,' responded Edmund grimly. He wrapped a strip of leather about his hand and reached for the knife

299

in the fire. 'You will have to hold him down, Felicia.'

She nodded and grasped Dickon's shoulders. A pulse beat in Edmund's neck as he gazed intently at the wound. Then he plunged the blade into the swelling. Dickon heaved up, gasping, moaning, and she did her best to force him back on to the pallet.

'Hold him still!' cried Edmund in a tense voice, glancing at Felicia briefly.

'Damn! Damn! Damn!' whispered Dickon through clenched teeth. His eyelids flicked open for a moment, seeing her face. 'Don't cry,' he gasped, before slumping into unconsciousness again.

'A cloth, and water.' Edmund raised his head and noted the tears on her cheeks.

She moved swiftly, holding the bowl as he dipped the cloth. She glanced briefly at the wound, easing the constriction in her throat. The flesh had been burnt back right into the healthy skin.

'Herbs!' he demanded, holding the cloth pressed against the bleeding wound. Felicia reached for the elecampane and he took them, bidding her fetch the bandages, while he replaced the cloth with the herbs once the bleeding had eased.

In what seemed no time at all he was tying the last knot of the strapping and stepped back, letting out a long breath. He and Felicia exchanged glances, and she was suddenly nervous about what they would say to each other.

'You did well,' he said softly. 'I could not have asked for a better helper.'

'I did what I had to.' She flushed slightly. 'Do you think ...?'

'I've done all I can.' He turned as Beatrice brought him a bowl of water, into which he plunged his hands. 'He will need careful nursing. There is a task for you to do that I cannot.'

'We shall take care of him, sir, don't you worry.' Beatrice gave a brisk nod, pulling the blanket up to Dickon's chin.

Edmund's lips twitched. 'Thank you. Er—it's Beatrice, isn't it?'

'Ay, sir.' She gave Edmund a beaming smile, delighted that he should remember her name.

'And how is Godric?' Edmund took the linen cloth from Felicia and dried his hands.

'He is well. The cough has almost gone, and Thomas and I are to wed at harvest-time. Your lady has given her permission. You are agreeable, sir?' Beatrice looked slightly anxious.

'I'm very agreeable.' Edmund handed her the damp cloth, bidding her empty the bowls and wash them before dismissing her. He looked at Dickon for a moment, pulling down his sleeves before turning to Felicia. 'You are well?' His voice was low and stiff.

'I am well,' replied Felicia, twisting her hands together in an ungainly embrace. 'And you? How goes the conflict?'

Edmund shrugged weary shoulders. 'Gloucester is ours. The Lord Edward controls the crossing of the Severn. We thought the Montfort would come to relieve the town, but he did not.' He ran a hand through his tawny hair, and scrubbed at the short golden beard on his chin. 'It is rumoured that he spent the last few weeks over the border in Wales consorting with Llewelyn.'

'Then Philip ...?'

'I don't know where Philip is,' he interrupted roughly, not looking at her. He had longed for her, missing her more than he thought he would, yet not knowing how much until he set eyes upon her. But now her words reminded him of how they had parted. ' 'Tis likely he is still with the Montfort, but who knows?'

'Then—Then the battle is still to be fought? Matters cannot rest so?' Felicia's voice was taut. She glanced swiftly at his lean weary face and away again, not knowing how to break through the polite conversation.

'No! It will come to a fight!' Edmund

gave a harsh laugh. 'If I get the chance, I shall surely fight your cousin. We march towards Worcester. It is said that the Montfort's son is coming from the south-east to join his father. The Lord Edward intends to take them one at a time if he can.'

'I see.' Her voice was uncertain.

'Tell me, Felicia, do you have anything to eat? I have not broken my fast and must go back today. I must be there if I am to have the Lord Edward's aid.'

'Today!' Felicia's voice was stark and shrill.

'Ay, today.' For a moment he thought he caught a flash of anguish in her eyes.

'You—You did see the Prince? Did he say that he would help us?' Felicia moved away towards the fire. Her hands shook as she picked up a spoon and looked into the cooking-pot to see what Beatrice had decided to throw into it to join yesterday's leftovers.

'I saw the Prince.' Edmund sat on a stool watching her as she stirred the contents of the pot. 'He seemed to believe me—said he thought I had a look of Sir Gervaise de Vert, but I could tell his mind was on defeating the Montfort more than on my problem.' He cleared a throat that was unexpectedly tense. 'What—What is there to eat?'

303

'Pork—and onions, with some beans thrown in.' Felicia longed to touch him, to see if being held by him was all that she remembered. She wanted him to kiss her ... and to go on kissing her.

'Felicia!' He rose, took the spoon from her hand, and swung her round to face him. She trembled in his grasp, unable to look at him.

'Felicia,' he whispered, nudging his bearded chin against her forehead before he kissed her eyelids.

She blinked and gradually lifted her head, letting her face slide against his rough beard until their lips met. They stood there close, not moving, their lips clinging. Abruptly their arms went about each other tightly. There was a hunger that needed to be satisfied. A heart's questioning that waited an answer. But in that moment words were superficial and could wait.

Edmund lifted his mouth from hers and saw her dazed face. He took her hand and led her up the ladder into the bedchamber, closing the trapdoor firmly behind him before reaching for her again. She scrutinised his features. He had been to war, and this was but an interlude before he returned. The world beyond the bedchamber started to slip away again as he began to undo the fastenings on her undergown.

There were just the two of them alone in an ocean of time. No tomorrow—no yesterday—only now. A man and his woman, knowing each other as Adam had his Eve.

He roused her to a pitch of expectancy that was exhilarating, wooing her with the hunger of his kisses and the urgency of his embrace on thigh and hip. Her need was desperate! The thought laughed in Felicia's mind as she made her husband welcome in her body. This time, when the fervency of his lovemaking threatened to overwhelm her, she clung to him, riding the storm with him until she reached a place of sweet delight. Never had she thought it could be like this!

Afterwards he slept, and if Felicia ached to hear words of love she brushed the desire aside, knowing that a man's priorities were somewhat different from a woman's. She lay for a while beside him, gazing at the contours of his face not hidden by the beard. Had he known he had pleasured her? He had said nothing, only kissing her hard and long before turning away to sleep. But she had seen his face and been glad that some of the lines of tension had eased. For now, she would have to be content.

Suddenly she sat up, remembering that she had left the cooking-pot over the fire. Perhaps, also, Dickon was awake and wondering what had happened to the two of them.

A door slammed as she came down the ladder, and she saw Joan walking slowly across the sweet-smelling herbage and rushes. Her cousin stopped short and looked up at her before her eyes went to the body stretched out on the table.

'Sooo—they have returned!' Joan's voice was loud in the silent hall. 'What has happened to the minstrel? Is—Is he dead?'

'No!' Felicia's voice was sharper than she intended. With Joan's arrival, she was suddenly depressed.

'Then what is wrong with him? Has there been a battle?'

'The city of Gloucester has been taken. Dickon caught an arrow in the shoulder.' Felicia voice was strained. Her legs felt weak, remembering the wound. What if it had been Edmund instead? She sat down on the bottom rung of the ladder.

'Is he going to stay here, then?' A shadow crossed Joan's face. 'Is the physician here, too?' Her voice rose. 'Of course he is! He must have brought him.'

'Edmund is sleeping. He has to return

to the Lord Edward's host.' Felicia forced herself to her feet and went over to the cooking-pot. She poured some more water into the simmering meat and vegetables. 'I shall nurse Dickon—do not fear that the task will fall to you, cousin.'

'He will enjoy that!' Joan's voice was bitter, and her hands clenched on the edge of the table. 'It is obvious that my help is not required. How many more men will you enjoy casting your spell on, Flissie?' Joan's eyes flashed brilliantly. 'You have been with the physician. All this talk of sleeping! And the minstrel ... You smile on him, and he—he is bewitched by you, though he would deny it!'

'That is not true! You talk nonsense!' Felicia exclaimed. What she had feared was happening. The sight of Dickon and the arrival of Edmund had roused in Joan all her former bitterness. Why it should be so, she could not understand.

'I do not! I have seen the way he looks at you and will not have a word said against you,' panted Joan. 'And what of Philip? You think you are free of him? You loved him once, and he does not forget that. He will claim you—he will come—make no mistake about that! He will destroy that bastard physician of yours, and his black hand will reach out and take you!' She laughed, a strange high laugh, and ran out of the hall.

Felicia's knees shook so much that she had to sit down or she would have fallen. How could her cousin say such things! Her mind must still be twisted by all that had happened to her at Philip's hands. What could she do? What could she do about Joan—perhaps it would be best to let her go into a nunnery. She would find the money somehow, and maybe the hands and prayers of holy women would help her—for she could not, it seemed.

There was the sound of footsteps on the ladder, and at the same time she heard Dickon stir restlessly. Felicia looked up towards Edmund and met his eyes. It seemed in that moment that she looked into the face of a stranger. A stranger she had met so many weeks ago.

'Is the food ready?' His voice was coolly polite as he approached her. 'I must leave soon.'

'Almost. It—It almost dried up. I shall get a couple of bowls ready. You will cut some bread?' She was babbling. She was babbling like a child caught out in a wrongdoing. How much had he overheard of Joan's words?

Edmund sat down and took up a knife and cut bread. There was a tightness about his mouth that had not been there before, and a strained expression in his eyes. Felicia wanted to speak, to talk about Joan's words, but somehow the sentences would not form in her mind.

They sat opposite each other, eating, not talking, not looking at each other. When Edmund had finished his food and drunk his ale, he got to his feet.

'You will remember to change Dickon's dressing daily?'

She nodded. 'Do you think Nell should be informed?'

'It might be best. She is certain to be anxious for news. Besides, if she comes to see how her brother fares, she will be able to help in the nursing of him.'

'I shall send one of the men.' Their eyes met momentarily, and there was something in Edmund's that gave Felicia pause in all her frantic thinking.

'Good.' Edmund picked up his gauntlets and went over to Dickon. Felicia followed him, watching him as he gazed down at his friend. Surely he did not believe Joan's words if he had heard them? She could not tell from his face. It was like a mask concealing his thoughts from her now.

He turned to her. 'No farewells, Felicia.' She was unable to speak for the tears that clogged her throat. He kissed her stiff lips—and was gone.

CHAPTER THIRTEEN

Joan ran and ran, her anger and jealousy forcing her feet on, oblivious of the curious stares of the peasants working in the fields. When she came to the forest, she pushed herself through the undergrowth that had thickened during the summer months. Angry tears slid down her cheeks. At last she could run no more, and she flung herself down in the tall grass. Her head ached unbearably and she had a dragging pain in her side. She lay there for a long time.

A rustling in the undergrowth caused her to lift her head at last. A figure stood before her, tall and handsome. The hair, though damp with sweat, was the colour of burnished gold. His eyes green, and wide set beneath finely arched brows. The nose was straight with slightly flaring nostrils with a full mouth above a dimpled chin.

Joan was instantly terrified that she would surely be struck dead. She had begun to think that she had imagined the angel, and doing good works had become tedious. Then she noticed that the figure was sweating. A wild hysterical laugh broke from her lips.

'What is wrong with you?' His voice was as harsh as she remembered it. His eyes narrowed. 'I know your face—are you not from the manor house?'

She made no answer, but continued to laugh. How could she have been so stupid? What did God care about her? No one cared about her—not even Felicia. And she was going to have Philip's child!

'Are you mad?' The man moved and grabbed hold of her arm, dragging her to her feet. 'Stop it!' He shook her hard, but she could not stop. 'By all the saints, will you stop it, damn you!' He brought back his hand and slapped her across the face. She gave a gasp, but still giggled. He slapped her again, harder this time, and the shock of the blow caused her to hiccup into a whimpering silence.

She stared up into his angry handsome face, and in that exchange of glances she began to wonder who he was. He was finely dressed in an under-tunic of red linsey-woolsey, over which he wore a blue linen cote-hardie finely embroidered at neck and hem. No outlaw, but what? She suddenly remembered the first time she had seen him.

'Are you from Philip?' Her voice trembled slightly, and her blue eyes were almost unbelieving.

'Philip?' The man's brows came together in a scowl, and his hand tightened painfully on her arm.

'I shall not tell on you.' Joan's voice was eagerly placating. 'I always knew he would come for her.'

'You did?'

Joan nodded. 'She should not have run away from him. Then—Then he would not have gone to Meriet.' Her fingers curled tightly, the nails digging into her palm. 'She loved him once. He could make her love him again.'

'Could he?' The man's expression changed, and his grip was not so painful. 'And how would he do that?'

'A love-potion!' she laughed once more. Then she remembered that the man did not like her laughing, and she did not want him to hurt her again. 'I could help you, if you wish,' she said, giving him a sly glance. 'I could put the potion in her drink.'

The man gave her a contemptuous look. 'Why? You must really want to get rid of your cousin! You are Mistress Felicia Meriet's cousin, aren't you?'

Joan nodded, a frown on her fair brows. 'She belongs to Philip. I—I love ... her, but she belongs to Philip, not to the physician.'

'The physician? There is someone else up at the house, a man?' He spoke quickly, hurting her arm again.

'No! The physician has gone—or is going to war. Only the minstrel is there now, and he is sick. He—He might die, perhaps.' The thought pained her. She did not want him to die. Did not want him to care for Felicia, either.

'You have a minstrel up at the house to entertain you? He is newly come?' Joan nodded, giving an exasperated sigh. Did he never listen?

'I see. You have been very helpful.' He loosened his hold on her arm. 'Does your cousin know you wander the forest alone? It could be dangerous to you. I doubt she would do it herself.'

Joan pulled a face. 'She is always talking of danger! She is scared that Philip might come. If I had a love-potion ...'

The man frowned. 'I shall get you a love-potion—but the time is not right to use it yet. I need to go away from a few days, but I shall watch for you again when you go walking. Go now! But don't speak of this meeting to anyone.' He gave a breathtaking smile that quite dazzled her. 'It is our secret.' The next moment he had gone between the trees, leaving her staring after him.

Felicia spread the linen sheet over the mattress of the truckle bed that Thomas

313

and one of the men had brought from under the bed upstairs. Dickon had woken once, and she had given him a drink, assuring him that his wound had been seen to. Now he slept again.

The door opened, and Joan came boldly into the hall. Felicia noted the tear-stains on her face, but she did not speak.

'How—How is Dickon?' Joan walked further into the hall and halted when she came to the table, gazing down into Dickon's slumbering face.

'I did not think you cared,' said Felicia brusquely, searching for the other sheet, and spreading it with some violence.

'I do not want him to die.' Joan's forehead wrinkled in thought. 'I shall help you to nurse him, if you wish.'

Felicia stared at her in puzzlement. 'Why?'

Joan gave a long sigh. 'I do not like to see him so.' She continued to gaze down at Dickon. 'Who is Nell?' she asked suddenly. 'Will she not be worried about him?'

'Nell is Dickon's sister. I stayed with her in Shrewsbury when I hurt my back.' She turned away, calling Thomas over. She wished to move Dickon on to the bed.

'His sister?' Joan's face was suddenly disconcerted. 'I thought ...'

'What did you think?' Felicia said impatiently.

Joan moistened her mouth. She did not like saying to Felicia what she thought. 'He did not tell me she was his sister.' She stepped back as Thomas came over to the table, sliding his arms beneath Dickon to lift him.

Dickon groaned, and his eyes opened. 'Edmund?' His voice was husky and pain-filled.

'He has gone.' Felicia stepped forward, brushing Joan aside. She smiled down at Dickon, and he attempted to smile back.

'Gone?'

'Gone back to join the Lord Edward. Poor Dickon—you are in our hands now. How do you feel?' She covered him swiftly with a blanket.

'As though the arrow were still in my shoulder,' he gasped, trying to sit up. 'How long have I been here?'

Felicia forced him down again. 'Only a day. Not even that. You must be good if you wish that wound to heal.'

'I'll try. Can I have a drink?' He moved his stiff throat slowly.

'I'll get it.' Joan could no longer bear to see him in such pain. She moved away and went to get the water. An awful realisation was growing within her, and she was not ready to face it yet.

For days Dickon caused both Felicia and Joan to worry. He did not seem to

315

respond to the herbs and potions that Felicia used, although she remembered dealing with wounds suffered by her father after a hunt or jousting. She accepted Joan's help as given, trying to forget the hurtful words she had flung at her the day Edmund had left for the second time. Joan seemed genuinely to want to help Dickon to recover, despite his offhanded manner towards her. Felicia also sent a messenger to Shrewsbury, thinking it necessary that Nell should know how ill her brother was.

The weather grew warm and sticky, oppressively so, as if it waited for something to happen before bursting into violent life. Then, almost a week after Edmund had left, Dickon began to improve and to demand something solid to eat. Felicia and Joan breathed the easier, and Beatrice was ordered to make some chicken broth.

'I shall do it with pleasure, Mistress,' Beatrice responded with a great beam. 'It is good to have the master's friend smiling again. I thought he would die that day the master brought him.'

'So did I.' Joan's tone was barely audible.

Felicia glanced at her. 'Perhaps matters will improve now.'

'Ay.' Beatrice turned to Felicia. 'Maud says she has seen an angel. An angel as

316

fair as the Archangel Michael himself, no less.' Beatrice rolled her eyes expressively. 'She thinks it a good omen ... perhaps it is. Perhaps the master will come home soon.'

Joan flashed Beatrice a glance, paling slightly. She had almost forgotten the man, giving him scant thought in the last week while nursing Dickon with Felicia.

'I wish it was a good omen,' murmured Felicia. 'Has Thomas heard any news, Beatrice? Did he go to market yesterday.'

'Ay, Mistress.' Beatrice chopped a leek with great deliberation. 'He mentioned that there's been a skirmish at Kenilworth over the border in Worcestershire. It's said that the fortress opened its gates to Simon the Younger, the Earl's son. But it wasn't much of a fight if Thomas's informant is to be believed—and the Earl wasn't it in.'

'I see.' Felicia's hands trembled. So it still went on and on. When would the waiting end? And where was Nell? If she had received the message, surely she should have been here by now? Or was she just impatient to see her? There would be things to arrange ... And what would she think when she heard of her own marriage to Edmund? Her nerves would snap if news did not come soon about him. Nell's arrival was really a minor event in

317

comparison to Edmund's return.

Another day slid by, then another. Dickon insisted on rising from his bed and sitting in a chair. He laughingly told Joan and Felicia some of the tales he used to sing when a minstrel. Of the conflict he made no mention, thinking it best to say nothing rather than to offer false platitudes.

Joan was suffering from a surfeit of confused feelings and only after great deliberation did she set off on a walk alone one afternoon. It did not take her long to reach the forest, and she was barely within the cover of its leafy branches when a twig snapped behind her and the man appeared. She turned to him. 'You have brought it?' she asked swiftly, wanting the meeting over with quickly.

'Ay, I have brought it.' He put a hand to his pouch and brought out a small phial. Joan snatched it out of his hand quickly.

'You must give it to her at supper-time. It is fortunate that you came today, because Philip will come for her tonight. You will make sure that the door is unlocked.'

Joan nodded, gnawing her bottom lip. 'I cannot stay. I—I shall be missed.'

He grabbed her arm, hurting her. 'You will do it?'

'I shall do it.' Joan wrenched her arm

out of his grasp. 'Now let me go!'

'Wait!' He pinched her skin as he tugged her sleeve. 'The minstrel ... He has gone?'

'He—He has gone,' she murmured, going from him before he could speak again.

As soon as she was out of the forest, she ran swiftly as she could to the house. She burst into the hall and immediately her eyes met Dickon's. Of Felicia there was no sign. She smiled at the man she had come to care for. 'Where is Felicia?'

'She has gone for a walk. I warned her not to, but she would not listen. I think the waiting and the weather are wearing her nerves to shreds.' He plucked a chord on his lute. 'I feel the same myself.'

'Would you like a drink? Then, if you wish, we could go for a walk too. I could find you a stick.'

Dickon gave a rueful smile. 'Our pace will be slow.'

'I don't mind.' Joan smiled back. 'I shall get us a drink.' She went over to the pitcher of ale and filled two cups. Then she took the phial from her pouch and poured the contents into Dickon's cup.

Felicia's undergown clung to her legs clammily as she walked towards the river. The sky was crowded with grey and black, yellow and night-blue clouds. When would the storm break? When would Edmund come—if he did come? Desolation gripped her as she watched the water slide swiftly over pebbles and skirt the boulders. A flurry of warm air hushed the tree-tops, stirring her hair. Then she heard the sound of footsteps, and whirled ... to confront Maud's angel. They stared at one another. She had seen him before.

'So you are Maud's angel? Why are you on my manor, sir?' Felicia's voice was surprised but haughty.

'An angel?' His voice was just as surprised, but he grimaced. 'Hardly an angel, Mistress Meriet.'

'You know me?' Felicia clasped her hands tightly to still their sudden trembling. 'You are an outlaw, then—or a fugitive from the conflict?'

'A fugitive? Perhaps. Rather I would call myself a spy, Mistress Meriet.'

'A spy? For whom?' Felicia's heart began to beat with heavy strokes. She glanced about her, hoping to see someone—anyone. But most were working in the fields or gardens at this time of day.

'I think you know,' he said softly. 'I wait for him now.'

Felicia turned and would have run, but the man stepped forward and grabbed her by the waist, swinging her off her feet. She screamed and hit him across the face, as there came a splashing in the ford to her right.

The man covered her mouth with his hand, swearing softly as he spun her round to face the horseman coming through the water. Over his fingers Felicia stared in growing horror into the face of her cousin Philip.

For a moment no words were spoken, and then a dark delight glinted in his eyes. 'By the devil, Beaufort! You have worked faster than I thought you would—but has the potion not worked?' He reached down and tilted Felicia's chin as Beaufort took his hand from her mouth. 'Give my sweet cousin to me.'

'My money first, Meriet.' Beaufort dragged Felicia out of his reach. 'I have dealt with your sort before,' he added in that harsh voice so at variance with his good looks. 'It was pure chance that I caught her. The sleeping-draught I think she has not had.'

'Your money—of course.' Philip's eyes narrowed slightly. 'Tie her up for me first, then. I do not put it past my dear coz to jump from a moving horse just to cheat me!'

'Please!' Felicia wriggled in Beaufort's hold. 'Do not let him take me. He means to kill me.'

'Kill you?' Beaufort paused as he

twisted cord about Felicia's wrists. 'Hardly, Mistress Meriet. 'Tis marriage your cousin has on his mind.'

'Then he is in for a disappointment,' she cried, staring up at Philip with sparkling eyes. 'I am already wed.'

Beaufort was suddenly still. 'What's this, Meriet? Another man's wife was not the bargain.'

'She lies!' Philip's face twisted with sudden fury. 'It is a trick! She plays for time, hoping someone will come along.'

'It is no trick,' she declared, struggling as Beaufort tied the cord. Her blue eyes darted to his face. 'I wear a ring.' Her gaze went to Philip's face. 'I am wed to a de Vert!'

'You're lying, you bitch!' Philip's face darkened as he swung down from the saddle. 'There were no more de Verts.'

'He is a bastard—but he has proof of his birth and inheritance.' Felicia flung the words at Philip recklessly, not heeding the danger she was putting herself in.

'What is this?' Beaufort's harsh voice rasped. 'You killed Sir Gervaise and his sons, Meriet? I had heard rumours that they were murdered!' He twisted Felicia to one side and faced Philip. The two men eyed each other.

'You would question my actions, Beaufort?' hissed Philip in a furious voice. 'You forget who is your paymaster.'

'I haven't been paid yet—sir,' responded Beaufort sarcastically. His fingers curled on the hilt of the knife at his belt.

'Edmund would pay you more to protect me,' cried Felicia.

'Edmund?' Beaufort started and flashed a glance at Felicia.

In that moment Philip swung his mailed fist and caught Beaufort a stunning blow across the side of his face, sending him and Felicia toppling to the ground. Philip was at Felicia's side in a flash, dragging her to her feet by her bound wrists. He looked down at Beaufort as he attempted to get to his feet, blood pouring from the cut on his face. Then he kicked him savagely in the head thrice, and Beaufort slumped to the ground.

'That will keep you, pretty boy, for daring to obstruct me,' muttered Philip, a nerve twitching at the corner of his eye.

'Brave as usual, Philip, hitting a man when he's down!' shouted Felicia, trying to pull away from him. 'That is, when you are not raping and killing women!'

'Shut your mouth, sweet coz, or I shall shut it permanently now—and that would be a pity. There's so much I want to do to you.' Philip's dark eyes glistened with a greedy triumphant light. He lifted her struggling body and flung her with a mighty heave over his horse, knocking all the breath out of her. Then he climbed up behind and dug his heels into the horse.

'Where ... are ... you ... taking ... me?' gasped Felicia, fear drenching her body.

'Where?' sneered Philip. 'Not far. We shall be there this day—and then will come the moment I have savoured in my dreams since you slashed my arm and went with your lover, leaving me bereft of your company.' He rammed Felicia's head down, and his horse splashed out of the ford and into the cover of the trees on the other side of the river.

There was barely any breeze as Joan and Dickon walked with slow steps down towards the river. The sky had darkened and a flash of lightning suddenly flared across the sky.

'Not the ... right time to come for a ... walk, I think.' Dickon gave a wry grimace and looked up at the sky. He yawned.

'Just—Just let us go as far as the river,' suggested Joan anxiously. 'We can always shelter among the trees if it comes on to rain.' She wanted to get him as far away from the house as possible, thinking that soon Philip would come.

Dickon gave a low laugh. 'You are set on this walk, aren't you?' He swayed slightly, and Joan grabbed his arm, suddenly worried. Perhaps the walk was too much for him in his present state. Why had she not thought of that before? 'Perhaps we can take shelter in the village if you tire. Thomas will help you back to the house later.' She kept hold of his arm, urging him on. She could see the river gleaming ahead.

'Maybe ... Maybe ...' Dickon gave another yawn, and his eyelids drooped. 'Maybe we should go back now, Joan. Right now!' He halted, and rammed his stick into the ground. 'I wonder where Felicia is? I hope she has got home.'

'I hope so too,' agreed Joan, gnawing her lip. If she had not, then Philip might come looking for her and catch them.

'Let us go back.' Dickon's words came out in sleepy muffled tone. Then, as Joan looked at him, he crumpled slowly to the ground.

'Oh, Dickon!' she cried, sinking to her knees beside him. She gave a sob as she tried to lift him. 'I did not mean to hurt you. Don't die!' She stared down at him. His face was drawn, and it looked yellow in the eerie twilight brought on by the threatening storm.

'Dickon, wake up! Please don't die.'

But he did not answer her.

The sound of splashing water caused Joan to look up. Fear seized her and she let out a tiny gasp. She attempted to lift Dickon again, heaving desperately, thinking that perhaps she could drag him under a bush and hide him. She felt sick and her stomach ached.

'Who's there?' The voice was sharp, and a cold dread joined her former fear. But she knew for a certainty that the owner of the voice would help her.

'Edmund!' Her voice wavered and sank. 'Edmund, help me!' A horse loomed up, and a dark figure slid from its back.

'Is it Joan?' Edmund knelt beside her, and a frown crossed his face as he stared down at Dickon. 'What is he doing here? Where is Felicia?'

'I don't know! Philip was coming for her. The man gave me a love-potion for her, but I gave it to Dickon. I wanted him to love me,' wept Joan, breaking down completely. 'I'm sorry. So sorry. But I am having his child, and I wanted Dickon, and he loves Felicia.'

'My God! What have you done, Joan! What nonsense you talk!' Edmund seized her by the shoulders and shook her. 'What man? Tell me!'

'A—A man. He came from Philip and he gave me a love-potion to give to Felicia, and said Philip would come for her.' Joan stared up at Edmund with wide eyes. 'I was scared, so I brought Dickon here, but he—he fell, and I cannot wake him.'

Edmund's face was suddenly bleak. 'Dear God! I could kill you myself at this moment with my bare hands, you poor fool!' He felt Dickon's face, listening to his breathing. 'He's asleep. They most likely gave you a sleeping-draught. But if Felicia hasn't taken it, she must still be up at the house.' He sprang to his feet.

'No! I do not think she is there. We would have seen her. She went for a walk,' cried Joan desperately.

Fear clutched Edmund's stomach. No, dear God, don't let him have her now! Not now when I am coming home to her! In the sudden silence there came a groan. Edmund glanced swiftly at Dickon, but he still slept. The groan sounded again, and then a voice called his name. Edmund peered about him, his eyes scanning the ground. Where was the noise coming from?

'Edmund.' The whisper came again, and suddenly he pinpointed its direction and saw the shape of a figure dark against the ground near the ford. Swiftly he went over, followed more slowly by Joan. He knelt in the grass and touched lightly the ugly wound all down the right side of the man's face.

'Who did this to you?' he rapped, a frown marring his face.

'You don't recognise me, Edmund?'

327

Beaufort gave a weak harsh laugh.

'It's the man! The man who gave me the love-potion. But what has happened to his face?' cried Joan in astonishment.

'Steven?' Edmund said incredulously. 'Not you! How?'

'A long tale, Edmund. If I had known she was yours ... But he spun me a yarn ... and I needed the money.' Beaufort winced and gave a groan.

'Dammit, Steven, what happened? Where is my wife?' Edmund grabbed the front of his cote-hardie, almost choking his old friend.

Steven coughed and tugged at Edmund's hand. 'Let ... me ... speak,' he gasped. 'You ... have a chance if you will listen. There is a hunting-lodge not far from the border with Worcestershire. Listen closely.'

CHAPTER FOURTEEN

It was barely an hour since Felicia and Philip had arrived at the hunting-lodge, but already it was getting dark in the room.

'Look at me, sweet coz,' commanded Philip in a taunting voice. 'I want to see the pain in your eyes.'

Felicia pretended to take no heed of him, but from the corner of her eye she caught the gleam of the flickering tallow candle as he moved it. She stifled a cry of pain as the heat seared the hairs on her bared arm as he ran the flame slowly up to her naked shoulder.

'Such courage!' he exclaimed, a tinge of admiration in his mocking voice. 'What a pair we would have made if only you would have wed me.' He weaved a pattern in the air an inch from her bared breasts.

Felicia gasped, and shrank from the flame, struggling against the bonds that tied her to the carved oak chair. 'You're mad,' she whispered in a seething voice. 'Quite mad!'

'I like fire.' Philip stared narrow-eyed at the candle, seeming not to have heard her words. 'I achieved enormous pleasure from setting your house at Meriet alight. I wish my father could have been there to see his old home burn. He never stopped talking about Meriet, and I grew to hate it.'

'Then why did you want Meriet? You destroyed something beautiful—but I shall build it again, and more beautiful this time! Edmund and I shall do it!' she exclaimed in a defiant voice, seeking to hide the icy fear that threatened her rigid self-control.

'I burnt your bed, you know, imagining

you in it, sweet coz.' He lifted his head. 'I suppose your cousin told you so? I meant her to. You still believe that it was Meriet I wanted? Perhaps I wanted your lands, but they were not that important—it was always you, Felicia, believe it or not, that I loved and desired more.'

'I don't understand! How can you say you love me, and hurt me so?'

Philip smiled. A smile that glistened like frost on a pond in winter. 'But you hurt me! You refused me! How did he do it? How did he get you away from me, that de Vert bastard?' He pouted, moving away to a table. He picked up a pitcher, filling a goblet with wine. He took a gulp, then came over and held the goblet to her lips. 'Drink! It might loosen your tongue.'

Felicia shook her head. 'He drugged your wine—my husband is a physician,' she murmured.

'Devil take him! Did he indeed, the cur?' He grimaced as he took another gulp, rolling the wine round his mouth before swallowing. 'A physician, you say?' He put out a hand and seized Felicia's chin, turning her face up to his. He let out a hiss of breath. 'You would prefer a physician to me!' He pressed his fingers hard into her cheeks and kissed her. Her stomach retched, and she retreated inside herself, not struggling, not intending to give him the satisfaction of seeing her fear.

Philip lifted his mouth from hers and stepped back; he drank again from his goblet. 'Aren't you going to plead with me, Felicia? I intend coupling with you first, before ...' He picked up the candle and singed a torn-off scrap of her gown. 'I want your last memory of me—not of a de Vert bastard. The skirmishing is almost over. The battle—I presume you will fight me?—is about to begin.'

Felicia made no answer, but his words caused her heart to leap painfully. Had there been a battle? If so, how had Philip reached Chipbury before Edmund? Had the Montfort triumphed? Was Edmund dead? She wished she knew—if he were dead, then gladly she would go to her death!

'What, still you will not plead with me? Damn you, Felicia!' He flung the wine down his throat, then tossed the cup away. Picking up a knife from the table, he slashed the cords that tied her to the chair, holding each wrist as he released it.

Felicia stamped on his foot as he started to drag her from the chair, but he laughed, and kissed her. Immediately she was still, and in that moment there came the sound of thunder.

Philip paused, then he lifted her and

flung her over his shoulder before she could escape. Panic surfaced, and she beat at his back with her fists.

'Now that is better, sweet Felicia,' he giggled, kicking the solar door open with his foot. He walked into the chamber with her still struggling, and flung her on the bed.

Rain suddenly sounded loud on the roof, beating against the closed shutters and the walls of the lodge. The room was almost completely dark except for the glow from the candle, but that threatened to be blown out with the gusts that forced their way beneath the shutters. The noise was deafening. The trees outside swept the roof with their branches, their rattling seemed to build up with the cascading rain into a crescendo of thunderous music.

Philip stood like a statue, staring at the roof, his face twisted with anger. Felicia rolled off the bed and began to laugh. 'So! You will not get all your own way, Philip. I shall not burn this night! Fire and water do not mix.' She ran to the door, clutching the remnant of her gown about her.

He moved swiftly and seized her arm just as she pushed the door open. 'We shall see about that, bitch!' He began to drag her back inside, but she clung to the edge of the door. He hit her clenched fists, causing her to gasp with pain, but she held on.

The sudden crash would have gone unnoticed if it had not brought with it such a gust of cold air and sweeping rain straight through the hall and into the solar. It caused Philip to look up. He was not expecting anyone, so he had not thought to lock the door.

Edmund walked forward and stood in the hall. His white surcote with the green tree of the de Verts clung to his mail, and rain dripped from his mane of tawny hair down his forehead. His grey gaze swept over his wife's face, and for a brief moment there was desolation in his eyes.

'Edmund!' Felicia cried, her voice breaking on a sob. 'You have come in time!'

Then the corner of his mouth lifted slightly and he looked into Philip's furious countenance. 'I looked for you on the battlefield, Meriet, but you were not there. So I came in search of you, wishing to renew our acquaintance.' There was a lilt to his voice as he drew his sword.

Philip gave an ugly laugh. 'The odds were too great, so I thought it best to withdraw—as you should now, Physician!' He released Felicia and walked slowly towards Edmund. 'Who left the battlefield the victor? Not the Montfort, I presume?' His smile was but a travesty.

'The Lord Edward. I presume that is your sword on the table, Meriet?' Edmund moved his sword slightly to the right. 'You may get it. Felicia, you will stay in the solar.'

Felicia stared at him, still clinging to the door, her knees shaking. How he had known where to find her she had no idea. In truth, at that moment she could not think clearly at all ... But one thing was certain: she was not going to stay in the solar to wait while the men fought over her. That Philip was a good swordsman she had no doubt, and she could only pray that Edmund had learnt much about fighting during his time with the Lord Edward's host. Still unsteady on her feet, she moved stealthily along a wall until she could lower herself on to a stool. She doubted if either man noticed her, so deadly was their concentration as they began to fight. In Edmund's face she saw the coolness and sternness that she remembered from when they had first met, yet the grey eyes had a sparkle, a dancing light that somehow gave her heart a lift as steel clashed on steel. He was the younger man, slighter in figure and experience, but he was quicker on his feet. She felt her own wrist brace as he turned a stroke and swung aside Philip's blow, taking himself out of danger.

A stool went over, and the table was rammed hard into a corner as Philip once again pressed hard, driving Edmund back and back. Edmund parried a determined thrust to his chest, twisting Philip's sword almost out of his grasp, but with a mighty heave Philip gained leverage and now it was Edmund on the defensive once more. Felicia gnawed on her knuckles, her lips moved silently. The danger passed for Edmund and now he was meeting Philip stroke for stroke, the metal rasping again and again as they stepped about the hall in this most deadly of dances. Suddenly Edmund had the advantage. He thrust forward, forcing Philip against a wall, until Philip's sword shivered and he went sliding against it as the blade fell apart, leaving him clutching only the hilt. Edmund stepped back, panting, allowing him to rise.

Philip laughed suddenly as he got to his feet, and pulled a dagger from his belt. 'Unevenly matched, de Vert?'

Edmund stared at him from lowered brows and tossed his sword aside, taking his knife from his girdle.

'Definitely a de Vert,' hissed Philip, his dark eyes glistening. 'Chivalry always was one of their failings. That is why you will soon be dead, Physician.'

'And over-confidence is yours, Meriet,'

335

said Edmund, his chest rising and falling rapidly.

Felicia bit back a moan as she straightened on the stool. Why had not Edmund killed Philip while he had the chance?

The men circled each other warily, looking for an opening. The rain still battered against the roof and shutters, but now its intensity seemed to be slackening as the fight reached its climax. Blood trickled down Edmund's cheek, and Philip's sleeve was darker now. Suddenly Edmund slipped and went over. Philip was on him, his dagger raised, bringing it down to Edmund's throat. Felicia sprang to her feet with a horrified scream and reached for the nearest thing to hand. She flung the pitcher at Philip's head. Her aim went wide, but the flash of silver distracted him. Edmund heaved and rolled over, thrusting upwards with his knife. She began to tremble as he rose to his feet. His surcote was stained. He began to stagger towards Felicia, whose feet moved of their own volition towards him. His arms went about her, even as hers did about his weary body. They held each other, his cheek resting against her hair.

'Oh, love, don't ever do this to me again,' Edmund said in a muffled voice, 'or I shall beat you within an inch of your life.'

'And you ...!' Felicia sobbed. 'Why did

you have to be so noble. I—I thought he would kill you!' She pressed her cheek against his chest, hearing and rejoicing in the great beat of his heart.

'Such faith in me,' he mocked in a weary voice. 'You disobeyed me, but I am glad.'

'Do you think that I could have sat calmly in the other room, waiting? I—I had almost given up hope of ever seeing you again in this life, so I was not going to let you out of my sight.' She looked up at him. 'You are hurt.' She touched his cheek, where it bled, with a tender hand.

Edmund seized her fingers and pressed them to his lips, kissing each one. Suddenly he noticed the searing red mark down her bare arm. Already it was blistering. 'What has he done to you?'

'It will heal.' She shuddered as she said the words, and for a moment the fear was with her again. She glanced down at Philip's huddled body. 'Let—Let us leave this place. I care not for storm or weather, for he would have set fire to me and this house.'

'Dear God!' Edmund's arm tightened about her shaking body and he lifted her into his arms and carried her out of the lodge.

The rain had almost stopped and the sun was trying to break through low-lying clouds in the western sky. Thunder still rolled in the distance, and to the east black and grey clouds banked the tops of trees.

Felicia took a deep breath of air laden with the sweet scent of rain-washed flowers and grass. Edmund gazed down at her and raised a dark gold eyebrow. Instantly she was aware of her semi-nakedness and her womanliness in a way that was possible only when she was with him. The look in his eyes brought a warmth to her body, but she did not glance away or attempt to cover herself. A horse whinnied and came towards them from its shelter beneath a great oak. It tried to nudge between them, but Edmund pushed its head firmly away.

'You have not asked how I came here, wife,' murmured Edmund, setting her on her feet but immediately taking her into the circle of his arms.

'You came on my prayer,' she said earnestly, snuggling up to him once more. 'Its fervency reached out and touched you.'

He grinned. 'You expected me to come to your rescue?'

Felicia shook her head and smiled back at him. 'Wanted you most desperately, but I could see no way of your knowing my need. I could only pray that my thoughts could touch yours.' She was serious once more.

Edmund kissed the tip of her nose. 'Perhaps they did. I was conscious of a need to get to Chipbury in the aftermath of the battle of Evesham. But perhaps an angelic-looking rogue is the real reason—and the answer to your prayer.'

'The angel?' A shadow crossed her face. 'I thought Philip might have killed him. He would have fought Philip for me, I think. My cousin misled him, although he was wrong in trying to abduct me.'

'I think Steven is regretting his mistakes at this moment. He will have a scar for the rest of his life, I shouldn't wonder,' said Edmund in a grim voice.

'Steven?' Felicia leaned away from him and looked up into his stern face. 'You know him?'

'Steven Beaufort is that old friend who followed the Montfort; but, old friend or not, I could have throttled him when I found out what he had been about. And Joan, as well!'

'Joan!' Her unsteady finger traced the bloodied outline of the tree on Edmund's surcote. 'What has she to do with this?'

Edmund scowled. 'I don't know the whole tale—I had no time to find it out. But she had been seeing Steven and, still thinking in her crazy way that you belonged to Philip, she asked him for a love-potion. She meant to give it to you

339

so that, when Philip came, you would fall in love with him and out of love ... with me.' He paused a moment.

'Ay,' murmured Felicia, flushing slightly. 'She wanted me to stop loving you?'

He chuckled, and kissed her cheek lightly. 'Instead she gave it to Dickon so that he would fall in love with her, thinking that he was in love with you, and she had fallen in love with him. He fell asleep while they were out walking, and she thought he was dying. She was horrified and saw her actions for what they were, I think. It sounds confusing, but I think Joan was more than confused for a while.'

'I cannot blame her. She suffered so at Philip's hands. If you had not come, Edmund ...' She shuddered and clung to him. 'She thought I loved Philip, but I was only a child in love with the idea of love when he came on a visit a long time ago. I soon discovered he was none of the things I thought him.'

'And what of me, Felicia?' Edmund tilted her chin firmly, forcing her to gaze into his face. 'Am I any of the things you thought me?'

She could not think of a word to say for a moment—not when he looked at her so. She attempted to clear the constriction in her throat. 'I have thought you many things,' she whispered. 'Imperious, unbelieving, ingenuous, infuriating ...' She smiled, and placed a hand across his mouth as he tried to speak. 'Kind, noble, humble at times, brave—but most of all I think of you as—as my most beloved physician. Does that answer you, husband?' She took away her hand.

'It is enough,' said Edmund huskily. 'But I am still a bastard physician, as your cousin so put it. When I first told you that my name was Edmund de Vert, it was the first time I had called myself that name out loud. Before I was always called Edmund the Physician—Edmund the Healer—Edmund the Herb-gatherer. When I asked you to wed me, my name was all I had to offer you, but it was so important to me, Felicia.'

'I understand that—and it is enough! Whether the Lord Edward has given his consent or not to your lands, I do not care.'

'Hush, wife.' He smiled. 'I pray that you no longer believe that I married you to gain your lands?'

Felicia shook her head. 'I flung those words at you only because I wanted to be more to you than a means of possession.'

'You always were more than that—and more than a pawn in a game of revenge. Yet, if I had not sought revenge—if Philip had not ...' His voice tailed off. He hugged her.

'I know,' she murmured. 'It is strange that good can come out of such evil.'

'Ay, for now we have a chance to have a good life together. God willing, we shall have sons that will bear the name of de Vert.'

'I would like that,' said Felicia softly, understanding his pride in his name and rejoicing that, between them, the gulf that his father and mother could not bridge could be vanquished.

Edmund laughed exultantly and swung her off her feet. 'My wanton wife! Have I never told you how much I love you?'

'No! But I would never tire of hearing you,' she cried as he lifted her high against his heart, burying his head against her breast before letting her slide down between his hands.

'It will have to wait, love.' He touched her cheek gently. 'There is Dickon to see to, and Steven is in a sorry state. Joan complained of not feeling well, and I am concerned. Do you know she carries Philip's child?'

'Oh no!' Felicia exclaimed in dismay. 'What can we do for her?'

He squeezed her hand comfortingly. 'Let's wait and see.' He lifted her on to the horse and, swinging up behind her, turned its head for home.

Joan was frightened. The dull nagging pain in her stomach was worse, and she did not know what to do. Several times she had tried to revive Dickon, but to no avail. No help could be expected from the angel, for he had swooned just after Edmund departed. If only Dickon would wake! Despairingly she stared up at the threatening sky and, as she did so, the first drops of rain fell on her upturned face. It soon turned into a downpour, and within minutes Dickon's eyelashes flickered and he began to stir. He sat up with awkward haste, blinking against the rain.

'What are we doing here?' He tossed back dripping hair and wiped a hand across his wet face.

'It is too long a story to tell now, but it is good that you are awake at last,' gasped Joan, hunching over, her hand to her stomach.

'Are you not well?' He placed a hand on her shoulder and stared anxiously into her face, which was drawn with pain.

'Can you help me to get up, Dickon?'

He nodded, and putting an arm about her waist, somehow managed to hoist her to her feet. She drew in a shuddering breath.

'What is it? Tell me, Joan.'

'I can't! You will despise me even more.'

'Despise you? What nonsense you talk!'

'That is what Edmund said,' she cried in a trembling voice.

'Edmund! Has he been here?'

She nodded miserably.

'Where has he gone? Where's Felicia?' He stared at her intently, his arm still about her waist.

'You will hate me, because you love her.' She sniffed, and wiped her face with the back of her hand.

'I love Felicia? She is the wife of my closest friend, and if ever there was a love affair, it is between those two!'

'You mean ... you don't love her?'

'No!' He grimaced. 'There is someone, but she's as prickly as a hedgehog— although, lately, I have begun to wonder if she might be fond of me after all. What do you think?'

'I ... I would say she is more than fond ... That she might ... even ... love you.' Tears welled in her eyes. 'But you don't know the things she has done. If you did, you would change your mind!'

'Joan, am I so perfect?' he teased. She nodded, giving a watery smile. He kissed her. Almost she could ignore the pain.

At the sound of voices and a splashing in the ford, Dickon lifted his head, surprise in his face. 'By the saints, that sounds like my sister!' Still holding Joan's hand, they walked towards the ford.

'Nell! Is that really you?'

'Dickon! I feared, when Felicia sent for me, that you might be dead by the time I arrived.' Nell slid from the horse and flung her arms about him, bursting into tears against his shoulder. He patted her awkwardly, murmuring words of comfort. At last she lifted her head and stood back, looking up at him. Then she noticed Joan.

'Who is this?' Her brow wrinkled.

'This is Mistress Joan, and we are going to be married,' said Dickon simply, holding Joan's hand.

'Married! Felicia and Edmund ... and now you!' she exclaimed, the slightest of smiles on her face. 'Well, you can tell me all about it when we get to the house. I am tired and soaked through. You have no horses?'

'We walked.' Joan gasped in sudden pain.

'Love, what is it?' Dickon put his arm about her. 'Nell, I'll have to borrow your horse and take her to the house. You follow on.'

'But, Dickon, what is wrong?' cried Nell, moving out of the way quickly as her brother lifted Joan on to the horse.

'Is that Henry you have with you?' he rasped. 'Quick, man. Give me a lift up.' Within seconds he was kicking the horse into action.

'Well!' Nell stared after him. Her feet were sinking into mud and she felt quite annoyed. 'I don't understand all this. Henry, help me up on your horse. We shall double up.'

It was as she placed her foot in his looped hands that she heard her name called. Puzzled, she turned.

'Nell!' The croaking voice was louder this time.

'Over there, Mistress!'

Her eyes followed Henry's pointing finger, and she saw a man kneeling in the grass. He staggered to his feet, but before he had moved a few yards he fell sprawling on his face. Then they both ran, and Henry rolled him over on his back. Nell drew in her breath sharply.

'His face is covered in blood!' She swallowed. 'Who could have done such a thing?' Kneeling, and without looking at Henry, she added, 'There is a napkin from dinner. Bring it, and make haste.'

With great effort, Steven opened his eyes. 'Nell?'

'That is my name, but how ...' Pausing, her eyes scanned the features she could see. Her hand went to the golden strands of hair sticking to the drying blood.

'I'm not surprised you don't recognise me, Nell.' His fingers clutched her sleeve.

She cleared her throat. 'Steven! I don't believe ...! Not after all this time to meet you again!'

'Not so handsome now.' He coughed. 'How's married life? I hope you are happy.'

'Seisdon's dead.' Her voice wobbled. 'What happened?'

'Long story,' he muttered. 'Take all night.'

'Tell me anon.' Lifting his head, she cradled it on her damp skirts. Then, reaching up, she took the napkin from Henry. Gently she began to clean his face, her lips as tightly compressed as Steven's.

'Do you know this man, Mistress?' Henry gazed down at them both, puzzlement clear on his pleasant, ruddy countenance.

'Ay,' Nell murmured. 'Henry, it might be best if you go up to the house and bring help.' He nodded and was gone.

'I was thinking of you just before I heard your voice, and thought I dreamed,' muttered Steven. 'I've never stopped thinking of you, Nell. I've been no good without you.' His mouth sought her fingers and he kissed one.

'Haven't you?' Her voice was husky,

and her whole body trembled. She had an overwhelming urge to burst into tears.

'I suppose it's too late for us?' He attempted a smile.

Nell took a deep breath. It was not in her nature to throw caution to the wind, but she, too, had dreamed and never forgotten.

'It's never too late to try, Steven,' she whispered, lacing her fingers through his, and holding his hand tightly against her breast. So they stayed, until Thomas came with Henry.

'I hope the ford is not swollen with rain.' Anxiously Felicia peered through the trees.

'We could always swim. Look at that moon!' Edmund caressed her cheek with his lips.

She smiled, flushing at the remembrance his words conjured up, but despite her fears, they suffered no misadventure in crossing the river.

'It appears that they got back to the house. No one is here,' said Edmund thankfully.

Golden light showed at the windows, a welcoming sight, she thought as Edmund helped her down. She felt a sudden lifting of her heart. Perhaps everything was going to be all right, after all!

EPILOGUE

'Joan has made a swift recovery,' murmured Felicia as she walked through the orchard with Edmund. 'It was best she miscarried, I think.' It was two weeks later, and the next day there was to be the harvest celebration, as well as three weddings. She reached up and plucked an apple from a tree, crunching into its cool flesh and then offering it to her husband.

'Steven and Dickon are looking well, too,' said Edmund, after biting the apple and handing it back to her. 'He'll never be as handsome, of course. And Dickon will always have a weakness in that shoulder. But we've come through the last few months amazingly well, all things considered.' He chewed thoughtfully.

'There have been times when I thought this moment—alone, just the two of us, loving each other—would never come.' Felicia smiled at him.

'Alone!' He laughed. 'With that crowd in the house, and all the bustle and noise of the preparations for the weddings? Beatrice is as jumpy as a frog, but enjoying it as much as the other participants. But after tomorrow we really shall be alone, and then I shall show you what loving is all about,' he teased.

Felicia came to a halt. 'What if I said I couldn't wait until after tomorrow?' A smile played about her mouth. There was a silence.

'I know a place along the river,' he said unsteadily.

'I think I know it,' she murmured. Their eyes met, and there seemed to be a singing in the air.

'Shall we go?' asked Edmund softly.

They went.

The publishers hope that this book has given you enjoyable reading. Large Print Books are especially designed to be as easy to see and hold as possible. If you wish a complete list of our books, please ask at your local library or write directly to: Magna Large Print Books, Long Preston, North Yorkshire, BD23 4ND, England.

This Large Print Book for the Partially sighted, who cannot read normal print, is published under the auspices of

THE ULVERSCROFT FOUNDATION